D0097458

A BRUSH WITH DEATH

ALI CARTER

POINT BLANK

A Point Blank Book

First published by Point Blank, an imprint of
Oneworld Publications, 2018

Copyright © Ali Carter 2018

The moral right of Ali Carter to be identified as the Author of this
work has been asserted by her in accordance with the Copyright,
Designs, and Patents Act 1988

All rights reserved
Copyright under Berne Convention
A CIP record for this title is available from the British Library

ISBN 978-1-78607-276-4
ISBN 978-1-78607-277-1(ebook)

Printed and bound in Great Britain by Clays Ltd, St Ives plc

This book is a work of fiction. Names, characters, businesses,
organizations, places, and events are either the product of the
author's imagination or are used fictitiously. Any resemblance to
actual persons, living or dead, events, or locales is entirely
coincidental.

Oneworld Publications
10 Bloomsbury Street
London WC1B 3SR
England

Stay up to date with the latest books,
special offers, and exclusive content from
Oneworld with our monthly newsletter

Sign up on our website
oneworld-publications.com

MIX
Paper from
responsible sources
FSC® C018072

For Sam

I'm sorry for breaking our pact.

Prelude

It occasionally crossed Alexander, Earl of Greengrass's mind that his past would come back to haunt him. A perfectly human thought, but one which came in the night and was always dispelled by the first ray of light through the gap in his bedroom curtains. He congratulated himself these days on conquering his demons and never letting his convivial character be dragged down by the silly mistakes any attractive young aristocrat might make.

The radio hummed as the alarm set it off; Radio 3 gently stirring this seventy-five-year-old man from a particularly sound night's sleep. He stretched out an arm to turn the violin strings down; his ears weren't ready for a deaf man's volume quite yet, and long gone were the days where his faithful wife's leg would give him a nudge to go and make her a cup of tea. Sharing a bed was an occupation they'd mutually given up long ago, and now he was no longer Chairman of the Game Conservancy, other than helping his eldest son learn the ropes of running the estate, Lord Greengrass's day began with a distinct lack of urgency.

On this particular Sunday morning in November, he rose from his pillow only to be hit by a rush of light-headiness. Something last night must have upset his sugar levels and just as he was going over his movements the cry came along the landing.

'Alexander! Alexander! What the heavens are you doing. We have to leave *right now*.'

Maybe it was the effort of travelling the length of the corridor, but Diana, Countess of Greengrass, rarely made the trip to her husband's bedroom.

He knew there was no need to answer, time wasted in speech would set him back a second or two, something he couldn't afford when he suddenly remembered today was a commemoration service, church was an hour earlier and his wife's role as organist demanded her presence.

His Lucozade tablets were on the bedside table, but in a flash of forgetfulness Lord Greengrass, now immaculately dressed in a three-piece tweed suit, forgot to put them in his pocket. An unforgivable mistake if his wife should find out.

She was already in the car pulled up to the door, furious Butler Shepherd was nowhere to be seen; one could tell by the great speed she achieved down the beautiful drive of Beckenstale Manor into the village of Spire. The sky was yet to fully lighten in that dragged-out way only a winter sky can.

Lady Greengrass took little notice of her husband as he followed her into the church. Not a soul to be seen. All those years of rushing assured her a life ahead of time.

'I'm going to rest in this pew,' he said, just inside the

west door, assuming his wife might wonder where he was if she couldn't see him in the front row.

He sat down, crossing his legs in that masculine way only the aristocracy can, and his shoulders drooped with the lethargy of missing breakfast. He blamed himself and only hoped the glass of water and everyday vitamin he'd taken at his bathroom sink would tide him over for the next hour of ceremony and a little bit of mingling with the community afterwards.

Spire church was large and austere for such a modest village, but today all that space might actually be needed, thought Lord Greengrass as he saw the villagers file in. Had he been of a less simpatico nature he would have minded that his son and grandchildren weren't here. As it was, what truly mattered to him was his and his wife's presence. Not every village boasted an Earl and Countess on their doorstep, and so all enjoyed, whether they liked them or not, seeing this pair in their finery.

Looking up towards the altar, he could see his wife's shoulders had begun their work-out, rising and falling rather more exaggeratedly than the music. Getting in the spirit was, for Diana, what church was about and Lord Greengrass certainly didn't use the doctrine as a wager for his morals; attending the Sunday service was a duty instilled early on in his traditional English upbringing. His family had been coming here for several generations and this thought gave him a warm feeling of pride as he slipped a large note into the collection basket.

With the service in full flow, and feeling a pinch in his bladder followed by the resulting desperate need to spend a penny, Lord Greengrass slipped out and headed round the back of the church, down the mossy side where no one went, confident his wife wouldn't have time to notice in the organ mirror that he had gone to relieve himself.

It was liberating to get a good breath of crisp air and he felt glad of a little space to himself. So glad in fact that he took his time finding a quiet concealed spot between two flanking walls at the back of the church. He fumbled with his flies, old fingers clumsy with the tight buttons and stiff tweed cloth. There it was. And holding it with two hands, Lord Greengrass raised his chin, crunched the back of his neck and gave a wink to the stone sculpture of Christ above him. Immediately he was overcome with wooziness and a sudden caterwaul from the congregation sent the old man toppling to the ground, breaking his fall with a blow to the head.

One cheeky wink and Lord Greengrass was flat out on the ground, deliriously gasping for life, his eyes flickering with a sparkle of hope that the shadow on the wall had come to help.

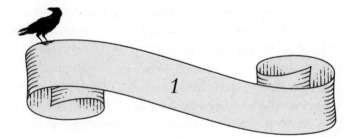

1

Home is an eighteenth-century white weather-boarded cottage under the Downs just west of Lewes. Within thirty minutes on foot from my front door I can be at the height of Ditchling Beacon, looking out over vast swathes of southern England.

A country full of houses ... and pets. Pets their owners adore like children – sometimes more than children and sometimes replacing children. I know a woman in her seventies, chain smoker and gin drinker. Her only child may get a smile of welcome, but no kisses left – these are given in abundance to a small, white, short-legged poppet. This dog replaced the last one, taken too early, run over, damn extendable leads. A reckless invention for beloved pets. There's another couple I met recently who live in a rambling house in Berkshire. They have five dogs, five children and a parrot. Every morning Mrs Finnes opens the kitchen door to let the dogs race out into the garden. When it's time for them to come back, she whistles just once, and then Percy the parrot takes up her whistle until Macy, Darcy, Ivy, Benji and Bridget come bounding back in.

Short-legged, long-limbed; stout, minute; smelly, hairy, fluffy; obedient, disgraceful, greedy, neurotic – the British love their pets.

I grew up thinking a house is not a home without a pet. Now just turned thirty-two and with a place of my own, I've lost the need of such an outlet of affection. I don't have it in me to love an animal enough to pander to its needs and routines. However, despite what I may think, ignorant friends and sometimes the odd stranger will come to my house, observe my country living and almost immediately exclaim: 'You don't have a dog?' and on realising this to be true suggest, 'Well, perhaps a cat is the answer?'

The presumption that currently without boyfriend, husband or child I must be lonely, irritates me. People don't often think in advance that a pet is a tie, and with it comes the need of routine and long periods of time spent at home; a recipe for loneliness and less of a social life. I am and always have been happy in my own company and relish the peace and quiet of having no one around when I am at home. My job enables me to run to my own routine and go away whenever I want.

I'm an artist, a painter really, and that's how I'd like to be remembered, but I have a side-line cash-earner drawing people's pets. It's not that I intended to be a pet portraitist, but through my own doing, I'm ashamed to say, I fell into it. I had been drawing people's four-legged friends on the front of my thank-you cards: an acceptable alternative to the conventional two-sided letter, with the bonus that I could write less in thanks.

Soon my cards were scattered across enough mantelpieces in the south of England that pet portrait requests started rolling in. 'Oh, the Burlington-Smythes were here for a shooting weekend, simply adored your sketch of Trigger, and are just dying for you to draw Bumble, you know, their naughty black Lab?'

I was quite taken aback by the surge of commissions and very quickly realised that I'd stumbled upon a profitable business.

I tend, particularly in the winter when my deckchair is hung up and watching cricket is over, to spend my weekends with people who have mantelpieces towering above upholstered fire fenders. I entered this social sphere five years ago with my good-looking then boyfriend Geoffrey, and was introduced to the glamour of the rich and dazzling grandees. Geoffrey was dumped within a year, being unsuitable long-term material: ten years older and very much on the wagon. He's now pitied by friends, drowned in booze and living with his mother on their heathery estate in the north of Scotland.

I, on the other hand, have been kept on by his southern circle, and enjoy many a house party, filling a spot as the single, eccentric artistic friend. The upper-classes love a token misfit at any gathering, someone who makes them feel they are in touch with modern life. It's either me, or a confirmed bachelor: we each add in our own way a colourful touch to their conventional set-up. It occurred to me early on that these society grandees have a combination of adored pets and money.

Some of you might have come to the macabre conclusion that there is guaranteed repeat business in drawing pets, and that's why I do it. But the pure truth is that I do it for the money, or at least enough money to subsidise my penchant for expensive underwear. As a single woman there are few things which give me a greater boost of self-confidence than knowing that underneath an outer layer is designer seduction. My lacy, red-hot twinset – and I don't mean the cashmere sweater and cardigan kind – or my midnight-blue real silk G-string or leopard-print push-up cleavage enhancer, all studded with sparkles, give me that little oomph that a woman on her own needs.

The process of picking what to wear each day, and admiring myself in the mirror before getting dressed, gives such pleasure that the more underwear I can buy the longer the whole decision-making process lasts. As soon as there is any fraying, fade in colour or tethering then the piece is relegated to a painting rag and I begin the major save. When I have enough money to cover the cost of returning to *L'Hôtel* for a night and indulging in the lingerie boutiques of *Saint-Germain-des-Prés* and *Rue St Honoré*, I set off on the Eurostar with an empty holdall and a wodge of cash. Bliss.

2

Beckenstale Manor is one of the most beautiful houses in the Purbeck Hills, two miles as the crow flies from the rugged Dorset coastline, nestling in a sheltered coombe. A large Georgian Manor, whose tall, sash windows line up as if to greet you by standing ovation as you gently wind your way towards them, traversing approximately two hundred acres of undulating parkland scattered with old oaks and pin-pricked with hornless Kerry Hill sheep, and bedding a large lake so close to the house it bounces back a magnificent reflection.

I was here for the August bank holiday weekend, staying with the Earl and Countess of Greengrass, and at Monday morning breakfast it was suggested that before leaving for home I must be introduced to the lovely young couple who had just moved in to the Glebe House, in the nearby village of Spire.

Diana, the Countess, began to explain the connection, 'My dear friend and neighbour in London for years, Lady Penelope, rang two weeks ago to say that her goddaughter and husband had bought the Glebe House in our village, and knowing we live so close suggested we might make our acquaintance with them.'

As I was eating my penultimate mouthful of a dark brown hen's egg, musing on the fact that Lady Greengrass, as she's known outside of formal introductions, had a bit unexpectedly felt the need to explain a viable connection, it crossed my mind that this new couple must be about the same age as Viscount Cornfield, the Greengrasses' eldest and only son, Arthur.

I was spot on.

'Rather nice to have a couple in their thirties nearby, especially if they are of a similar age and stage as Arthur. Coincidentally they are called Codrington, of Codringtons the private bankers who Arthur would have taken a job with had he not left London so soon after marrying Asquintha.'

Lady Greengrass's chest rose considerably as she let out a sigh. 'Arthur only left London to give Asquintha the opportunity of having a home of her own and finding stability in her life. We know she'd struggled on that front, uprooted aged fourteen when her parents divorced.'

With a resigned shake of the head Lady Greengrass, as she often does, blamed Asquintha for any decisions Arthur took that she disagreed with. Asquintha was middle class, without assets of her own and with divorced parents; none of the boxes the Greengrasses had wanted ticked by a future daughter-in-law. In the five years I have known them it is clearly apparent that they have been bound by their upbringing and are thus incapable of treating Asquintha as an equal, as if in some way doing so would lower their social status.

'There is a lot of responsibility involved with the running of Beckenstale and I do worry that Asquintha, having never grown up in a large house with servants, will not know how to treat them and where to draw the line of respect.'

I attempted to stand up for Arthur's wife, Lady Cornfield. 'She seems an astute woman, and so I'm sure she'll manage.'

But Lady Greengrass had little hope. 'When she first arrived she asked the servants to call her Asquintha. Fortunately her name is unpronounceable for them so they have in fact stuck with 'My Lady'. Much to our relief, wouldn't you say, Alexander?' She looked down the long table to her husband, the Earl of Greengrass, who was sitting at the other end reading a crisp copy of the *Telegraph*.

When no reply came she snapped, 'Alexander!?'

Raising the bridge of his nose above the centrefold of the newspaper Lord Greengrass, as he's referred to in conversation, stared up the table at his wife and me. After forty-five years of marriage the mild expression on his charming face no longer had the desired effect.

'Do you ever listen to what I am saying?' said his wife, in an irritated tone.

'Of course I do, darling,' he replied and then smirked at me as he sunk back behind the newspaper.

Aristocrats have a right jumble of different surnames, which makes following family lineages confusing for us common folk.

What you have to be clear on with the Greengrasses, who run and own Beckenstale Manor and its estate, is that the family surname is Russell. At the head of the family are Alexander and Diana, the Earl and Countess of Greengrass. Their eldest son Arthur and his wife, Asquintha, use one of his father's courtesy titles, Viscount and Viscountess Cornfield, 'Lord and Lady Cornfield' in conversation. All sons and daughters of a viscount put 'The Honourable' before their names. So Arthur and Asquintha's sons, so far, are The Honourable Michael Russell and The Honourable James Russell.

I felt the rules of lineage meant the Greengrasses were deluded in thinking that Asquintha would in any way detract from their aristocratic placement in society. Instead, my theory of why Arthur and Asquintha moved out of London with haste upon their marriage differs from that of Lady Greengrass.

You see, there were originally two Greengrass children: Arthur and his younger sister, Amelia. Tragically Amelia died aged only seven, when there was a mishap and she drowned in the lake. Of course this was a terrible and unforeseen circumstance, although one hears of enough grand houses with lakes and drowned children to be left wondering why these houses have lakes. But they do, and Beckenstale Manor is no exception.

Likely due to this accident precious Arthur has been treasured even more than most eldest sons or only children, although somehow he is remarkably unspoilt. I am sure the Greengrasses have subconsciously warmed to me as a surrogate daughter, and true to his nature, Arthur has never once shown any jealousy of me for this even though I have spent a lot of time at the family pile over the years.

Those who know Arthur pity him for the visible burden he carries, wanting to bring happiness back to his depleted family. It therefore came as no surprise, to me at least, that he returned to live at home so soon after finding a wife.

With a large furnished annex of the main house, a two-thousand acre estate to take on and enough money to run it, anyone can see that it was a tempting proposition. And by moving home early in their marriage Arthur and Asquintha, in their four years of being at Beckenstale Manor, have brought new life and a certain amount of pleasure to Lord and Lady Greengrass.

Their young sons Michael and James will be followed by more grandchildren, I am sure. There's plenty of room and Asquintha is energetic, young and more than capable of running a large household.

I get on with her very well, and I like that she has a sharp sense of humour, even if at times it is rather too pointed.

It is no secret that Asquintha is longing to take over the running of the whole place, endlessly throwing suggestions on her mother-in-law's deaf ears. 'Have you ever considered putting a shower in the house? Far more practical than a bath, I always think.' 'I could easily get the gardeners some new wheelbarrows. Plastic ones are so much lighter than tin.' 'Shall we have a garden party this summer? Nanny and I can make cupcakes, and there's no need for cucumber sandwiches nowadays. Far too dated. And as for sponge fingers, I haven't seen them for years.' (Lady Greengrass was rather fond of sponge fingers.) Asquintha was robust and without compromising her manners was well able to give as good as she got from her mother-in-law.

Breakfast was drawing to a close and Diana continued

with her reasoning for our visit to the new young couple in the Glebe House.

'I thought it best if you and I go and meet the Codringtons now before I drop you off at the railway station. I will then follow up with an invitation to dinner so that they can meet Arthur and Asquintha here first.' Justifying the unsaid, she continued, 'With Mary in our kitchen it's no trouble.'

'Are you sure you don't mind taking me to my train? I can easily get a taxi,' I said.

I almost always drive to weekends away, however far it is. I like to get there under my own steam and be able to bring my travelling paints and sketchbook, so that if the weekend extends I can always do some work at the same time. I am lucky not to be bound by a nine-to-five office job although it does mean people often try hard to persuade me to stay on Sunday night too.

This particular bank holiday I had come directly to Beckenstale Manor on the train from London. I'd been visiting my parents and if I'd gone back to Sussex to pick up my car I would have never arrived in time for dinner on Friday, and Lady Greengrass does not like her schedule to be put out. 'If I ask someone for the weekend, I expect them to arrive on Friday with time to change and have a cocktail before dinner, and only leave after we've had lunch on Sunday. It does make it difficult catering for the casual younger generation who pick and choose when they arrive and when they leave. People have no manners nowadays. I do hope Asquintha will insist the grandchildren know properly how to spend a weekend away.'

Telling me to get a shuffle on, she got up and walked

straight out of the room without giving me a chance to say anything else.

I went down the length of the table to say goodbye to Lord Greengrass.

'Thank you Alexander, for a lovely weekend. I have so enjoyed spending the bank holiday with you both.'

'Susie!' He stood up, opening his arms and placing his hands on my shoulders. 'Diana and I much enjoy your visits. Please come again soon.' He kissed me on both cheeks. 'No need to leave it for a year.'

'Thank you,' I smiled and left the room.

'Coo-eee! Susie! Hang on a minute,' shouted Alexander, a little too loudly.

I poked my head back round the door. 'Yes?'

'Don't forget to sign the visitors' book, it's on the hall table.'

'Of course.' I smiled and raised my hand to say goodbye.

The traditional visitors' book, hardbound in luxurious calf leather, lived on the round table in the centre of the large hall, its gilt-edged pages catching the light of the enormous chandelier dangling above. It would be difficult to leave without signing it anyway, as Diana always opens it the evening before a guest, or 'visitor' as she likes to say, departs.

'Susie, please sign the book, no comments,' instructed Diana, whose size was diminished by the looming figure of Butler Shepherd standing behind her, all ready and waiting to hold open one half of the enormous front door.

As I wrote the date '29th September – 1st August' and signed my name 'Susie Mahl' with a certain amount of pressure applied to ensure a legible signature on the thick, woven cream paper, I couldn't help but notice that the last person to stay at Beckenstale Manor was Robert Hatch back in February. This visit must have coincided with Alexander's retirement as Chairman of the Game Conservancy, and Hatch's appointment.

It surprised me that two elderly people living in a big house furnished with servants had not had more visitors over the summer. But then again I had rarely met anyone other than immediate family in all the times I'd stayed here, and as a small party is far more relaxing than a houseful I had never questioned it. But now, confronted with this almost empty page, various theories ran through my mind, then, before I got carried away as I am wont to do, I purposely stopped myself nosying into other people's business.

I have a knack of paying a little more attention to detail than is needed at times. It's not malicious, but I just enjoy matching things up and making sense of situations.

Avoiding the faux pas of closing the book and smudging the wet ink, I laid down the fountain pen and put my right hand into my skirt pocket, ruffling around to find a bank note for Butler Shepherd.

Tipping is a custom in a grand house that you as a visitor should abide by. Servants rely on tips. Their basic wage is the minimum and it is only through the accumulation of houseguests' tips that they can afford treats, whether that be a present for a loved one or a holiday away from the estate. The general form is to leave money for each night under the lamp on your bedside table, an equivalent amount on your dressing table in an envelope labelled 'For the Kitchen', and a sum of your choice slipped into the butler's hand on departure.

The front door was opened and sunlight cast a golden triangle onto the porch and, as I passed Butler Shepherd, in a smooth transaction I slipped the note from the cup of my hand into his.

'Thank you Ma'am,' he said bowing his large head. 'Your luggage is in the boot.'

There's something about Shepherd that disconcerts me. I think it's his eyes, which stare without the slightest flicker. He's been with the Greengrasses a long time and on one occasion I've witnessed him hovering in a bedroom doorway as Mary, his wife and also the housekeeper, unpacked a visitor's suitcases. Unpacking is not unusual; all guests on arrival have an opportunity to request their belongings not be touched, but if they don't, Mary hangs up pressed clothes and neatly folds the others into a chest, leaving the drawers ajar for the visitor to see where everything has been put.

There is ample opportunity for servants to frequent bedrooms throughout their daily routine as rooms are tidied in the morning, and after six in the evening shutters and curtains are closed and beds turned down. If Shepherd had a tendency for light-fingeredness I am sure he would no longer be here, but it's well known that rich people can be careless with their loose change.

I stepped down from the porch onto the gravel of the yard and within moments Diana and I were gliding in her Volvo estate down the drive, through the parkland and past the ornamental sheep, headed for the village.

Spire is half a mile west from the end of the Greengrasses' drive. The small village is stretched out along one big bend in the country lane. We flew through it, and just before the last house on the left Diana turned right and bumped down a private drive running along-side the low flint wall of the graveyard.

I was sure that she had been longing for an excuse to call in on this new couple, and I was a little concerned that introducing me was a rather feeble one. I was nobody to the Codringtons, and by the size of their house they were clearly somebody. With the wheels of the car crunching the gravel we drew up adjacent to their front door.

The Codringtons were clearly very much still getting settled after moving in; the garden was half mapped out with twine, a concrete mixer was almost secured to the patio with its own residue and the windows were curtainless.

Lady Greengrass stretched an arm behind her seat and reached for a clematis in a small pot. Before we were fully out of the car the front door edged open and there stood a real stunner: elegantly thin, snappy short hair and compelling female attractiveness. At moments like these I think I should be wearing my underwear on the outside. Back at you, Keira Knightley. Lady Greengrass thrust the clematis towards her hopefully soon-to-be new friend.

'I'm Lady Greengrass – Diana – from Beckenstale Manor and this is Susie Mahl, an artist friend we have staying for the weekend.'

'Antonia Codrington, pleased to meet you.' After which, handed the clematis, came a genuine thank-you and then there was a fraction of a pause before coffee was offered.

Following in line, through the cold porch and tip-toeing over piles of outdoor kit we soon found ourselves in a remarkably tidy and rather jazzy kitchen. A door opened, through which came an unsurprisingly attractive, very tall man. 'I'm Ben, Antonia's husband,' he said, as Diana and I both received a firm handshake.

'Benji, will you make coffee, please? Come, Diana and Susie, have a seat.'

Antonia perched on the arm of a chair at the head of the disconcerting glass-topped table, which cut a transparent dash across the centre of the kitchen. Diana and I sat on either side of her.

This was the very first posh house I'd been inside that had a modern, individual style. The lights hung from the ceiling on retractable strings, the sink was one curved continuation of the surface into which it sank, and little details such as a see-through toaster and revolving fridge caught my eye. But there was something undeniably comfy to the kitchen that made me think there wasn't a whiff of interior designer or lighting consultant. Antonia, or perhaps Ben, had enviable taste. There was evidence of a child but no noise to be heard, and a dog-less basket in the corner.

Ben brought mugs of hot coffee to the table and, while the Aga took the chill out of the air, we listened to Diana's run-down of the village. She knew virtually everything, helped in no small part by being the organist of the flint-spired church that could be seen through the kitchen window.

As I listened, a snide comment of Asquintha's echoed in my ear: 'She's the first and only organist I've ever met with one deaf ear and a bum too big for a piano stool'.

As Diana went on at great length the poor Codringtons soon began to deduce what they were in for. Here was a woman who once a week would be at the end of their garden, peering over the yew hedge desperate to be asked in with a 'Oh, why thank you, just a glass of sherry and I'll be on my way.'

With my train to catch, there was just enough time for the Codringtons to have learnt more than enough about us from Diana, and for us to know no more than meets the eye about them.

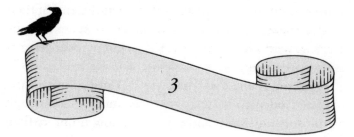

3

As these things tend to come about, no sooner had my thank-you card arrived at the Greengrasses than Diana was off to drop in on the Codringtons, suggesting that if they ever wanted their dog or horses drawn then they really should consider contacting me. 'Such a pleasure to have around, and really rather a good artist' was how Diana put it, apparently.

Five months later, on the bright end of a November lunchtime, my home telephone rang unexpectedly. I crossed the kitchen into the studio and grabbed the receiver.

'Hello.'

'Susie?'

'Yes.'

'It's Antonia Codrington. Sorry to call out of the blue but I got your number from Lady Greengrass who has been encouraging us to have a drawing done of our dog, Situp.'

'Oh, that is nice of her to have suggested it.'

'We've often thought of having him drawn but we've held out until we got a recommendation from a reliable source. There are many average artists dashing out pet portraits but when we saw your drawing of the Greengrasses' Harriet we really did think you had a style unlike anything we'd seen before, and we love it.'

'That's very kind of you.'

'I mean it, your drawing not only shows the character of the dog but to choose such a humorous pose without ridicule is very talented. Would you come and draw our dog?'

Not yet knowing Antonia nearly well enough for chit-chat, the conversation didn't diverge in any way from the subject of commission. I was delighted to agree, and followed on with the usual questions, beginning with the inevitable, 'What breed of dog is Situp?'

'He's a Deerhound. Big chap, about four and a half feet long, two feet high when standing and three and a half feet tall when sitting upright. Ash-grey, fit and lean.'

It is such a help when I get a client who predicts and answers several questions at once without using any infantile pet terms, either to me or the animal in the background – 'oochy coochey' being a particular favourite with some of my clients.

I continued talking Antonia through the process: 'I will carry out the final drawing at home in my studio but to begin with it would be ideal if I could come and spend two days with Situp in order to get to know him. During this time, I'd like to do a handful of preliminary drawings and take several photographs.'

'Yes, I thought you'd be wanting to visit. I could tell from the life in your drawing of Harriet that you didn't just copy her from a photograph.'

I find it impossible to get atmosphere in my work if

I have not sat in front of the subject, and I was encouraged that Antonia had liked the pose I had chosen for Harriet. No matter what it is, a living being or an inert object, I have the need to spend time in the same place as my subject before I can fully understand and engage. For me painting and drawing is half heart, half hand and eye; and without one, I can't use the other.

I asked Antonia if she could email me some pictures of her dog. 'They would be very useful in helping me have an image of him in my head. Quick snaps would do fine. I don't want to take up your time.'

'Of course I will. There are plenty already on my iPad. Just ignore the hideous orange ball he almost always has in his mouth.'

There was a small pause.

'Now, I suppose we ought to discuss price,' said Antonia with her pleasantly straightforward approach.

Helpfully I have a flat fee for pet drawings, which removes any awkwardness of discussing amount or timescale, particularly as people rarely realise quite how long it takes to create a work of art. Almost the better it is, the easier it looks to do but the longer it may take to achieve this.

I talked Antonia through my terms of business. 'Extra costs include travel and framing, if you'd like me to organise that.'

Antonia, faultless in her decision-making, answered, 'Don't worry about a frame. Ben shall sort that.'

I explained that I like to be left alone to decide the pose of the pet and composition of the drawing, on the agreement that the client only pays if they like the final picture.

'That sounds good to me, but how does it work with those who want a particular pose?'

'Interesting question,' I said. 'In those cases I think I'm probably not the right choice for them. I can't draw something truthfully unless I have composed it in my head, and therefore it is important for me not to be bound by preconceived poses or input from the owner.'

Although I was possibly going into too much detail, I wanted to try and explain what spurs me on as an artist. It is difficult to express this without sounding pretentious but I tried. 'I have to look and look until I am captured by a subject. It could be anything from a pose to a shaft of light falling on the pet, but I need to allow something to grasp my attention before I am given a way in to recording what I see on paper. I don't mean to sound inflexible but it frustrates me when people ask me to draw something and then they tell me how to do it.'

'I completely understand. Ben is the creative one in our family and I've found it is never a good idea to question his judgment as it just throws him in to a total spin. You've put it so clearly.'

Understandably Antonia wanted to be at home when I come to visit Situp so we had to find a mutually suitable weekend. This wasn't that easy. Her high-powered job as a 'contract risk and security consultant' – no, I'm not one hundred percent sure what that is either – required her to be in Switzerland every three weeks. How much consulting can a consultant do?

But, after a bit of discussion, and her kind offer to stay, we settled on the forthcoming weekend.

'We,' said Antonia, and quickly tagged on, 'and Situp

of course, look forward to seeing you. Why not arrive around 6pm on Friday? I'll send you that email with photographs now. Thanks, Susie.'

I put the receiver straight down on the desk, slightly hoping I'd forget about it and the battery would run flat. I hate telephones; haunted by those silent moments during adolescent calls to the opposite sex, I still get nervous.

Even my best friends know not to call me.

Talking of which, I remembered I owed Nancy a letter particularly, since she's pregnant again and in need of distraction.

Kemps Cottage
6th November

Dear Nanc,

I hope you, Peggy and Adam are well. Not long to go till the next one arrives. How do you feel? Still eating lots of canned sausages? I hadn't heard of that craving before but then again you've always been slightly dated in your guilty treats. Remember when you were still eating Cremola Foam in powder form long after dip-dabs came out?

Life in Sussex is as happy as ever. I really do enjoy the fact I can come home, spend days in the studio, walk for miles on the Downs and rarely get interrupted. You must come and visit again soon. I know it's not ideal sleeping arrangements but my neighbour Cecilia con-tinues to say she will happily put my friends up.

I'm currently painting very large seascapes from the small oil sketches I did in the summer. Do you remember that day we picnicked at Cuckmere Haven and I painted the cliffs? Well, that one is almost finished. Peggy could walk in to it, it's so big!

I'm off to the West Country this weekend to draw a dog. Not the usual, as this one is a Deerhound. Staying with a posh young couple so will give you the full run down of a weekend in luxury when I am back home.

Lots of love Nanc and to the other two,

Xxx Susie

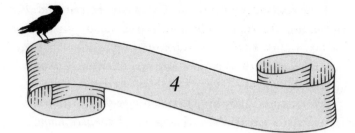

4

Friday morning arrived. It was early but I wanted to finish my still life of a tangerine before I headed off to the Codringtons. If I left it until Monday morning, the delicate green leaf I'm struggling with will be all dry and crispy by the time I'm back in the studio. I got out of bed and only woke up fully under the gush of the shower as I pondered what underwear I was going to put on. A twinset would give a little bit of confidence for a weekend with new acquaintances.

The stairs creaked as I tiptoed on wet feet back up to my bedroom, which slopes with the gentle slump of the cottage. I went straight for the chest of drawers which sits at a jaunty angle to the right of my bed. That's where I keep carefully folded and delicately layered brassieres and bottoms. I am not half as prescriptively tidy with the rest of the house but these scented-paper lined drawers deserve extra special care. I chose a bright pink, lacy twinset to slip into.

I was pleased to have another commission. I needed more pennies in my *Rue Saint Honoré* pot, and I was all too aware of Christmas drawing near and the presents to be gathered.

I always spend Christmas with my parents in London in the home I grew up in, south of the river. Rare bookshops, blue-and-white-awninged butchers, furniture restorers and friendly neighbours, Cleaver Square and its environs has a gentrification of its own.

My parents, Joseph and Marion, are old and crabbity. In the two years I've lived here they've hardly ever visited me in Sussex as it's too big a step from train to platform apparently. Most of their good friends have passed away, partly their fault for not mixing with their own generation, instead preferring the company of older people; while I, their only child, have so far failed to produce any offspring.

I have often wondered why parents crave grandchildren. Is it because they can have a second shot at being Mummy and Daddy, cleaning their conscience on the next generation? Or maybe it provides compatible conversation with their contemporaries for years to come, now that their own children have learnt to walk, speak, go to the loo alone, been educated, are in full-time employment and (hopefully) married to the one person out there for them.

To be fair, my parents are more broadminded than most and have always supported and encouraged me whichever way I have wanted to go. We are fortunate to have brains. Proper brains, I don't think I am boasting to claim. Interests growing up lay in sustainable hobbies, like reading and classical music, and we were surrounded by quality from door knocker to washing-up brush. Not often the most effective, but always tasteful. My father took the second half of William Morris's mantra: 'Have nothing in your house that you do not know to be useful, or believe to be beautiful' to such an extreme there was no leeway to fulfil the first.

I love my parents for the enlightenment they brought me and the sophistication ingrained in their make-up. I've always wanted to spoil them and this Christmas I had in mind to give them what they have been on the hunt for for over several years now: an inlayed maple and rosewood antique chessboard.

As I mused on this I packed my bag for the weekend so that I would be all ready to go as soon as I'd conquered the two-tone green leaf conundrum. As the day progressed and the painting didn't, I sacrificed lunch for more time at the easel. Finally, minutes before I had to leave, I cracked the perfect combination of greens for topside and underside of the tangerine leaf. I was filled with the great feeling of joy in getting the interaction of colour just right.

Colour theory is an area of painting that fascinates me and something which I am pretty sure will preoccupy my mind and be the drive of my artistic practice forever. For me the fact that any single colour changes in our perception depending upon which colours are next to it, is simply magic.

To get the combination of greens for the topside and underside of the leaf correct it was important that I held up the colour I'd mixed to the orange of the tangerine skin. Had I looked at it against the blue of my shirt or the white of my palette I would have seen it as a different green. You may have never realised before that none of us ever see a single colour. They are all in continuous flux, determined by their neighbours.

I rarely ever buy a pre-mixed colour of paint which is why the trolley in my studio basically only has tubes of warm or cool blues, reds and yellows. From these primary colours I know that, with trial and error, I can make almost any other colour. The problem with pre-mixed tubes of paint is not knowing the exact combination of primary colours within them, and therefore making modifying the hue very difficult.

To get the colour of the tangerine leaf just right I mixed varying amounts of lemon-yellow, cobalt-blue and cadmium-red to make dark green, a little of which I held up on my pallet knife to the orange of the skin. Only then could I see that I'd mixed too vivid a green and needed to add a lot more cadmium-red to tone it down.

There are various different threads of colour theory. The Impressionists applied small dots of yellow and blue paint, which become mixed in our perception giving an impression of green. This technique gives a rough texture to the surface of their paintings which, like eating the skin of a kiwi before the delicious fruit, doesn't appeal to my taste.

Hardly even glancing at my finally finished painting I hurriedly cleaned my brushes in vegetable oil and popped my palette into the fridge to keep the leftover oil paint from drying out over the weekend.

My mobile started to buzz on the floor of the studio. 'Mum' was flashing on the screen. I picked it up without bending my knees.

'Hello.'

'Susie, everything okay?'

This was my mother's way of indicating she wanted a quick conversation.

'Yes everything's good. I'm about to set off to Dorset for the weekend.'

'How lovely. With friends?' She tried to be casual but I knew her too well and could picture the hope in her expression that a suitor was in tow.

'A dog commission for a couple called Codrington. I don't know them well.'

'Well done, sweetie, you're really taking off with these. It's so clever of you.'

Mum is a great support but she doesn't like to spend too much time on the telephone, and so she quickly got in her latest technological problem she wanted my help with.

'I can't do it now,' I replied, 'I have to leave but will do it as soon as I'm back next week.'

'Thank you sweetie, I don't know why my computer plays up so often. It infuriates me.'

I had tried to help with her computer before; neither of us, it seemed, were technologically savvy.

Stepping out of my boiler suit, leaving it in a wrinkled heap on the floor, I rushed through my not very big house and placed my overnight bag, sketchbook, camera, outdoor kit and a gift box of smellies in to the boot of the car. The engine started and Smooth FM instantaneously blared out an embarrassing old favourite.

Dammit, only fifteen miles in and the petrol light came on. Thankfully I was in luck, a cheap fuel station appearing almost in response to the warning light. Why is it that the price of fuel wavers from country lane to motorway? Surely there should be a set price countrywide?

As I was drawing up to the pump, a man leaving the

kiosk caught my eye. I always think there's something tantalising about an athletic man in a finely cut suit (that's one with two slits in the jacket, not one).

I find I have to be careful not to get caught out staring at people. Recording the things which catch my eye is part of the process of getting to know myself better, the chemistry of inside and outside meeting. Indeed, this is the essence of what, as an artist, I attempt to convey in my paintings and drawings. I'm not sure pet portraits fully utilise this intuition, but as commissions tend to do, they take me away from my personal interpretations and force me to portray what it is I think the owner of the beloved animal wants to see.

Mulling on the good-looking stranger I'd pretended not to be looking at, with a full tank of fuel and a greedy packet of liquorice to perk me up, I set off on the remainder of the journey.

I think I hide it well but I do get a little nervous going to stay at places I have not been to before. You never quite know if you've packed the right clothes or got a generous enough present. It is at times like this I really could do with a wingman. Not that Geoffrey was ever any help. He had no clue about the fluster girls get into worrying about what to wear and who might be there, and he used to tease me rather than attempt to settle the nerves. Nevertheless he was with me as my companion on those occasions, and that is something I miss.

It was very dark as I bumped along the Codringtons' drive. I looked at the clock on my dashboard: six o'clock on the dot, which meant that I was bang on time, as I always am. Even if I try to be late I am never even a second out. The nightmare guest, but at least I'm consistent.

As I went through the ornate house gates the church bells were striking the hour, particularly eerie on such a cold, moonless winter night. My headlights lit up an unfamiliar car in the yard: a Saab that I was pretty sure hadn't been here last time. I was certain I would have remembered as it's a car our family always wanted. When life seemed too much my mother used to joke, 'A Saab and servants – that's all I ask for.'

The thought that there were others staying this weekend caused my nerves to jangle a little more.

As I turned my engine off the outdoor light immediately came on. Antonia appeared on the front step, together with a dog the size of a horse – Situp, I assumed. She was followed by her handsome husband. Do we kiss hello? I wondered. It's easy to kiss another woman hello without too much deliberation, but kissing a man can either be interpreted as a sign of flirtation or an over-familiar, slightly unmannerly act. But before there was time for me to come to a conclusion, Ben had crossed the gravel and relieved me of my suitcase.

'Hi Susie, I hope your journey was okay?'

'Yes, thank you,' I replied a bit stiffly.

Antonia stood on the porch holding on to the dog's collar, 'We're so pleased to have you to stay for the weekend. This is Situp,' she said. I patted him and then followed my hosts into the warmth of their home.

Crumbs! In the kitchen was the man from the petrol station. My heart gave a flutter of juvenile excitement.

'Henry Dunstan-Sherbet,' he introduced himself.

Here was a double-barrelled, wedding-ringless hunk.

You can't be too sure with the upper classes that no ring means no wife, but I was happy to assume that in this case it did.

'Susie.' I gave him just my first name.

'Yes, you've come to draw Situp, I hear. Nice to meet you.' He leaned in to kiss me on both cheeks. I was flattered he'd initiated it and I didn't mind at all.

Situp had been 'at school' when Diana and I had dropped over previously, and despite seeing photographs Antonia had emailed to me, I'd kept an open mind as to what a Deerhound would look like.

Situp was table-height, svelte, two tones of grey and he was more characterful than most 'trained' dogs. He'd be out of place in a shooting line, that's for sure, being far too calm-natured for ratting out pheasants; with legs almost as long as Antonia's he'd be a comical sight amongst the smaller spaniels. Not that this mattered, as Ben didn't seem the type to be shooting every weekend – too soft a voice and no signet ring – and as for Antonia, she's certainly not the type of woman who would relish a weekend in the company of other wives, however nice they are.

I assumed that Situp had been sent away to gundog school mainly to understand the full meaning of his name rather than be ordered into adopting country-pursuit behaviour.

I liked him. He was hovering at my knees, ever so slightly leaning against my shin angling for a pet. I rubbed the top of his head and smiled down at him. I am going to enjoy drawing this one, I thought.

Fighting a wave of tiredness from driving in the dark, I sat on the arm of one of the corduroy sofas, an addition from my last visit. Almost immediately I was handed a cup of tea. 'Thanks Ben.' It was as if he could read my mind.

Joining Henry, he sunk into the sofa opposite me, while Antonia stood between us warming the backs of her legs against the wood-burning stove. On command, Situp retreated to his basket. 'Don't let him annoy you Susie, if you give an inch he'll take a mile.' Antonia smiled with genuine companionship.

There was word of a child aged two named Arabella, but no one dwelt on her for long. Presumably it was a case of out of sight, out of mind, as she was being taken care of by Antonia's childhood nanny who Henry referred to as 'May the Muncher.' I wondered if he was joking, but his easy manner here made me think Henry had known the Codringtons a long time.

Over the course of tea, I learned that Antonia and Ben had been undergraduates at Oxford a few years before I was studying at the Ruskin School of Art. We reminisced about the beauty of the colleges. Ben had been a scholar at University College and Antonia told the story of how, when he first took her back to his room, he had paused en route at the Shelley Memorial to recite 'Love's Philosophy.'

> *The fountains mingle with the river*
> *And the rivers with the Ocean,*
> *The winds of heaven mix for ever*
> *With a sweet emotion;*
> *Nothing in the world is single;*
> *All things by a law divine*
> *In one spirit meet and mingle.*

Why not I with thine?—

See the mountains kiss high Heaven
And the waves clasp one another;
No sister-flower would be forgiven
If it disdained its brother;
And the sunlight clasps the earth,
And the moonbeams kiss the sea:
What is all this sweet work worth
If thou kiss not me?

There was something unashamedly pretentious about Oxbridge students, I thought. But I could see that although I wouldn't like to include myself in this opinion, others might if I were to talk about our art school parties. Parties had almost always been fancy dress, with themes such as 'Your favourite character from a Brueghel painting', or worse. And then there was our regular after-dinner party game (plenty of opportunity as there were many dinner parties) of 'Gather your team-mates and recreate a scene from a nineteenth century masterpiece.' The nights had gone on too late to remember in detail quite how it all played out, and with the distance of time I could only hope we maintained a sense of humour about it all.

Henry looked exhausted and gave little to the conversation. He was from the other side of the fence, a Cambridge medical student coincidentally at the same College as Alexander Greengrass. Only those in the know could pronounce the 'keys' properly in 'Gonville and Caius.'

'None of us know how he got in there,' said Ben. 'It's not like he had the grades.' He turned to his friend, smiled and said, 'Our Henry can charm the pants off anyone when it comes to getting something he wants.'

'Ben!' said Antonia. 'Lay off him.'

Henry smiled. As the conversation progressed I found out he'd known Ben since birth and they'd even shared a pram. 'Our mothers are best friends,' said Henry, 'have been since they were twelve.' He looked at Ben, presumably alluding to the secrets both generations must share.

There was plenty of time over the weekend and so I didn't embark with Henry on the boring, although I've always thought rather interesting, questions of occupation and habitation. He was dressed in a suit, and I wondered if perhaps he'd left medicine for the gold rush of hedge funding.

Antonia began to draw down the kitchen blinds, and said, 'Let me show you to your rooms.'

Henry gallantly picked up my bag together with his.

Upstairs the house was far bigger than it looked from the outside. Much like the Codringtons, it was tall and narrow, going up four floors. Henry and I were being shown to our respective rooms when Situp came horsing up the stairs and blasted through the partly opened door of a bedroom on the second floor that had wooden letters spelling 'Bella' on it.

Henry and I both tensed up but there was no need as Situp soon came sulking back out, having been barked at by Antonia for misbehaving. 'Sorry for that,' she said. 'He's a big softie really and would never hurt our darling Bella but I feel I should tell him off.'

Situp, tail between his legs, slunk off down the stairs in that hangdog way guilty canines have.

'Now, you're in here, Henry, and there's a bathroom

just round there,' Antonia pointed to a little staircase, which went back on itself. 'And you're upstairs,' she told me.

Henry handed me my bag and I followed Antonia up another flight. 'There you go, there's a bathroom under that arch. We'll eat in the kitchen about seven-thirty so bathe if you want.'

Quietly I closed the door and smiled to myself. Not often do I end up somewhere so relaxed that I can put drawing out of my mind and just look forward to the evening ahead. There were shutters on the windows but I drew the curtains all the same. They made the room look softer and told a dream-like tale of stags racing through a forest full of berries. The bed was very comfortable, with a topper and a hot blanket. Luxury. In the en suite bathroom under the arch there was a bottle of pine bath-essence, the vibrant green of which was lodged in my long-term memory, back to those happy times of three baths a day at Granny B's house, anything to keep warm. Pine bath-essence, if you haven't come across it before, is like washing powder: something you think you can smell from outside the packaging. I always think this is similar to the sensation of simultaneously secreting saliva at the back of your teeth when you say the word 'lemon'.

I poured a good slug of green liquid into the running bath. The water was absolutely baking, as it often is in great big houses with great big boilers, so whilst I left it to cool I unpacked my suitcase. A surprisingly homely touch for Antonia, I thought, was that inside each draw of the clothes chest was a little lavender pillow. Perfume for my panties. How nice.

I slipped out of my clothes, leaving them in a pile on the floor, and flicked through my book until I reached the dog-eared pages that denoted 'Mrs Packletide's Tiger' and then bathed in the deep water, indulging in a bit of humorous alone time.

I do enjoy the fact that my job plunges me straight into other people's lives. If I'm being honest I am a bit of a nosy parker. I always have been. Not in a deceitful way, it just interests me to see how other people live. What they surround themselves with and how they interact with one another. Unfortunately my curiosity sometimes leads me to a truth I would rather not know. Only two weeks ago did I come across an old schoolfriend's husband getting it on in a bathroom with her sister. It was very late. The sister had unfortunately forgotten that her room and mine had an interconnecting jack-and-jill bathroom. When I woke by coincidence in the early hours of the morning and saw a light shining through the keyhole I couldn't stop myself getting out of bed and having a peek through the crack. I seriously regret doing so, as I am left bearing an abhorrent guilty secret. For there, right in front of me and very close, was the provocative younger sister wrapped round her brother-in-law in a position I would rather not describe.

I was toasty warm and a little wrinkly when I got out of the bath and my hair, although thick, had gone rather flat. My fringe needed a puff up and my ponytail end was a little damp. I gave it a right go with the hairdryer and got such a bouffant effect I decided to leave it down. No time for make-up, I put on my pretty pink under-wear, a casual jersey, a cotton miniskirt and fashion tights. Lucky Henry, you might well think.

Taking with me the box of soap I'd brought as a gift I headed downstairs. The smell in the corridor promised a good dinner and my tummy gave a gentle rumble.

'You look nice Susie, great tights!' said Antonia who was in the kitchen holding her daughter.

'Thanks,' I said and handed her the box of soap. 'This is a small gift for having me to stay.'

'How kind of you. Lovely soap is so nice to have and what pretty packaging.'

Antonia had received my present with her one free arm and introduced me to the occupant of the other. 'This is Arabella,' she said, looking down at her young daughter. 'Bella, say hello to Susie.'

The little girl, who was wearing pretty, floral pyjamas, looked at me with a stern stare, clearly weighing up the newcomer. Podgy-limbed, hair as dark as her father's, red-cheeked and full of alarming potential, this was a child with a gaze like none I had ever met before. Finally, maintaining a heavy brow, she turned to her mother and said, 'Susie.'

'Yes, Bells, that's right,' beamed Antonia. 'Sorry Susie, she's a little tired and about to be whisked off to bed.'

At that precise moment the kitchen door creaked and in waddled the nanny.

'May, this is Susie,' introduced Antonia. 'She's with us for the weekend as I've asked her to draw Situp.'

May stuck out her hand, which I shook with as much of a grasp as I could get.

'Hello May.'

'Hello Susie. Lovely dog, Situp. Lovely dog.'

Bella was promptly taken out of the room by May, and the boys entered in a cloud of Henry's aftershave.

Effeminate as some men think it is, I do love a whiff of aftershave. (Next time you pass a string of male bicyclists in France, inhale deeply, you won't be disappointed.)

'What's for supper, Anty?' asked Henry.

'Very funny. You know I can't even boil an egg.'

'Just teasing. Fish pie's my bet, Susie. Conservative man, our Ben.'

Dinner was unfussy and completely delicious. When it came to pudding Ben jumped up and rapidly cleared the plates into the dishwasher, reaching up into the cupboard high above the kettle to produce a large bar of dark chocolate. 'Ice-cream and chocolate sauce anyone?' he asked.

I waited for Henry to answer and in doing so he turned to me and exclaimed, 'You have to have Ben's ice-cream-chocolate-sauce-delight – it's the best ever.' He turned to Ben. 'Yes please Benji, I'll shout for Susie too.'

There was no need for Antonia to answer, her smile told us all she was definitely in for some.

'I think he likes you,' said Antonia, peering through the table to Situp who'd lain on my feet most of the evening.

'Seems to,' I said.

'It's not often he makes friends so quickly. He's yet to fully warm to Henry,' said Antonia, smiling in good humour at their friend.

By the time we'd finished pudding it wasn't anywhere near 11pm, but it was clear all the same that none of us wanted to stay up late. I had a day of drawing ahead, the sooner Henry could lay his head on his pillow the better, while the parenting would kick in for Antonia and Ben at seven the next morning. May does nights, I'd been told, and parents do mornings. Nancy would certainly have a less exhausting life with an arrangement like this.

I was first to say 'Goodnight' and then quickly made myself scarce. No doubt they would soon be having a little tête-à-tête about the newcomer. Any of us would do the same. 'Footage' is what my family calls this, as if someday one of us might write a novel.

Within moments I was snuggled between the perfectly-ironed, luxury cotton sheets of the double bed. The comfort reminded me of those extraordinary years in my twenties house-sitting and PA-ing for the rich and famous. The last thing I counted was eleven strikes of the church bells, before sleeping deeply as if there was not a thing in the world to worry about.

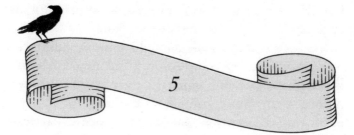

5

It was only 8:30am but I was the last up. There was a note on the table written in biro.

Help yourself to anything, I'm down at the stable – will be back by 9
  A.

Antonia was obviously cleaning out Minty, Bella's horse. A true sacrifice, if you're the horsey type, is to wait for your three-year-old to grow up a bit before you can ride together, and be rid of the long walks spent watching your little poppet jiggle up and down, and from side to side.

I flicked on the mesmerising see-through kettle and helped myself to a bowl of muesli from the table. I ate it standing up as I looked out of the tall bay window. Ben and Henry were moving the chicken coop onto slightly fresher grass. It was an amusing sight. Ben is so tall that in order to keep the coop at a flat level when they were walking, Henry had to use all his strength and hold up his end as high as his chest. The poor chickens were shut in their nesting box and even standing inside

I could hear a sound so frantic I'd be surprised if any eggs were laid over the rest of the winter.

I sat down at the table and added more milk to my bowl. As with every commission, I find myself in a privileged house spending time with the pet and its owners. A forty-eight-hour visit of walkies and spontaneous photographs. It's a key part of my process. I have to capture – intuitively and accurately, hopefully – the character of the pet in my drawing. If I sense the words 'Good Boysies' going through the owner's mind when they admire the finished picture, then I know that I've cracked it. I am lucky enough so far not to have had a drawing refused.

In every commission I am attempting sensitively to portray that look of loyalty that passes from pet to owner. The knack of capturing this is not always simple. There are two parts to it. The first is to get the pet looking straight at me. Then the animal in question must adopt an expression which shows its character: a pricked ear, cocked head, raised eyebrow. I must get at least one photograph with both these things happening at the same time. Two days is almost always necessary to get the little so-and-so to stop looking confused and trust me enough to show some characterful charm.

As I swallowed my last mouthful of muesli, in came Ben followed by Henry. 'Morning,' they said in unison as Situp crept in behind them with a slightly anxious expression and scurried to his basket.

Henry plonked himself down opposite me and poured cereal into his bowl as if it had no bottom to it. Ben pressed the button on the coffee machine, and over the sound of grinding beans Henry looked at me, his spoon mounded with cereal and bellowed, 'Very good stuff this.'

I smiled back at him, briefly taking in his strong and modestly hairy forearms as he rolled up the sleeves of his distressed woollen jumper and Tattersall shirt; this high-quality and well-worn clothing being a sure sign of a true gent. Fortunately, Henry did not carry the two less attractive common features of the aristocracy: buck-teeth and a large triangular nose.

'Coffee?' Ben asked as the grinding stopped and he raised his eyebrows, or eyebrow in his case, at us both.

'Yes please,' I replied. 'The kettle's just boiled.'

Henry, mouth full, was nodding too. The cafetière steamed as Ben poured in the water, half watching it and half turned towards us.

'Susie, if I can be a help with Situp today, just say. If you need somewhere quiet there is room for you both in my office above the garage. Henry and I are going to leave you alone. I've recruited him to dig manure into the flowerbeds while it's dry out there. He's fitter and stronger than all of us put together.'

'Going to be dry all weekend, according to the fore-cast,' said Henry, ignoring the compliment.

'That's great,' said Ben. 'It's so difficult to get any out-door jobs done at this time of year. These short days of good weather are few and far between.' Without sitting down he continued talking at the same time as he began to lay the wood-burner in advance of the next fire. 'When the sun's set I always feel it's time to go to bed. If Anty and I are both at home in the week we struggle to keep working when it's dark.'

Ben got a firelighter out of the box and practically

put his whole head inside the wood-burner whilst nestling it amongst the kindling. I could only just make out what he was saying. 'Must be bad for an artist, the winter light?'

'Yeah,' I agreed as his head reappeared. 'It's not great for painting. I do have a daylight bulb in the studio, which makes a difference to drawing, but artificial light is no good for mixing a warm colour. My day at home is over once I've lit the fire, and so the temperature dictates the timetable.'

Ben sprung up and came to sit at the head of the table. He poured us all a cup of coffee and finally sat still for a bit.

'You're lucky, you two,' piped up Henry, who had finished his cereal. 'I'm totally at the will of others and if I stopped when I felt like it, I could be putting someone's life on the line. My responsibilities are not something I can bat about willy-nilly.'

Slightly taken aback, no longer assuming he was the city slicker I'd put him down for, I asked Henry what he did.

'I'm a cosmetic surgeon,' he said with a broad grin.

It took me completely by surprise. I hadn't come across one of these in the flesh before.

'No ordinary cosmetic surgeon, Susie,' said Ben seemingly over-excited by the turn of conversation. 'Henry's one of the most successful on Harley Street.'

This would explain the finely-cut suit he'd arrived in yesterday. He must earn a packet and I guess being on the right side of forty and good-looking pays off in his trade.

I blushed, remembering my first glance of him

coming out of the petrol station kiosk. In my head I did a quick suitability calculation: knee-weakeningly handsome, very rich, similar age, probably unmarried, reassuringly scruffy out of work clothes…But before I convinced myself he was The One in that slightly eager way any single person of a certain age does, Ben distracted me. 'He's normally booked up for months with no time for weekends away but now he's on secondment and only works three days a week,' he explained.

'Oh,' I said, not entirely sure what 'on secondment' meant.

'We've got him here for an extra-long weekend.' Ben smirked at Henry. 'Eager to invite yourself to stay, weren't you, Henry?'

'C'mon Ben, you make it sound like you didn't want to see me.'

'Well, you weren't quite so eager on visiting us in Notting Hill.'

Obviously not keen to keep this banter going, Henry hastily swung a question in my direction, 'Where do you live Susie?'

He was interested in me, and that could only be a good sign!

'East Sussex.'

'Really?' he said as if he was genuinely pleased to hear it.

'Yes, just north of Brighton.'

'What are the chances of that? I'm lecturing three days a week at a Sussex university in Brighton.' He quickly added, 'Well, Hove actually.'

I laughed at his in-joke and very nearly let slip that I'd seen him on my way here.

'What area of cosmetic surgery are you in?' I was intrigued to know.

'Female body-reshaping.'

'If you Google him he's top of the listings,' said Ben helpfully.

'I've got the record for the highest number of breast augmentations performed in the shortest amount of time,' Henry boasted. 'Five before lunch; that's one an hour on a good day, or two an hour if you get what I'm saying.'

Ben laughed. His friend amused him.

I, on the other hand, was feeling a bit sensitive about the way the conversation I'd initiated was going.

'But it's not like that any more,' said Henry. 'Five years ago I retrained in labiaplasty and now I seem to have hit the jackpot. Who'd have thought that would be the next big thing.'

'Henry! You don't know Susie nearly well enough for this conversation and so I'm going to stop you right there,' said Ben, in an effort to prevent his friend embarrassing himself. 'Let's just settle for the fact you're very good at what you do.'

Henry, now with modest intentions, justified Ben's comment. 'I reckon it's because I don't let my feelings get involved. Most male surgeons give up the job because they can't cope emotionally. They fall in love with their clients and as soon as this happens they lose their surgical skills, as they're too busy worrying about whether the perfect body they're operating on is ever going to wake up again. I never suffer from this problem.'

'So, no surprise you can't make a relationship work,' said Ben. 'You have to let your heart out of its cage one of these days, my friend.'

'You know me too well,' said Henry, seemingly unperturbed by Ben's directness.

'Right, Susie, what's the plan?' asked Ben.

Relieved at the thought of getting up and out of the kitchen I suggested we could go for a walk so that I could get to know Situp.

'If you don't mind hanging on for half an hour or so until Antonia's back, then we'll all go together up the chalk path behind the house to the standing stone on the hill. I'm not sure she'd forgive us if we went without her.'

'Of course, that sounds great. If it's okay I'll do some drawings of Situp before we go. Can I take you up on the offer of your office? It would be good to be somewhere quiet.'

'Sure.' Ben jumped up from the table, 'Come on boy,' he said to the basket in the corner. Reluctantly Situp came towards him, snaking around Henry's outstretched arm trying to pat him.

'Come on doggy, liven up,' said Ben. 'He's not usually this sullen, Susie, I'm sorry.'

'Don't worry, we've two days to cheer him up.'

'When you've got your things from the car just go across the yard, up those pine steps.' Ben pointed out of the window. 'And straight into the office. I'll take Situp and his basket there now.'

'Thank you,' I said as they left the kitchen. Henry began clearing the table and by the time I'd come back downstairs with my car keys he'd gone and everything was put away. Such good manners for someone who's had a privileged upbringing.

Ben's office was sparse. It was kind of him to let me

into his private space. His laptop was open on his desk although not on. By its side was a stress ball and a notepad with various page-references scribbled down. Most likely from the tome which lay by its side. The Codringtons had not lived in the Glebe House long but, still, there really was very little in here. No distraction, I supposed, from Ben's incomprehensibly dull occupation of writing the definitive history of private banking. The only one of four walls without windows had a long bookshelf with a row of financial guides stretching the length of it. Not even I was tempted to look in them.

Situp was curled up dozily in a wicker basket in the centre of the room.

I bent down to look closely at his features and decided to rest on the floor and study his muzzle. He didn't even stir. Maybe he'd had a bad night's sleep as dogs do, you know.

I began with some very quick sketches and then settled in to a more detailed drawing, which involved immense concentration. As it tends to do, this led to a complete annulment of time and I got the fright of my life when, quick as a flash, Situp braced upright and the office door was flung open.

'Hi Susie, that's us ready to go up the hill,' announced Henry with gusto.

Situp scurried outside so quickly it was hard to believe how calm he had been only moments ago.

Henry hovered in the doorway as I packed up my things. It was very thoughtful of him not to come in. It's a natural reaction for most people to wander up and look over your shoulder, rarely asking whether you mind or not. Most stare as if they have the right to do so, disregarding the fact this is your hard work. I don't often take offence, as I accept that it's just part and parcel of being an artist. But there is quite a large bit of me that's relieved when people don't mosey over, half-pretending not to look.

Together, Henry and I descended the steps and met up with the others in the yard. I sprung the boot of my car open, and swapped my drawing things for my outdoor kit. Henry offered his arm to stop me wobbling on one foot as I squeezed the other into a Wellington boot.

'Morning Susie,' said Antonia who was looking county in jodhpurs and patent riding boots, with Bella sitting atop a small ochre-coloured pony. 'I hope you slept okay and the bells didn't wake you.'

'Nothing would have woken me in that incredibly comfy bed.'

'Oh, I'm so pleased.' She turned to wipe a tear from po-faced Bella's cheek. There had obviously been a tantrum.

'Right let's go,' said Antonia, and then on realising her husband wasn't there, shouted, 'BEN!'

On cue he came out of the house. 'Alright Anty, I was just locking up.'

I slipped my camera into my pocket and all together we set off round the back of the house and up the chalk path.

The Purbeck Hills are one of my favourite stretches of downland in southern England. Ancient and riven with mystery. We followed a route up through a cavern of green fields. Antonia led Minty, with Bella wobbling precariously from side to side in the saddle, although Antonia didn't seem the slightest bit worried by that.

Ben and Henry marched on up front and I lagged behind, taking in Situp's motion as he raced up ahead and back down to us again, tail wagging at last. Calling him he bounded towards me, full of the thrill of being outside in the crisp winter air.

I snapped away with my camera as we walked for over an hour. The November sky was the pale blue colour it goes when the air is cold and the sun is blazing. And while it was easy to get this delightful dog to express the endearing qualities of its character, frustratingly in almost every shot he had his tongue hanging out. A difficult thing for a dog to put away when he's hot and well exercised.

It wasn't until we were back in the yard, Situp sitting tall, left ear raised ever so slightly, legs ready to spring at any moment and eyes looking at me with adoration that I snapped a picture with lightning reaction, catching his pose. I knew at once that it was 'the one'.

Pleased that I'd got the perfect photograph I now had the remaining twenty-four hours to get to know Situp's character as best I could. It's important to allow time for this as it enables me, when I'm back at my easel with the photograph in hand, to strike up conversation as if the pet were in my studio, bringing the drawing to life.

After a hot, buffet-style lunch prepared by May, the men went to the rubbish dump, followed by the pub. I trudged back to the office along with Situp, leaving Antonia, Bella and May making Christmas tree decorations in the nursery. Antonia and I had arranged to join the others later for a quick drink before Saturday evening Catholic Mass.

There are many good reasons for being a Catholic,

not least the fact you can go to Sunday Mass on Saturday evening. This 6pm service doesn't keep you in with the social posse, but it's quick and convenient, which often suits me. It is a great shame that none of the pretty English village churches are Catholic any more as it means that wherever you are you almost always have to get in the car to go to mass.

Spire is no exception; we had to go all the way to a much larger town and I wouldn't have gone had it not been mentioned. But surprisingly Henry announced at lunch that he was definitely going, and Ben said he'd keep him company, and so I asked if I could come too.

Having spent most of the afternoon drawing I wasn't sure where Antonia was when it approached the time to leave, so I lay on my bed having a rest until I heard her call, 'Susie! Ready to go.'

I met her in the kitchen, and she said, 'Sorry I'm late but I've been working on something so dull I won't go into it. Male chief executives can be such bulldozers.' I wouldn't know, but I smiled back at her with sympathy.

There was no time for a drink but she offered to hop in my car and show me the way. Antonia was clearly in high-powered work mode so I took the easy option and accepted despite the fact I knew exactly where I was going.

We arrived at the Dorset Horn to find Ben and Henry up at the bar. The ruddy-faced publican spotted Antonia immediately. He tipped his head at Ben, who turned round and smiled at us over the crowd. Antonia and I stood just inside the entrance and, as the boys walked towards us, to my suprise Lord Greengrass crossed their path.

Ben stopped to say hello and spoke loud enough for us all to hear, 'Good evening, Lord Greengrass.'

Alexander looked up with a, 'Good evening Ben.' Then he smiled hello in my direction.

Ben said, 'I'm so sorry we are in a bit of a rush, but do pop in tomorrow for a drink after the Sunday service.'

'Many thanks, I'm sure we will.'

Henry was now by my side. 'Who's that?'

'Lord Greengrass. He's the one who introduced me to Antonia and Ben. Such a nice man.'

'Really?'

'You don't think I can be friends with someone more than double my age?'

'I'm pulling your leg, Susie. I'm just jealous you're expressing affection for another man.'

Was Henry flirting with me?

With no time to waste we piled into my suddenly rather small car, Henry going straight for the front seat, which pleased me.

As soon as we were off Ben announced from the back, 'We'd better be careful or we'll be going to another church service here tomorrow.' He enthusiastically reeled off what the publican, Ronnie, had told them earlier. Apparently there's a commemoration service for the flood of 1963. There were newspaper cuttings pinned up in the pub saying most of the village was underwater, several cats whose owners were away from home died unable to get of out their flaps and it was three weeks before the main street was clear of debris.

'Ronnie says the community gets together every ten years, and in his words, "Say particularly special prayers to Noah", in the hope that it won't happen again. Do you think we should go, Anty? We don't want to set the village against us,' Ben said.

'Of course not, Benji. Diana will stick up for us tomorrow if our absence is mentioned, I have no doubt about that.'

'Well, that's that,' said Ben, mocking his wife's forceful manner. 'Ronnie's not going either – says he can't stand the excessive faith in this village.' He leaned forward and tapped me on the shoulder. 'Draw up here, Susie, so Anty can hop out and walk home through the graveyard.'

I stopped the car and waited until I was sure she could see her way through the rough ground. As her elongated figure faded into the dusk, towards the glimmer of light from the house, I'm sure I heard her call, 'Situp?'

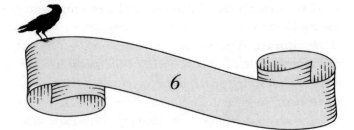

6

Slightly later than most we slipped into a back pew just before the organist's playing accompanied the priest and altar boys down the aisle. St Giles, although an ugly modern building, was pleasingly full of flowers. There must have been a wedding here recently.

Ben and I joined the congregation singing 'Hail Queen of Heaven', one of the very few good Catholic hymns. Henry obviously wasn't the singing type. It niggled at me, the fact I hadn't spotted he was a Catholic. Usually I'm pretty good at that, but there was something about Henry that set me off-kilter. It was the seeming lack of depth when he talked about his job, although right now he was so absorbed in the service it would be hard to argue otherwise. He didn't glance at Ben and me once during mass and looked pensive to the point that I thought he could be genuinely troubled.

Ben and I were out of the church swiftly after the last hymn but Henry got stuck behind a gaggle of tottering old ladies. He towered above them, smiling at last towards Ben and me standing by the car. As soon as he'd seen us we got inside; it was another cold, dark night.

'Great to see a full church,' said Henry, climbing into the back seat.

'Yes,' agreed Ben. 'I wasn't expecting that, although I don't come here often, only when my family are staying really. Not very good of me.'

'It's hard to go regularly when you're not married to a Catholic,' said Henry as if speaking from experience.

'You're right. Antonia almost prefers it if I don't go. Sunday morning's our lie-in and Saturday evening's about our only other "us" time.'

'Best marry a Catholic if you can, Susie,' joked Henry from the back.

I made an amused sound of agreement from the back of my nose and then concentrated on my driving. The road to Spire was full of blind bends, humpbacked bridges and the chance that a badger could be lumbering across at any moment.

As we got back to the yard of the Glebe House I knew from the clock on the dashboard there would be no time for a bath. It would have to wait until after dinner.

We went into the kitchen to find Antonia sitting in an armchair pulled up to the Aga, engrossed in P.D. James's *Death Comes to Pemberley*.

'What on earth are you doing with that?' exclaimed Henry with a giggle in his voice. Antonia swung round to find him pointing at the Aga.

'Oh that thing.' She reached over the hot plate, picked up a pale, white object, which looked a little like a cockatoo's cuttlefish, and handed it to Henry. I moved closer to him to take a look. Ben was already crouched down at the wood-burner piling on more logs. It was nice to see that Antonia's lack of nesting never upset him.

'Situp brought it back,' she said, 'I'm drying it out as I thought it was rather an interesting thing to draw and that maybe you'd like it, Susie?'

Wow! 'How thoughtful,' I said, 'Yes that would be great.'

Henry was twirling the bone in his fingers. 'Yeah, I'm sure Susie would like a bit of human skull knocking about her studio. Not to worry about the law and all that.'

'What?' cried Antonia with a snap of surprise.

Henry held up the bone. A few bits of dry mud dropped to the floor.

'This is a temporal bone from a fully-developed human skull,' he said. Ben was now looking in our direction. 'Afraid Situp's got you in a bit of a pickle. He must have dug up a very old grave.'

'What do we do?' asked Ben, standing upright.

'Lucky for you it has no flesh on it,' said Henry.

'Oh *please*,' said Antonia.

'It's been in the ground a long time.' Henry turned the piece of bone in his hand again. 'I'd say it's at least a hundred years old. We could probably bury it again without too much of a problem.'

I didn't feel it was my place to voice an opinion even though I thought Henry's approach breached the law. They all agreed that the bone needed to be re-buried wherever it was dug up from, and Ben was all for getting the job done right away.

Antonia contradicted him, and with reason: 'I think we have to wait until it's light so that we can be absolutely sure we're putting it back in the right place.'

Henry backed her up. 'We also need a bit of daylight to make sure that we don't leave a trace.'

Henry crept towards Situp's basket. 'Who's a naughty boy then, diggy, diggy in the graveyard?'

But Situp was not amused and drew back further into his bed, determinedly looking the other way.

'Let's eat,' Ben said, bringing a large pot to the centre of the table and resting it on a slate.

Antonia picked up a green salad and a bowl of crushed new potatoes from the sideboard.

'Henry, sit down next to Susie and we'll go opposite you,' said Antonia.

I smiled at the convention. No upper-class house sits down to a meal (or to 'eat', as they would put it, 'meal' being terribly non-U) without a table plan. Breakfast, lunch and dinner visitors are placed boy, girl, boy, girl, with a sigh or frantic telephone call to a suitable neighbour if numbers are uneven, sexes unbalanced or there are thirteen for dinner.

'Right, you go first, Susie,' said Ben lowering a ladle into the pot. 'It's Guinness and venison stew.'

They were very generous with their wine, the Codringtons. The previous night we had Sancerre before dinner and were offered a bottle of Chablis with the main course, although neither Henry nor I accepted and so Antonia and Ben abstained. Tonight there was a magnum of Chambertin on the table and not one of us held back. We drank the whole thing over the course of the evening and completely forgot that someone had to be up early to bury the bone before the commemoration service began.

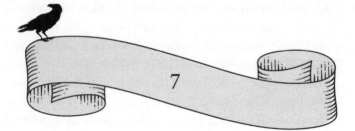

7

The bells of Spire village church chimed as my feet trod down the stairs. Again I was the last up, but only just. There was a smell of fresh coffee as I entered the kitchen.

The room was silent until Henry saw me and said, 'Morning, Susie.'

'I've made some coffee, Susie, but if you'd rather tea just say,' said Ben.

'Coffee's perfect, thank you.'

Maybe it was the effect of all the red wine but it was a breakfast to forget. The temporal bone still sat on the Aga and neither Antonia nor Ben joined Henry and me at the table. I felt a bit of an atmosphere.

'Susie, will you be staying for lunch?' asked Antonia, who was putting something pale, solid and unrecognisable in the fridge. Maybe she was a baker at heart.

A part of me wanted to disappear right now, as it's always difficult when strangers drop their guard in front of you. But, overall, I was enjoying a lovely weekend and in any case I didn't want them to think I'd picked up on a tense feeling in the room. 'I'd love to stay for lunch, but will head off straight after if that's okay?'

'Perfect,' said Antonia as she went through the open door into the nursery. 'Come on Bella, let's go clean out Minty.' She hurried back through the kitchen with Bella on her slim hip.

'Shouldn't have stayed up so late,' said Ben. 'When May chooses to take a Sunday off it robs us of our lie-in and that makes us all a bit grumpy.'

'I'm going to bury the bone now,' said Henry. 'If either of you want to come that's fine, but the sooner we do it the better.'

'I'll go and get you a shovel,' said Ben, wriggling out of taking on the job himself.

Henry grabbed the bone from the Aga and followed Ben outside. I was now the only one left in the kitchen, and I realised the bone was probably the cause of tension in the house as much as the red wine and May's night off. Clasping my cup of coffee I watched the boys through the kitchen window.

Henry sauntered across the gravel carrying a shovel, and then Ben marched purposefully across the yard and straight through the gate in the thick yew hedge into the graveyard.

I suddenly felt a pang of guilt that I was not doing anything to help. This isn't an unusual response for a Catholic, but it was one that needed to be acted on. I could at least keep watch or something. With this thought, I raced out after them.

At first glance, opening the lych-gate, there was no one to be seen. I faced the north wall of the church and decided to walk round anti-clockwise. As I was turning the corner with the porch I walked smack bang into Ben.

'Susie, I'm so sorry,' he said, embarrassed by our proximity before his eyes focused on something behind me. I turned around to see Situp bounding towards us; he must have sneaked out of the house.

Ben grabbed him. 'Will you hold him while I get the lead out of my pocket?'

I grabbed hold of Situp by the collar.

'Have you seen Henry?' asked Ben.

'No, but I haven't looked far.'

'Henry!'

No answer.

'Henry!' Ben called in a louder voice. Situp looked up at him and began to whine.

Still no answer.

'He's not out the front and there are no graves on the south side so there's no point us looking there.' Ben was making a start in the direction I'd come from. 'Far more likely he's round the back, that's where the old graves are.'

It was as we were approaching the wall of the north transept that I caught sight of Henry, ducking out from underneath a large bowing branch of an old yew tree.

'Did you find the grave? Have you re-buried it?' called Ben anxiously.

'Course I have,' said Henry coming towards us. 'Easy peasy. I knew the bone was of some age and figured that old yew could have grown up over some graves. Took me a while to find it – a neat digger your dog, but it's all buried and back where it came from now.'

From inside the church the organ sounded, 'Guide me, O Thou Great Redeemer'. Henry joined in with the congregation using the shovel as a comically large microphone and Ben and I both laughed at him.

'Shhh!' I shushed firmly, certain I'd just heard an unearthly sound coming from near by. Ben and Henry looked a bit taken aback, but within a split second there it was again: a faint but deep gurgle, and this time we all heard it.

Henry sprinted off round the corner of the church. Ben held Situp's lead tight as we followed, Ben and Situp first, with me close behind.

As we rounded a sharp corner with a supporting wall, bent back into a nook, right in front of us was a shocking scene. I felt as if someone had punched me in the stomach.

Henry, with his back to us, was straddling a man whose brogues I could see pointing in my direction. Ben thrust Situp's lead into my hand, gently pushed me back and then stepped round to the man's head.

'Leave it, Ben,' said Henry sharply as he stretched his arm out to stop him bending down. 'He's a goner, I fear. His pulse has stopped but I'll try CPR, although I don't hold out much hope.'

Henry slid off the rigid body, and he began to pound on the man's chest.

Aghast I looked down on a pitiless figure whose withered penis was popping out of his flies. As Ben removed Situp from the scene, saying that he would telephone for an ambulance, Henry stopped the CPR briefly to preserve the patient's modesty.

After a while Henry stopped what he was doing.

'You all right, Susie?' he said as he stood up. 'Quite something seeing death first hand, I know.'

What a thing to say at such a moment. But then what

do you say? I'd been unable to utter a word, and then my worst fears were realised as I saw the dead man's face. 'That's Alex, Alexander, Lord Greengrass,' I stammered.

'Sorry?' said Henry.

'He was the man in the pub yesterday,' I said. 'He's always been very good to me, and I'm very fond of him.'

'Oh goodness. I'm so sorry, Susie.' Henry gripped my shoulder firmly.

'What happened?' I asked in a voice that sounded to me as if it were a long way away.

'I'm not sure yet.' Henry began drawing me away. 'We'd better go and sit on that bench over there.'

I wriggled out of Henry's clutches, overcome with emotion. 'Is he definitely dead?'

'Yes, he is, I'm afraid.'

The whole world was silent. I couldn't even hear my feet touch the ground as we walked slowly to the bench. Henry and I sat side by side.

The creak of the gate roused our attention and we swivelled and saw Ben walking towards us with a mobile to his ear. He ended the call. 'Officer Moss is on his way,' he told us.

We fell into shocked silence. All I could think about was Diana. The service must be nearly over. What a complete tragedy.

Ben, now pacing back and forth behind the bench, was the first to break the silence. 'Did you see that mark on his forehead?'

'Yes, I think he must have banged himself as he fell down,' said Henry. 'Looked some age, so I expect he had a cardiac arrest. How old was he?'

'Seventy-five. He only stopped working full time last

year,' I said. 'He never wanted to step down as Chairman of the Game Conservancy as he missed travelling the country.'

There was another silence.

Unanswered questions rushed through my mind and I desperately prayed that no one in the congregation would want to leave the graveyard by this path. The chatter of the faithful drifted from the west door, and then the dreaded cry came.

'Alexander! Alexander! Alex!' Diana sounded irritated as she appeared around the corner. 'Susie!' she spotted me, and made a B-line for us. I hurried towards her, straight past the nook in the church wall where her dead husband lay.

We kissed on both cheeks as she said, 'Is Alexander with you? I can't think where the devil he's gone. It's unusual of him not to return at the end.'

As we drew apart Diana went straight in to shake Ben's hand, not leaving a moment for anyone else to say a thing. 'Hello Ben. And who's this handsome young man?'

'This is Henry Dunstan-Sherbet.'

'How do you do, Henry, I'm Lady Greengrass. You won't know me but I used to know your mother. Princess Violet?'

'Really?' said Henry in a surprised voice.

Then, with admirable calm, he gently explained. 'Lady Greengrass, I am very sorry to tell you there has been a shocking incident during the service. It's my sad duty to tell you that your husband has lost his life.'

Diana didn't seem the least bit upset. It was as if she had misheard Henry.

'How can you be so sure?' she asked forthrightly.

'Henry's a doctor,' I said. 'There was nothing he could do by the time we came across Alexander. I am so sorry, Diana.'

'For heaven sake, there's obviously been a mistake,' insisted Diana. 'Show me where he is.'

I grasped her now slightly trembling hand. 'An ambulance is on its way and so I think we should wait for it to arrive.'

'No. I'd like to see my husband.'

I could see Antonia was striding towards us with Bella dangling off her arm and Ronnie by her side. Ben set off at high speed to shoo them away as I reluctantly took Diana to the spot where Lord Greengrass lay.

Silent tears streamed down her cheeks as our hands slipped apart and her entire body heaved. Diana looked at her husband's lifeless body but she didn't attempt to touch him. Softly, I put an arm around her shoulder and without resisting she let me lead her back to the bench.

We sat side by side and I let a lump burn its way through my throat as my heart went out to the Greengrasses.

Ben and Henry made their way back to the bench, accompanied by a policeman who looked a bit younger than me. Large feet, gangly body and a goofy expression. Crouching down to our eye level, quivering as he did so, he spluttered out what he had to say, 'I'm Officer Moss. Detective Inspector Grey will be here any minute. In the meantime I'll carry out a few routine procedures.'

'Where's the ambulance?' blurted Diana.

Officer Moss immediately stood upright and pointed over the low, flint wall which ran along the south side of the graveyard. 'There it is. It's going to park at the Glebe House.'

Ben, Henry and I were distracted by the morbidly comic sight of two paramedics rushing through the graveyard, slightly crouched and with legs bent as if in someway they would be less visible in this position. Any one of us could have easily let out a giggle, one of those inappropriate outbursts that brew up just when they are not meant to. Thankfully we were saved by a short, balding, cylindrical man, dressed in lay clothes and repetitively pushing the bridge of his glasses up his nose, walking towards us. His legs didn't allow him to move at any great speed but his voice was loud enough to write off the last few steps.

'Detective Inspector Grey.'

'Hello, Inspector,' said Ben. 'This is Lady Greengrass, Susie Mahl and Dr Henry Dunstan-Sherbet.'

'The deceased is your husband, Lady Greengrass?' asked Inspector Grey.

Diana nodded.

'I am sorry we have to go through this straight away but I have a few necessary questions that must be answered before I can let you all go.'

'Thank you, Dr Dunstan-Sherbet,' finished Inspector Grey a while later, having ascertained Henry's medical credentials, which Officer Moss verified. Henry had described the incident from beginning to end including, in a whisper so that Diana was spared, the fact that Alexander's privates had been exposed. Nodding respectfully, Inspector Grey shut his notebook. 'Always handy to have a doctor on the scene,' he concluded. Then he swivelled on his heel, and asked Ben exactly the same questions.

'Susie and Henry were the only other people here. I had my dog Situp on a lead but he's back in the house now,' said Ben.

'Anyone else around before we got here?' asked Inspector Grey.

'My wife and daughter and Ronnie from the Horn came as far as the gate, but I sent them away before they got any further. There was no time to explain so I just whispered to Antonia that there had been an incident and I would be back home as soon as I could.'

'Who has been near the body?'

'Henry, Susie, me and Lady Greengrass.'

'Anyone else?'

'No.'

Ben answered with confidence and clarity. I was impressed with both his and Henry's handling of the situation.

As Ben strode towards the lych-gate I was struck with the thought of how peculiar it was to have seen Ronnie accompanying Antonia and Bella. Yesterday Antonia had made it pretty clear that he was not her favourite person when she said to me, 'Ronnie's a gossiping old flirt. I've told Ben to socialise with him in the pub and never at our house.'

Diana sniffed, her interview had begun and I was apprehensive about Inspector Grey's approach. He fired questions one after the other.

She replied with a weak voice but there was not

much she could add to Henry and Ben's statement, and his questions ceased when she said, 'I was inside the church for the entire service, Inspector. I AM the organist.'

It was now my turn and I couldn't help but notice that Inspector Grey's attention seemed caught on my woollen mini-skirt.

'Susie Mahl.'

'Is that Susan or Susannah in full? Any middle names?'

I explained that my middle name is Susan and my first is Victoria.

Diana looked at me with surprise as I had never mentioned this to her.

'I've always preferred the shortening of Susie rather than Vicky.'

'How do you spell your surname?'

'M.A.H.L.'

'Thanks, Vicky.'

'Susie,' I corrected.

Inspector Grey had a string of questions: Age? Occupation? Home address?

As I answered, neither policeman took any notice of Diana, who sniffed and snivelled into her handkerchief.

I was longing for the interview to be over so as I could offer her some comfort but Inspector Grey didn't draw breath.

'Where was the body when you first saw it?'

'On the ground.'

'Did you interfere with it in any way?'

'No.'

'Who else has seen the body?'

'Henry, Ben and Diana.'

'Are you acquainted with the deceased?'

'Yes, I've been friends with the family for five years.'

I put a hand on Diana's knee with the intention of stopping the interview going on any more. It worked.

Inspector Grey looked down on Diana. 'Right, My Lady.' He listed the next steps, using his fingers.

Forefinger: 'The body will be taken to the mortuary after we have examined the scene.'

Middle finger: 'There will be a post-mortem.'

Ring finger: 'You can expect a telephone call by the end of the day.'

Pinky: 'And a medical report within the next few days. There will also be an inquest.'

Then Inspector Grey thanked Diana and me, and made his way towards Henry, who was still wandering amongst the graves. Officer Moss followed and the three of them stood talking.

I let the silence settle us both, and then I offered Diana a lift home.

'That would be awfully kind, Susie.'

As the two policemen and Henry went to stand before Lord Greengrass, Diana and I walked down the path and through the gap in the yew hedge to the Glebe House.

I opened the passenger door of my car for Diana to get in, before I rushed inside to grab my stuff.

'Susie!' Ben and Antonia were sitting at the kitchen table looking uncomfortable.

'I'm so sorry,' I said, 'but I am going to have to pack my stuff and go. Diana's in the car and I've offered to drive her home. Thank you for everything. It's just terrible it's ended like this.'

'Would you like me to come with you?' asked Antonia, as she made to get up.

'No it's okay, thank you. Diana is remarkably calm under the circumstances.'

I raced upstairs, stuffed everything in my suitcase, and trotted back through the kitchen with a final 'thank you' and a wave that indicated that they shouldn't get up to see me off.

As I padded across the gravel towards the car I could see Diana in the passenger seat looking miserable and with her head hung low. She sat up a little when I got in but said nothing.

I adjusted the rear-view mirror, which had been knocked askew, and started the engine. As I turned my head to reverse I tried to catch her eye to give her a little smile but she wasn't looking. She'd disappeared into herself and I knew I had to get her home as soon as possible.

It wasn't until we were drawing up to the front of Beckenstale Manor that I broke the silence to ask if there was anything I could do to help.

Diana's answer took me by surprise. 'Susie dear, it would be a tremendous comfort if you could bear to spend the night.'

I parked the car as close to the front door as possible. Turning off the ignition I looked across at Diana, and with a small smile, I said, 'Of course I will spend the night.'

Diana looked relieved. 'Thank you, Susie. I knew you'd say that.'

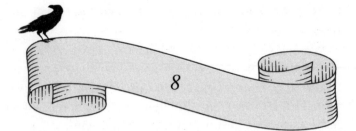

8

News had already reached Beckenstale Manor. Mary, the rather too-old-to-be housekeeper, and long-standing Nanny were right in front of us as we walked through the black and white tiled porch into the unlit hall. They stood comfortingly close to one another.

'My Lady. I'm so sorry,' they spoke at the same time, both glancing down at their feet as they did.

Diana walked straight past them and on through to the drawing room without any sign that she had heard.

I secured my handbag over my shoulder and said, 'You've heard the terrible news, then,' as they clearly had.

Mary was most shaken by the circumstances. 'Me and Nanny were having our Sunday morning coffee at mine as we always do, when the phone rang and Ronnie was on the other end. He told me his Lordship had died in the graveyard. Said police and ambulance were there.'

Nanny stood by Mary's side but didn't ask me for any details.

'Yes,' I told them. 'Lord Greengrass died this morning in the graveyard during the commemoration service. I think it would be best if you both go back to your house, Mary. Lady Greengrass has asked me to stay the night and so I'll be here with her this afternoon and evening.'

Mary nodded, and then said, 'Lunch is all prepared on trays in the kitchen and there is a pan of soup which just needs heating up. Would you like me to do that for you? The bed is made up in your usual room and there are fresh towels in the bathroom.'

'Thank you very much,' I said. 'There's no need for you to do anything further.'

Nanny finally spoke, with dread in her voice. 'Who's going to tell Arthur and Asquintha?'

'Lady Greengrass will if she isn't doing so right now. I think we must all keep Lord Greengrass's death to ourselves for the time being as that will be kindest on the family.'

'Of course,' they agreed.

I could see that Mary was about to lose her composure and I didn't want there to be any risk of Diana seeing.

'I'll call you both if anything else is needed,' I said, and took a small step in their direction to chivvy them on their way.

'Thanks, Susie,' said Nanny, leading Mary towards the kitchen, headed for one of several back doors.

I crossed the hall into the drawing room. Diana was sitting in the corner of one of the sofas fumbling with a white handkerchief. I placed my handbag on a chair by the door and sat down next to her. It was as if death had chained itself to her, dragging her through reflective thoughts and confronting her with the unbelievable fact that yes, Alexander, her husband of many, many years, had died and was never coming back.

If I sound brutal, this is because I know how deeply painful the thought is of someone never coming back. No goodbye and no warning. Poof, and a loved one is gone. The cruel fact that the deeper one's attachment to that person is, the greater the pain, does not bear thinking about.

I shouldn't exaggerate Diana's love for Alexander, now that he'd gone. They'd been married a long time, but he wasn't an easy man. They had shared companionship, I sensed, rather than romantic love and ferocious passion. But Diana would be bound to miss Alexander, as anyone would who lost a partner they'd lived with for forty-five years.

I was worried though how their son Arthur would take the news. I guessed that as he hadn't been in the hall or come to find us, he didn't yet know.

'Susie,' Diana said as soon as she saw me. 'Can you pass me the telephone from over there; it's on the table by the door.'

Once I'd got it for her, she took a deep breath, pressed speed dial, and held it to her good ear. 'Arthur, dear. Please can you come through to the drawing room as there's something important I have to tell you.'

It was not unlike Diana to telephone the annex and prey on Arthur and Asquintha's good will. Her tactic, which I have seen quite a few times before, is to ask whoever picks up the telephone to come through. Then, having got them on her turf, she asks whatever favour she wants, which is impossible for them to refuse.

This time I knew that poor Arthur was in for an almighty shock, one that I didn't want to witness.

'Diana, I'll go and sit in the conservatory for a while.'

'Thank you Susie,' was all she could muster.

I felt something of a coward as I moved quickly out of the room and across the hall, keen not to cross paths with Arthur. I was pleased to remember that I had a pencil and sketchbook in my handbag, as I felt I needed to draw something in order to take my mind off the haunting recurring image of Alexander's prone body. Fortunately there was the most spectacular pink Phalaenopsis orchid in the centre of the conservatory's marble-top table, which for a time absorbed my concentration and dispelled conscious thought.

'Susie,' said a quiet voice twenty minutes later. Arthur was standing in the doorframe.

'I am *so* sorry,' I said as I stood up.

'Yes, it's very, very sad. Mother said she has asked you to stay. Are you sure you are happy with this?'

'Of course, although I don't want to intrude on family privacy.'

I didn't know Arthur well but his ability to conduct this conversation without so much as a tear was the first time I'd seen any of his mother in him, apart from that wickedly curly hair.

'I think you will be a great comfort to Mother. She has always spoken so fondly of your kind manner. Asquintha is not as comfortable as you are with her company,' he replied.

'I will happily stay a couple of days, but you absolutely must send me away if at any point you feel it is inappropriate my being here.' I put my hand on the back of my chair trying to relax the distance between us.

'Of course,' said Arthur, who was twisting his signet

ring on his finger, one way and then another as if what he was about to say was making him nervous. 'Mother and I discussed that it might be best for you to sleep in Nanny's spare room.' He looked up at me. 'She lives in Rose Cottage, which I am sure you have been to or at least passed in the walled garden.'

'Yes, I know the one.' I was relieved, thinking this was a much better arrangement than me sleeping in the house.

Back and forth Arthur's ring went, round and back round his finger. 'If you are able to stay until Mother feels stronger then I would like to pay you for your time.'

I was rattled by this unexpected offer. Of course I would stay for Diana's sake, but I would never ever expect, nor want, to be paid. I was a bit shocked he'd even suggested it. How can he possibly think of genuine comfort as a service that could be paid for? Then I told myself that he was a good and kind man who must have suggested it with the best possible intentions.

I tried to answer without showing any offence had been taken. 'It is thoughtful of you to offer payment but I absolutely won't accept. It's a privilege to be asked to stay. Your parents have been so kind to me over the years, and so I would like to do all I can to comfort your mother.'

'If you insist,' said Arthur. 'Thank you very much. It is so kind of you and I need hardly say that it means a lot to all of us.'

Despite the fact I'd been coming to Beckenstale Manor for five years, the last four of which Arthur and

Asquintha have lived in the annex, I was still very much Diana's friend rather than Arthur's or his wife's. I am much closer in age to Arthur and Asquintha but our difference in lifestyle and their children made me feel more akin to the older generation. I'd only ever been through to dinner with them once and would describe them as acquaintances rather than good friends. Right now this conversation felt a little sticky, particularly as what I really wanted to do was throw my arms around Arthur and console him. But I knew that such an action would be inappropriate on several levels, so instead I packed my drawing things back into my handbag and followed him to the hall.

'Would you like me to carry your things to Rose Cottage as Butler Shepherd has a day off today?'

'No, don't you give it another thought. I saw Nanny not that long ago and I know she's with Mary, and so I'll pop in there on the way and let her know I'll be staying.'

'Please can you ask Nanny when you see her to come immediately to our annex?' said Arthur. 'Once I've broken the terribly sad news to Asquintha we shall both return to Mother and the boys will need looking after.'

'Of course. Just so you know, Mary has left lunch in the kitchen.'

'Thank you. I doubt we'll eat it but do help yourself if you'd like.'

I smiled at his kind offer.

'Mother and I have discussed that it would be best for you to spend the afternoon making yourself at home in Rose Cottage and if it is okay with you that we shall all reconvene in the morning.'

Arthur seemed terribly anxious not to take advantage of me, and so I replied, 'Yes, of course. But please let me know if there is anything I can do to help.'

I had completely forgotten until I stepped outside that my car was pulled up quite so close to the front door. I re-parked it at the end of the row of others in the yard. I had never been too sure why this small family needed quite so many cars but I knew that most large country estates had what they refer to as 'an old banger', a spare car to lend if anybody breaks down.

I popped the boot of my car open and took out my suitcase. I'd only packed for a weekend and was going to have to be inventive with my outfits if I was here longer than the one night. I certainly didn't want to revisit the memory of those fourteen years of drab school uniform, wearing the same thing day in, day out. I'd hated school and every little thing that went with it.

Housekeeper Mary's husband is Butler Shepherd and together they live in a very pretty two-up two-down Purbeck stone cottage at the back of Beckenstale Manor, conveniently only steps away from a back entrance that leads straight into the scullery and on into the kitchen. Like the majority of country houses, Beckenstale Manor has a front door for family and visitors and several discreet back entrances for servants.

Shepherd and Mary had, I knew, been with the Greengrasses thirty-five years. Both ten years younger than Diana, who is seventy, their working lives had meant they looked a similar age. Mary is both cook and housekeeper, with only Miss Jenny under her, while Butler Shepherd waits on everyone, yo-yoing between the main house and Arthur and Asquintha's annex. Even the grandchildren don't carry their plates to the dishwasher or their outdoor kit to the car.

'Susie!' said Nanny in a slightly surprised voice when I knocked.

'Hello Nanny. Were you expecting someone else?' Nanny looked a bit awkward, and so I explained, 'Arthur has asked if I can remain here until his mother is calmer. He suggested I could stay in your spare room. Would that be ok?'

I was a little nervous asking such a favour, outside of my comfort zone, and hers.

There was no need, Nanny looked at me with a broad smile. 'That would be just great. I'd enjoy the company. I never have people to stay.'

Nanny was full of chatter and didn't seem at all perturbed by Lord Greengrass's death. 'No surprise she wants you to stick around. She's always favoured you. All us staff have noticed that, ever since you first came.'

I smiled but wasn't sure what to say.

Nanny turned on her heels. 'I'll just say to Mary and then I'll take you to me house.'

I stood on the doorstep listening to their hurried chatter. Then Nanny re-appeared with a duffle coat on and we set off together back round the front of Beckenstale Manor, across the yard and following the curve of the red-brick garden wall, until we came to a pretty cast-iron gate letting us in to the rose garden. Nanny's bungalow was in front of us as we turned to our left.

'Lovely location this, don't you think, Susie?'

'Romantic, that's for sure.'

'Well it's yet to have an impact on me love life, but

maybe you'll have more luck.' Nanny chuckled as she unlocked her Beckenstale-Estate-blue front door.

'It's about time I did, that's for sure.'

'Oh Susie, I can't believe you don't have a stream of young men proposing. With that blonde hair, they'd be after you before they'd even seen your pretty face.'

I liked the fact Nanny treated me as a companion. Butler Shepherd and Mary were different. They'd had to wait on me when I'd come to stay, but Nanny's position lay somewhere between the Greengrass family and their staff, and frequently she had dropped her guard in front of me. Whether it be raising her eyebrows behind Diana's back or asking me to join her for tea and biscuits in the nursery, I had taken these overtures as a compliment, and so we had built up a rapport over the years.

'Arthur wanted me to ask you to go to the annex and look after the boys so he and Asquintha could spend time with Diana,' I remembered to say.

After giving me a quick tour, Nanny returned to the big house.

She was so calm and adjusted about Lord Greengrass's death that I wondered if she had known it was coming. Perhaps he had been ill? I doubted he had died through old age, as although advanced in years he wasn't *that* old.

Now that I was on my own for the first time the thought of never being able to say goodbye to him made me feel sad inside. And, I am ashamed to admit, it also crossed my mind that my days as a guest at Beckenstale Manor may well be over.

Very soon Arthur and Asquintha would move in, and Diana would move out. That's how it goes when the head of an aristocratic family dies.

I was suddenly conscious of making the most of my time here while I still had some, and with this opportunistic thought I decided to go for a walk down at the nearby coast. The unbroken horizon and crooked limestone coastline were two of my favourite views round here. I always much prefer a day with a walk in it and a blast of sea air would help me sleep tonight.

By the time I got back to Rose Cottage it was almost dark. I hadn't eaten since breakfast and so, after warming up in a bubbly bath, I made myself a bowl of pasta and ate it standing up in Nanny's 1960s kitchen. The room was dimly lit by one overhead light obstructed by a slightly wonky lampshade which I was unable to straighten. There were no chairs although there were a couple of stools, while the extended window ledge of the single window doubled as a breakfast bar. I was just finishing my washing up when I heard the latch on the front door.

'Home at last,' Nanny said with relief, 'Susie?'

'I'm in the kitchen.'

Nanny appeared in the doorway.

'How are they all?'

'Sad, Susie, so sad. I had to try me hardest to keep me emotions at bay looking after those boys.'

'Well done. It must be such a great help to Arthur and Asquintha you being there.'

Nanny said the whole business had upset her much more than she thought.

I was able to distract her by pointing out she wouldn't want to miss the beginning of her favourite TV show, and before long she hurried to her front room.

I don't like watching telly; I never have – I'm not sure

why – and consequently I find it difficult to engage with. The idea of nodding off on the sofa in front of something I could live without could never replace the joy of being in bed for me, and so I told Nanny I was turning in for an early night.

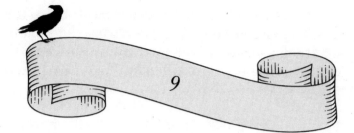

9

I t was a great relief when Monday morning arrived. Despite my conviction that my walk would send me straight to sleep, I'd spent most of the night awake with the realisation that when someone dies there is a dreadful limbo between death and burial. It's a nonsense period which until concluded gives no allowance for moving on and learning to live with the loss.

I got out of bed, almost tripping on my full-length nightie as I stood up. I crossed the small room to draw back the bedroom curtains and then wished I could do the same with the clouds. They looked particularly heavy, as if they were going to burst open at any minute and let cascade a downpour. I opened the window and put my hand out to test the temperature so I could dress accordingly. It was very cold outside, and thermal underwear was the order of the day.

I love my luxury thermal underwear, which consists of an ivory, soft silk, underwired bodice with knickers to match. Last time I was in Paris I found a boutique selling polo-neck bodices and at this moment I was very pleased I had then spent an extortionate amount of money and bought one. Admittedly, a bit of a palaver to get into, but this set never fails to keep me warm all day. Over the top I wore a red wool jumper, a mauve woollen mini-skirt and thermal black tights. You'd have had to take me to the North Pole to get cold.

I headed to the kitchen and called out to Nanny but there was no reply. She'd obviously gone back to the annex already. It was only 8am and too early for me to go over to Diana just yet.

I stood in the kitchen and for the first time in ages I didn't feel remotely hungry. I made a cup of tea and carried it through to drink in Nanny's front room overrun with spider plants. Its long window faced straight on to the rose garden. The herbaceous border – the upper-class's description of a flower bed – had been trimmed back for winter and its dark earth looked particularly desolate as the rain began to fall.

There was a copy of a trashy newspaper from yesterday on the trestle table beneath the window, so I picked it up and settled in one of the sunken armchairs. I rarely read a newspaper but now enjoyed passing a bit of time with a junky story of a minor celebrity's wife's devastation over her husband's affair with a hairstylist. It was plastered over the front page together with a picture of the couple; the editor of the paper obviously felt it was a vital bit of news.

I think I'd be more likely to read a newspaper if the majority of it were good news. Wouldn't we all feel better if it was? But then I supposed that wall-to-wall good news would be unlikely to sell many copies. I wondered if Lord Greengrass's death would be reported in today's papers – I very much hoped not just yet.

I took my empty teacup back to the kitchen, picked up my raincoat from the porch peg and flung open the front door of Rose Cottage. It was absolutely tipping with rain, so with my hand holding my hood tie tight, I ran for it. Out of the walled garden, across the yard in front of Beckenstale Manor and straight under the awning of the main porch.

It was only once I pulled my hood down and looked up that I realised there was a stranger standing right in front of me. He was a tall, thin man, with polished loafers gleaming from beneath a dark, flannel suit, and he looked to be as startled by my sudden appearance as I was his. I smiled at him. He composed himself, stretched out a cold hand and we exchanged a 'How do you do?'

'Martin Jenkins. I am sorry we meet for the first time under such upsetting circumstances.'

He must have mistaken me for Asquintha, I realised. 'Oh no, I'm not Asquintha. I'm a friend of Diana's, Susie Mahl.'

He apologised and explained he was the family's private client solicitor.

As I reached for the door handle to let us in I explained that Arthur had rung me the previous afternoon to say that the family solicitor was coming first thing this morning. 'I'm in the unusual position of being included in the family affairs despite being unrelated,' I added.

I hadn't realised that Martin had in fact rung the doorbell before we'd shaken hands and consequently Arthur was walking through the hall towards us as we entered. There was no sign of Butler Shepherd, which was odd.

'Good morning, Martin,' said Arthur, shaking his

hand, and then looking over the solicitor's shoulder to nod a greeting at me.

Martin offered his condolences.

'Thank you,' said Arthur. 'Let's go through. Mother and Asquintha are in the library. I'll take your coats.'

Martin removed his long trench coat and I took off my waterproof. Arthur hung them on pegs in the porch and then led the way to the library. He held open the door as we entered the musty room. Both walls either side of us were lined head to toe with books, and the cabinets that encased them were tall, thin and tidy; rather like Martin, I thought.

Diana and Asquintha both stood up on opposite sides of the oval mahogany table. It was the first time I'd seen Asquintha since being here. Her dress sense had always amused me as she so routinely wore provocative clothing for a member of such a conservative English family. Her leopard-print leggings were a particularly strange choice this morning, considering the circumstances, but at least her good figure minimised the excess attention they drew.

'Thank you for coming, Martin,' said Diana as she walked towards him and shook his hand.

I smiled at Asquintha to say hello. She had never been jealous of my relationship with Diana, and she didn't seem the least bit disapproving that I was included in this particularly personal family meeting.

Martin clasped Diana's hand in both of his and said, 'I am so dreadfully sorry that your dear husband has passed away.'

I could tell by Diana's stiffness that she felt Martin had overstepped an invisible line between solicitor and client.

'You must be the Countess of Greengrass,' said Martin as he turned to Asquintha, who was edging her way up the table.

Diana rebuked, 'Until my husband has been buried, we shall not be publicly using our newly acquired titles.'

Asquintha shot a knowing look at Arthur. He was clearly torn between mother and wife, and so he smiled at both of them in an obvious effort to avoid disloyalty to either.

Martin apologised for his presumption to Diana.

'Pleased to meet you, Lady Cornfield,' he then said to Asquintha, and without an ounce of inhibition Asquintha kissed him hello on both cheeks at the same time as shaking his hand.

'Please call me Asquintha,' she added as she drew away.

'I see you have met Susie Mahl,' said Diana in a snappish tone. 'I've asked her to stay with us for a while.'

Martin spoke to the room. 'This is a private meeting and therefore I must ask if it has been agreed by all members of the family present that Susie Mahl is in fact permitted to be present?'

'She certainly is,' announced Diana, without the slightest consultation with her son and his wife.

'Well,' said Martin easing the atmosphere. 'It's always good to have a close friend you can all call on.'

This was a nice way of putting it; I decided I liked Martin.

'She's a trustworthy girl and is a great comfort to me,' said Diana, to show that she had some personal differences with Asquintha.

'Let's sit,' announced Arthur with an authority I'd not

seen in him before. 'Martin, you take the head of the table; Susie, if you could be beside mother.'

I went around the table and sat down opposite Arthur and Asquintha.

I wondered whether on the death of the head of a family comes not only title and estate to the eldest son, but with this an embedded sense of leadership. It certainly seemed to be the case here, as previously I had always thought Arthur quite mealy-mouthed.

Martin laid his briefcase on the table. 'This is the most difficult part of my job,' he began, 'and I am sorry we all have to come together to discuss the late Lord Greengrass's affairs.' I thought he must be a bit nervous as he was pushing the top of his biro in and out against the table, but fortunately it made no sound. 'If at any point you want to stop the dialogue and continue at another time that is absolutely fine. I, as the executor of Lord Greengrass's will, have twelve months' grace from the end of this month to submit the inheritance tax forms. However, as there is going to be tax payable, and interest starts running on this sum from six months after date of death, it is advisable to submit the forms as soon as practical.' The pen-action stopped and Martin looked down the table at us all with a serious expression. 'In my experience the sooner legal requirements are conformed to the better it is for the peace of the family.'

Without a second's silence, Diana chivvied, 'Arthur and I are well aware of what you are here to discuss. We have come prepared.' She looked across the table and gave her son a nod. 'And we're hoping we can deal with the whole business today.'

'Right, let's begin.' Martin shuffled through the papers

in his briefcase, taking a large wodge out and dividing it up into two piles in front of him. 'The main purpose of us meeting today is to go through Lord Greengrass's will, trusts and any gifts he made. From this it will become clear how I calculate the inheritance tax due on his estate, as well as give you, Arthur,' Martin looked up from his foray, 'an understanding of the affairs in hand.'

I knew that the word 'estate', when used in the context of a will, referred to the sum total of Alexander's assets and liabilities, and not only Beckenstale Manor and its land.

'Lord Greengrass's affairs are reasonably easy to navigate,' Martin said as he passed the substantial piles of papers down the table to Diana and Arthur. 'He was a financially shrewd man and had no loans, debts or mortgages.'

Arthur placed the papers between him and Asquintha. Diana looked up and then did the same for me.

'Clarity is the most important element of our discussion,' said Martin, 'and matters of law are bound up with complicated conventions so you must forgive me if at times I go in to extended detail. I am afraid it is necessary for facilitating the paperwork which I will have to get in order soon after this meeting.'

Martin had clearly mastered the skill of being both sympathetic and to the point with a bereaved family. His was a job that, I surmised, would usually be reserved for those later in their career. I also noticed that although Martin's clothes blended in with his upper-class clients, his shoes gave away a more modest background. No gent would ever have countenanced brown shoes with a dark suit. Martin's were a light shade of unmistakable brown.

'Turning to page two of my summary of the position, you'll see, Lady Greengrass, that your husband signed a trust document naming you as the sole beneficiary of his pension. In the appendices, which begin on page 62, are the details of its investments as well as the contact details of your fund manager. The full value of the pension will be passed on to you inheritance-tax free, but you will have to pay tax on income taken.'

Diana seemed to know more about their personal finances than I gave her credit for, as she nodded knowledgeably.

Martin went on. 'Income tax is due on any withdrawals the beneficiary takes from the fund if the deceased was seventy-five or over at time of death. The beneficiary, in this case you, has to pay their highest marginal rate of tax, be it twenty, forty or forty-five percent as your financial adviser can explain. I should point out that you also have an option that instead of making withdrawals from the fund year on year, you could receive the pension as a single lump-sum payment, although this would be subject to a tax charge of forty-five percent.'

Diana continued to nod as I shuddered inwardly at the thought of such high rates of tax.

'Lord Greengrass's ISA fund follows the same instruction as his pension, left to his spouse, inheritance-tax free. To limit the inheritance liability I suggested Lord Greengrass left both these tax-sheltered investment vehicles to you.'

Diana said pointedly, 'My husband honoured me as

his wife, and I always knew he would have made sure I was well cared for in the event of his dying.' She clearly felt a bit put out.

The combined value of the pension and ISA, shown in the document on top of the pile of papers between Diana and me, I could see was a substantial amount of money to live off.

As a non-member of the family and non-beneficiary, I felt increasingly uncomfortable being at this meeting, finding it utterly extraordinary that these private matters were so exposed to me when I was neither an executor nor a trustee. The only explanation I could think of is that, in some tragic way, I was filling the void of Diana's deceased and much-missed daughter.

The meeting moved on to 'Dispositions'.

Martin looked towards Arthur, and then looked at the paper before him as he said, 'Your father's situation is not particularly straightforward. As you will have been aware, Beckenstale Manor was gifted to you during your father's lifetime. Aside from the house, the Manor comprises four workers' cottages, two gatehouses, several farm buildings as well as any additional structures for the housing of livestock and/or poultry; there are 1,410 acres of woods and 500 acres of parkland together with the lake, the gardens, greenhouses and follies. The gift when made was a "PET". However, because your father died within three years of the transfer, the full value of the Manor is included in his estate for inheritance tax purposes.'

Martin looked towards Arthur but only Asquintha returned his eye contact.

'Are you familiar with PETs and the seven-year rule?' Martin asked her.

Arthur turned to Asquintha who answered 'No.'

Diana took an exaggerated breath.

I looked closely at Asquintha, quite admiring her apparent total disregard of Diana's pointed behaviour.

'A lifetime gift is known as a "Potentially Exempt Transfer" because the donor has to live seven years without occupying or retaining any enjoyment of the property (unless he pays a full market rent for its use) in order for it to qualify as a gift on which no inheritance tax is payable,' Martin explained. 'In this case, Arthur, your father gifted his property to you on the fifth of September two years ago. But because your father, the donor, has died within three years of the gifting, the PET has failed. As a consequence the whole property will fall into the taxable estate and its value is aggregated with his other assets for inheritance tax purposes.'

Asquintha looked crestfallen. Both Diana and Arthur knew about PETs obviously, and they looked more calmly at the bits of paper in front of them.

It was all rather fascinating to me. I don't come from an aristocratic family or a family with assets, whether that be stocks and shares or multiple properties.

However, in the not too distant past, the Mahls enjoyed a brief spurt of fortune. Three generations ago my family made a lot of money by producing a savoury spread. They created a sensational anchovy paste to go on toast or crumpets at afternoon tea and quickly followed it up with a salmon variation. The money from these popular pastes enabled two generations of us Mahls to live in large houses with an array of servants.

As is the case still, people with money enjoy spending time with people who have money. Invitations flooded in, and my ancestors hopped from estate to estate, shooting in the winter, tennis and croquet in the summer, fishing in the autumn, while spring was usually spent in the Alps skiing in one resort or another. Despite the fact that our money was made in trade, a frowned-upon source by the highest classes, we had the lifestyle to match theirs and the money to boot.

It wasn't long of course before drink, reckless invest-ment and a futile attempt to branch out in America stripped us of our cash and soon after, our privileged circumstances and thus had us dropped from a very high height.

My father, the great grandson of the successful con-dimenteur, was close enough generationally to have had, in his infant years, friends with large country seats. So when aged eight I succeeded in a fully-funded scholar-ship into private education, acquaintances could be re-established and we were accepted back to the rich people's network. Now, the fact that I can talk about public schools, drop legitimate double-barrelled names into conversation and know not to write comments in a visitors' book, means my chances are improved of weekend invitations to beautiful country estates.

To be fair I have many genuinely kind, nice and loyal posh friends from school. Of course they are easily rid-iculed, but I do enjoy their company and would hate to seem bitter or ungrateful, even when very occasionally I am made to feel just for a moment something like a poor relation.

I collected my thoughts to find Martin still talking. 'We will discuss the inheritance tax calculation towards the end of this meeting but for now I must talk you through the most profitable transaction from the land in the last twenty years.' Martin flicked his tongue between his forefinger and thumb and, turning over the piece of paper in front of him, he continued, 'Taking into account capital gains tax on any profits made brings to the top of the list the sale of ten acres on the far western boundary of Beckenstale estate to a property develop- ment company eighteen years ago.'

Diana abruptly interrupted at this point to say, 'Yes, yes, my husband included us in his successful sale that brought in a million pounds, and so there's no need to go in to detail about the ghastly affordable housing we enabled.'

I knew the development they were discussing. It was three miles away from the Manor and there was 1,410 acres of forestry lying between it and the manor house, and so I didn't have a huge amount of sympathy. In fact, it does annoy me when grand people bang on about how idyllic where they live is and are reluctant to sell a tiny corner of their vast amount of land to allow other people the opportunity to live somewhere beautiful too. Actually, I thought Alexander had been clever to make a good financial return at the same time as helping pro- vide homes to those in need.

At this point Martin paid undue attention to his biro, pushing it in and out of the table again. Then he looked straight at Diana, 'I'm afraid I must go in to detail about this sale as it brought in a much larger sum of money than you have suggested. This sum was split in half, and part went in to the estate account, a quarter of which was spent on wood regeneration and the remainder into the Greengrass charitable trust.'

'Oh,' was all Diana said, clearly out of her depth, and without the knowledge to protest.

'Moving on then to the charitable trust. This is its own legal entity, governed by trust documents, which you both have a copy of in front of you. Lord Greengrass was the sole trustee and under his will he appointed you Arthur to be the sole trustee in his place.'

Martin clarified the position regarding the charitable trust, pointing out that it was unusual for a trust to only have one trustee, and he recommended that Arthur appoint two, ensuring no disagreements with the tax office.

After detailing the terms of the charitable trust Martin highlighted the largest donation to date, a considerable annuity to a Cambridge college. This seemed to come as a surprise to Diana as her head tilted sharply to one side.

I thought there probably was a good reason why Alexander hadn't appointed any trustees, but I couldn't prevent a small shiver of suspicion.

Martin told Arthur, 'My advice to you as beneficiary is to direct donations from Beckenstale Estate income into the charitable trust, therefore qualifying for an income tax deduction on the gift.'

'Yes, I see,' said Arthur who seemed to grasp exactly what Martin was getting at.

'If you retain the current annuities then there is no need to draw up fresh paperwork and we can proceed to other matters,' Martin continued.

Diana's high-pitched, little cough interrupted Martin at this point as a clear sign of interjection.

But then she noticed that we were about to move to a section with the heading 'Lady Greengrass's inheritance' and an awkward moment was averted.

Martin was looking down the table at Diana. 'As you are the wife of the late Lord Greengrass, you are what's referred to as an exempt beneficiary and therefore there is no inheritance tax due on anything he left you in his will.'

Interestingly, among such inanimate objects, as car and loose change was 'Susie Mahl's portrait of Harriet'. This amused me.

'It is worth mentioning,' said Martin, 'that all jewellery, described in detail on pages 53 to 59' – thank goodness, I couldn't help thinking as this meeting had gone on for a very long time, we were nearly at the end as appendices began on page 66 – 'has been left to you, Arthur. This has been the tradition in the Greengrass family over several generations with the unspoken understanding that it will pass together with the family title down the male line and therefore remain within the family.'

The annotated list of pearls, precious and semi precious stones, rings, necklaces, bracelets and brooches was endless, with each item described in elaborate detail. Lucky, lucky daughters if any are on the way.

'Martin, are you absolutely certain my husband stated that all these pieces of jewellery were to be passed on at his death rather than mine?' squeaked Diana.

'Yes, that is correct. On effect of your husband's death every piece of jewellery is directly inherited by his eldest son.'

I didn't dare look towards Asquintha. But Diana took out her handkerchief and flapped it around to distract us from her lack of generosity.

But Martin continued. 'You will need to forward me

bank statements, utility bills and other outstanding bills to date, Lady Greengrass. And Arthur, your next step will be to change all bills and servants' payroll into your name to become effective as of the 27th November.'

Arthur nodded.

'Now I will talk you through the distribution of the estate's assets,' Martin went on. 'It's simple, and is now wholly and solely in your name, Arthur.'

Arthur mumbled something in Asquintha's ear. It made her smile and she squeezed his hand in return. Diana noticed and tapped the table, thus giving Martin a cue to continue.

Martin leafed through the last few pieces of paper in front of him. 'As the executor of the late Lord Greengrass's will I am responsible for paying the inheritance tax on his estate.'

He explained the fundaments, and then he scribbled a few figures down in the margin of his note pad. 'Totting this all up I've come up with an approximate figure based on my provisional estimated valuation of the estate. This figure is included in the footnote.'

It was a staggering sum. I looked at Asquintha whose face had gone ashen, so much so it reflected brightly back at her as she stared down onto the mahogany table.

Diana seemed completely unfazed by the amount of inheritance tax owed. She was after all, aristocratic in her own right and therefore probably accustomed to sums soaring into millions. Arthur's eyes remained fixed on Martin, calmly acknowledging what he was saying.

At a mention of the gift of residue, Diana looked worried, and so Martin explained to her the Acceptance in Lieu scheme to clear the inheritance tax. 'On inheritance of the title every Greengrass Earl throughout history has bought a contemporary work of art. It remains in the family for a subsequent generation in the hopes it will increase in value enough to cover the inheritance tax bill on the estate when his first born grandson, assuming he lived long enough to inherit the family title, dies.'

'Did Alexander buy something?' questioned Diana. 'He never had an eye for art, we all know that.'

'It's not about having taste, Ma, it's about having the money to afford to buy it,' said Arthur.

'And where might this picture be?' Diana queried.

Martin, for the first time all morning, was silent.

'In the attic,' Arthur supplied. 'It's wrapped in the packaging it came in. We wouldn't want it on our wall, it's one big black canvas with a flick of what looks like Tipp-ex in the top right hand corner but it's worth a vast sum of money already,' he told his mother.

Martin wrapped up the final detail with, 'Your late husband's grandfather's American Expressionist painting will be submitted to the Arts Council England, who will assess the open-market value of the item and pass this to the minister who will then make the final decision whether to accept it or not. The Greengrass family throughout history have had a sharp eye for buying paintings before they become fashionable. With this rep-utation I am confident that the current gift of residue will be accepted into a national museum in lieu of inheritance tax.'

And then the meeting was more or less over, aside from a little further detail on what was going to happen, and Diana and Arthur signing some forms.

At last Diana turned in her chair and looked up at me. 'Susie, will you join me for lunch?'

'That would be lovely,' I replied.

'On your way out,' she dismissed me, 'would you be kind enough to let Mary know we will be ready to eat in the conservatory in ten minutes. Just the two of us.'

'Of course.' I stopped in the doorway to thank Martin for allowing me to be present.

'Goodbye Miss Mahl,' he replied without letting on whether he'd found my presence an imposition or a comfort to the family.

10

Grand houses almost always have a daily timetable and a similar one at that. Abiding to formality, and making no allowances for casual behaviour. Plans are made well in advance and usually by written invitation: '*I know the summer has hardly begun, but Humphrey and I so hope you will be able to shoot with us on the 15th of December. Usual form: arrive Friday evening in time for dinner, shoot all day Saturday, depart on Sunday after luncheon. With love, Priscilla.*'

And days with no formal plans follow a set routine: breakfast at 8am, coffee at 11am, lunch at 1pm, afternoon tea at 4pm, cocktails at 7.30pm and dinner at 8.15pm. Gin and tonics will be available at the drinks cabinet in the drawing room from 6pm onwards.

But now it was clear that under the dreadful circumstances of death, this daily routine goes awry.

Mary told me that Diana's lack of appetite had led to wasted food and her post-lunch nap yesterday continued for several hours, regardless of the fact that afternoon tea was prepared and waiting. Under the circumstances this was fair enough of course, but I did think that someone really should have requested the kitchen to hold back on food production.

Mary was delighted therefore when I asked for lunch in the conservatory in ten minutes. 'Oh Madam,' she confided. 'I've been in a fluster about where and if Lady Greengrass would like it. I have laid up the dining room, the conservatory, and that tray there,' she pointed at the table, 'as I wanted to cover all bases.'

'Thank you, Mary,' was all I said. It was not my place to start changing the routine, although I longed to for the benefit of the servants.

Lunch was hot minestrone soup, but the conservatory was decidedly chilly, and there was a dreadful racket of the rain falling on the glass roof. The watery, blurred view, out the windows almost convinced me I was crying.

But nothing, it seemed, was going to distract Diana, who furiously stirred her soup back and forth round her bowl with an enormous silver spoon, venting her frustration as regards Arthur's marriage outside his class.

'All those explanations, Susie, of laws and conventions, they took up such a lot of Martin's time. I found the whole thing frightfully embarrassing,' she muttered. Then she referred to Asquintha, although without mention of her name. '*She* really should go and look it up in a book and learn it, rather than shame us all in front of our family solicitor.'

Diana was being irrationally critical of her daughter-in-law, who, as far as I could tell, was behaving (clothing aside) demurely and as one should within a mourning household. Thankfully after one final stab, with a 'Countess Greengrass! Who'd have thought a middle-class girl from Kent would ever be in for a chance of marrying an Earl' the conversation took a more interesting turn.

'Henry Dunstan-Sherbet, Susie.'

She said it as if I knew him well. Maybe she thought I did.

'It's a different matter when women marry into the lower classes. You can see it with his mother, Princess Violet in her own right, don't you think? We used to know her but then we lost touch. Partly because their house isn't big enough for weekend parties and partly because quite frankly Graham is just not, you know, our type.'

'Ben Codrington and Henry are old friends,' I said grasping hold of what I did know.

'It was all Violet's money that sent Henry to that school. Graham didn't have a penny and Violet married him for love. Not that I'm saying you shouldn't marry for love, but money is far more useful. As for that surname, how embarrassing to invent your own double-barrel.'

'I didn't know that was the case.'

'Oh yes. You can tell by the awful nouveau hyphen; Dunstan-Sherbet is a combination of Graham's mother's and father's surnames. I don't think Violet would have eloped with him if she was to be plain old Mrs Sherbet.'

I didn't agree but knew it wasn't up for discussion. Instead I was happy (and hopeful!) with the thought that you could get married for love alone.

'Henry's their only child. And it turned out to be an unhappy union.' Crash! Diana had instantly shattered my illusions. 'I can be sure that if Violet hadn't come from

Catholic aristocracy she and Graham would have gone their separate ways years ago. People in his circle do get divorced, you know, Susie.'

Poor Henry. The misery of being an only child in an unhappy home.

'He is handsome, with that twinkle in his eye reminding me of Alexander. But don't let it tempt you, Susie. He's not good enough for you.'

'He's not my type anyway.' I wasn't entirely convinced by my own words but I wanted to make it clear to Diana that Henry and I were not an item.

Over the course of lunch there was hardly a mention of Alexander or his sudden death.

Perhaps understandably, given the session with the solicitor, Diana was far more concerned with herself and what was to come. 'I shall have to live alone and leave all these lovely things behind. What loneliness lies ahead for me, I wonder?'

We touched on the charitable trust and the substantial donation Alexander had given to his old Cambridge college. It didn't sit well with Diana, who said, 'To donate to a cause which gave no benefit whatsoever to the rest of his family was most peculiar.'

I was intrigued why Alexander, a man so seemingly straightforward, leading a pretty conventional and honestly rather dull life, would have wanted to keep aspects of his financial affairs from his family. I had a disloyal thought that perhaps it was deceit rather than discretion that had driven him to conceal certain out-goings. Could there ever have been another woman in his life?

We'd finished our bowls of soup and with no more

cutlery laid I saw that this would be the only course. I was half listening to Diana's disappointment at being left none of the precious family jewellery as I stared out of the windows, hardly able to see the lake it was so misty and wet outside. If Alexander was here no doubt he would have lifted the gloom as he had a pleasant way like that, but instead I found myself wallowing in the sadness of his death.

It was a relief when Diana sent me away with, 'Susie my dear, you seem tired. I think we should both rest this afternoon.'

'Yes, that would be nice, but are you sure there is nothing I can do for you?'

'You are such a dear girl to be here for me. I don't know how I would get through this transition without you. There is one small favour you could do if you wouldn't mind.'

'Yes?'

'The mortuary report,' Diana began, and I sat up as my body tensed at the mention of such an unfamiliar term. 'I was telephoned while you were speaking to Mary to say that it is now available to collect from the county hospital this afternoon. I didn't want to ask Arthur to get it, and Asquintha hasn't volunteered to help. I am hoping you wouldn't mind tootling off there after lunch.'

Good God, what a thing for her to have to ask.

I replied without a hint of reluctance, 'Of course not. That's no problem at all.'

'Marvellous. If I'm not up from my rest when you return, just pop it in the tray on the hall table. Thank you so much, Susie.'

Mary reappeared with hot coffee and before she'd even placed the tray on the table, Diana sent her back to the kitchen with a curt, 'Mary, you should have asked; neither of us are going to drink that, so you'd best take it away.'

Mary's bottom lip began to wobble but her back turned before the tears came.

I stood up, thanked Diana for lunch and left the room. The door to the library was wide open and from the hall I could see Diana's stack of documents lying on the table just where she had been sitting. A sudden, inquisitive impulse struck and I found myself flipping through the papers, heart racing for fear of being caught. I reached the section 'Donations to Date'; there was something about the charitable trust which had unsettled me. I whipped out my mobile telephone and took a photograph of the record in front of me.

Diana was in the hall when I stepped out from the library.

'Susie!' she said. 'Are you looking for something?'

As innocently as I could I replied, 'I thought I'd left my coat in there but it must be in the porch.'

'I do hope it is. If Shepherd hadn't disappeared this morning we wouldn't have this confusion. I am so sorry.'

'That's okay. I can see it, there it is hanging on the pegs. I'll be back later.'

'Thank you Susie.'

My mackintosh had raindrops clinging to it still, but most lost their grip as I pulled it over me. The keys were in the pocket so I made a dash for the car, deciding to go straight to the county hospital. As I drove, with the windscreen wipers waving, like a mother trying to teach her baby to do the same, I felt preoccupied about the job in hand.

By the time I returned Diana was still napping so, as she had instructed, I left the sealed envelope with the report on the hall table.

When I got back to Rose Cottage I was rather pleased to find Nanny still out looking after Michael and James. I went straight to my bedroom with good intentions of reading a book.

The almightiest crash of thunder bolted me upright in bed from a deep snooze. *The Age of Innocence* flew off my chest and for a split second I had no idea where I was. Flicking on the bedside light I realised I must have been fast asleep. A sheet of lightning lit up the window. It was spectacular. Whoever would keep the curtains closed with a display like that going on outside in the dark winter night?

I picked up my mobile phone from the side table to ring my parents.

'Hello Mum, it's me.'

'Susie! I've been wondering where you are. Called the house several times. Your father's been wondering if you'll come up and see us next weekend. We'd love the company. And we have Duncan coming for supper on Saturday.'

Duncan is my mother's godson. He's a poet and lives in Edinburgh but comes down to London occasionally, as he likes to put it, 'on business'. He always visits my parents and to be fair on him he is good company, if you don't let him stray into abstract poetical details; this can lead to a late night and much feigned interest in the intricacies of an overcast sky or a rippling puddle. Aside from this, he is in fact very entertaining and tells endless funny stories in a thick Edinburgh accent.

'Mum, I'd love to see you all too, but I am in the West Country for a while.'

'You're still there? But it's Monday night, I thought you were only going for the weekend to draw another dog or some such thing?'

'I was. But Mum, shockingly Alexander Greengrass died yesterday. I was there when it happened – he dropped down dead in Spire graveyard during the Sunday service.'

'Oh Susie, how awful,' said my mother. 'I do feel for his wife. It's not nice in old age when one goes before the other.'

Even though she does not know the Greengrasses, I was surprised Mum was not a little more sympathetic to the situation. She could at least empathise with the position I was in.

I angled for some motherly love. 'It's been such a shock seeing death first-hand, Mum.'

'Well, death happens to us all, Susie.'

This wasn't quite the response I was looking for. I know she would be miserable without my father, but somehow she seemed unable to draw a parallel between herself and Diana.

'I won't be able to come this weekend,' I said abruptly, though her silence made me follow up with an explanation. 'Arthur, Diana's son, has asked me to stay for a couple of days to comfort his mother. I would like to be here for her particularly as they don't know yet why Alexander died.'

'Susie, you mustn't let them blackmail you into giving up your time. It's the usual thing of people thinking artists always have time, as if they are permanently on holiday.'

Mum was protecting me but it wasn't what I needed. I wanted to talk about the ins and outs of death, and let out all the feelings I had bottled up over the last two days. But this conversation wasn't heading that way.

Resigned to the fact that little comfort was going to come down the telephone line, I continued without letting on that this had hurt me. 'Don't worry, Mum, they've given me a room in Nanny's sweet cottage in the rose garden. Arthur offered to pay me but I didn't accept.'

'Why on earth not?' said my mother, who was always wanting me to have a little more money than my art earned me.

'Mum. Diana and Alexander have been so kind to me over the years. It's nice to be able to do something for them in return.' My voice was agitated again. Parents are so good at pushing the wrong buttons. I tried one last time for some comfort. 'It is such a shock that Alexander just dropped down dead.'

'Yes. Well, we'll hear all the details when we next see you. Just give us a call when you are back home again and we'll make a plan. Oh, and please don't forget to order my rail card online.'

I didn't want our conversation to end just yet. 'How are you and Dad?' I said. But Mum had hung up.

I knew I shouldn't be surprised; my mother is worse than me about the telephone, using it purely as a means to make a plan and rarely as a medium to have a proper conversation, let alone give affection. I didn't dwell on that; it used to upset me but I'm grown up now and it's not like she's ever going to change.

Having left the Codringtons in a rush yesterday I felt I owed them a call. Particularly as it was looking unlikely that I was going to be able to keep to the terms of producing a drawing within two weeks of visiting Situp.

I got up from the bed and paced round the room with the phone in my hand as the dialling tone sounded.

'Hi Antonia, it's Susie.'

'Susie, how *are* you? And how is Diana?'

'It's been a long day, that's for sure. The family solicitor was here all morning, and Diana took to her bed after lunch and I wouldn't be surprised if she's still fast asleep.'

'Are you okay?'

'Yes, thank you, it's nice to be here for Diana.'

I sat back down on the bed, relaxed that we were now talking.

'Is there anything we can do?' asked Antonia.

'I don't think so.'

'And how is Arthur?'

'Poor Arthur spent the majority of yesterday evening on the telephone letting people know his father had died. Awful job to have to carry out.'

'It really is wretched. Ben has been quite knocked by the whole thing, and as for Henry, after inviting himself to stay he rushed off as soon as he could. I don't blame him but it's always a bore to have catered for people in advance and end up being left with far too much food in the house.'

'How annoying,' I replied, although without too

much sympathy as it was understandable Henry might have wanted to leave asap.

'We've all been wondering if you know how Alexander died?'

'I don't, but hopefully there will be news soon.'

'Something about it seems very strange to me.'

I was inclined to agree with her but not wanting to speculate I dodged the conversation. 'I'm going to stay here for a few days and so I was ringing to say I am sorry but I don't think I'll have your drawing finished within two weeks.'

'There's absolutely no rush, Susie, I really mean it. Don't begin to think about that right now.'

'Thank you so much for understanding. I'll start it as soon as I'm back in my studio. He's a lovely dog, Situp, and I have plenty of material to go on, and so hopefully you'll be pleased with the end result.'

'I've no doubt about that, Susie.'

'Thank you, I had such a nice time staying with you.'

'We enjoyed having you too. Please call if you need anything.'

'Of course. Bye Antonia.'

'Bye Susie.'

I hung up and pulled the rug from the foot of my bed over me. It was cold in my room, the windows were single-glazed and the magenta velvet curtains, although thick, were not double-lined. The rain hammered at the glass and I suddenly wanted to be back in my own cottage in front of the wood-burner with my sheepskin slippers on and a plate of hot buttered toast and honey. This was not an option, however, although the thought of the toast made my tummy rumble. I didn't feel as if I could be bothered to cook but I definitely had a craving for comfort food.

Extracting myself from under the rug, I picked up the hot-water bottle from the bedside table and went down the short corridor into the kitchen. The only thing worth looking at in here was the view, but it was dark now. I pulled down the pale-mint window blind and went to flick the switch on the kettle. The cupboard above it was ajar and to my delight a packet of dark-chocolate digestive biscuits winked at me. Perfect. I reached my arm up and rustled several out of the packet. When the kettle popped I filled up my hottie, made a strong cup of tea and returned to my room for an early night.

I had the most recent *Week* magazine in my handbag, and so once I'd slipped into my nightie, I lay in bed slurping tea, eating biscuits and reading it backwards as I always do. It's far more engaging this way round, leaving the drab current affairs to the end.

I heard Nanny come in at nine and flicked off my sidelight before she had time to discover I was still awake. I needed sleep and didn't want to embark on an inevitable late night of gossiping.

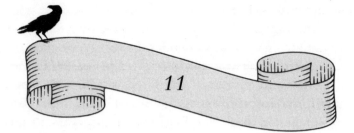

11

At 9am I was woken by a rat-a-tat-tat at my door.
'Susie?'

'Yes?' I scrabbled to find the bedside light switch.

'I'm going to make some porridge, and so would you
like some?'

'Yes please, I'll be up in a sec.'

Nanny's footsteps faded down the corridor as I rose
from the bed, pulled on some woolly socks and wrapped
myself in the towelling dressing gown hanging on the
back of the door.

I stared down the corridor into the kitchen at Nanny's
marvellous clashing skirt and second-hand woollen
jumper. Her back was to me, leaning over the cooker,
stirring a pot. I wasn't used to seeing her out of her blue
pinny uniform.

The floor of the corridor creaked as I walked down
it. Nanny swung round.

'Sleep well?' she asked.

'I was out for the count. Didn't hear a thing. I hope
you slept okay?'

'I always sleep well. As they say clear conscience,

sound night's sleep.'

I leant against the doorframe hugging the fluffy gown around me.

'Did you hear any news from Arthur last night?'

'They were distracted when they got home.' Nanny raised her voice above the sound of a wooden spoon violently stirring a rapidly thickening mixture. 'Only thing he told me was that they were still waiting on a confirmation of cause of death, and further tests would be needed. Very strange Susie. Never heard of a situation like this before.'

The stirring stopped, her shoulder rested and Nanny turned to look at me. 'When my mother passed away, at a ripe old age mind you, they were quick to diagnose a fatal aneurysm. Did it within a day.'

'I've been thinking,' I said. 'As Alexander died on a Sunday there may have been fewer doctors or pathologists on duty. I suppose the inquest will make things clearer.'

'I'm not sure, Susie. In all me years I've never heard of the like. It doesn't fit right for me. Everyone works on Sundays nowadays as there's not enough Christians left to fight for the right not to. Old age got him I reckon, and we won't know exactly what happened until we hear it.'

Despite saying this, Nanny's scepticism emphasised a niggly feeling I had that there was something sinister surrounding Alexander's death. I agreed with her that unless they were complete muppets over at the hospital, a clearer diagnosis of the cause of death should have been intimated to the family by now.

Nanny added a slug of milk to the saucepan and I

took my chance to divert the conversation. 'How long have you lived here?'

'This will be my forty-second year. I came soon after Arthur was born and was given this bungalow in the garden the day I arrived.'

'It's yours?' I asked with surprise.

'No, Susie.' Nanny laughed. 'What I mean is they gave it to me to live in and I have done ever since.'

'Goodness.'

'I'm lucky not to have been moved. Some other folks have either been sent on their way or had to move to another house on the estate. Mary and Shepherd lived at one time in the lovely gatehouse, you know the one with all the ivy growing up it?' I nodded. 'That was all Mary's hard work, and it had a big garden round the back too. But just like that, they were told to pack up and move.'

'Who by?'

'The Greengrasses of course. They wanted Shepherd and Mary closer to the Manor. That Diana would have Mary butter both sides of her bread just to make sure she was getting her money's worth.' Nanny smacked her hand over her mouth and froze. 'Oh, I've said too much. Please ignore me.'

'Don't worry Nanny,' I said, touching her shoulder. 'You're safe with me. We all like to rant about our bosses from time to time, and it doesn't mean we hate them. You've been here a very long time and so it's clear how much they mean to you, and you to them.'

'My situation isn't rare, Susie. Most family-nannies in the old-fashioned sense take on a job in their youth hoping to be employed by the eldest son when he grows up and has children of his own. It's a tradition that comes with the job.'

'I see. But what did you do for the years in-between Arthur's adulthood and Michael's birth?'

'Clever Susie, you're very thorough in your thinking, aren't you?' I smiled at Nanny, as she gave me the full rundown of her time at Beckenstale Manor.

'In between the births of children and grandchildren I took on household chores. Washing, ironing and flower arranging. Once the childless years passed, Miss Jenny was employed to fill my gap. Rotation you see. When Arthur and Asquintha's children have grown up Miss Jenny will have too, then she'll flee and I'll go back to washing, ironing and flower arranging, which, let's be honest, I can do till my dying day.'

'The aristocracy have got it all covered, haven't they?' I said, which amused Nanny.

She turned to stir the porridge and I looked out of the window. The boxed hedges framed triangular flow-erbeds filled with wintering rose bushes. The layout led my eye along the geometric lines of hedge and inter-secting gravel paths, lulling my mind into a sleepy haze.

'Ready!' exclaimed Nanny, which made me jump.

I turned around and there she was standing right behind me with a bowl in each hand.

'Come on sleepy head, let's go through.'

I followed her into the adjacent front room and we plonked ourselves down in the armchairs of the three-piece suite.

'What you going to do today?'

'I'll make my way over to the house and see if there is anything I can help with. Also I want to try and encourage Diana to let Asquintha do something helpful.'

'Poor Asquintha, she really does not get a look in. Never has.'

'I know.'

With hungry, morning stomachs the conversation paused for us to eat the majority of our honeyed porridge.

'Well, I'm going to take the boys to playgroup in a minute, and then I'll be having lunch with them and shan't be back here until late afternoon. Are you in for dinner tonight?'

'Yes. Would you like me to cook? I love cooking and particularly when it's for someone other than just me.'

'There's not much in the cupboard,' said Nanny apologetically.

'Don't worry about that. I should be able to find time to go to the shops today and, if not, I like a challenge.'

'Sounds good to me. Thanks Susie.' Nanny pushed herself up from the armchair. 'Right that's me finished. Shall I take your bowl?'

'Yes, please.' I stood up as she took it and went to have a shower.

Nanny had put on her blue pinny and gone by the time I was dressed and on my way out.

I met Sid, the groundsman, as I crossed the yard in front of the Manor.

He doffed his cap with a 'Mornin' Miss Mahl.'

'Morning,' I replied, thinking word must have gone round I was staying in Rose Cottage.

'It's nice to see you but I'm sorry about the circumstances of your visit.'

'Yes, it's very sad news.'

'Haven't seen Lady Greengrass today but I hear no one knows yet how his Lordship died.'

'Oh, I'm not sure that's true,' I answered slightly surprised by Sid's forthrightness. There's nothing like a country estate for gossip among the staff.

'It was just something I heard…and that he was in the pub on Saturday night. That's queer for sure, Miss Mahl, as he never does nowt like that.'

Where was this new gossip coming from? I attempted to quash it. 'Well, the family received a report last night and so I'm certain we will all be told the reason soon enough.'

'If you ask me, I reckon he passed out and knocked his head for dead.'

'Did he pass out often?'

'Once in the fifteen years I've been here. He was a thin man, Madam.' Sid looked at me with appraising eyes. 'You should put some weight on too, or you'll be passing out.'

I felt a little startled, but he was already turning to go with a 'Righty ho, I need to rake the gravel in the back yard. Got fair ruffled up in that storm last night.'

'See you Sid,' I said, but he'd turned and gone, whistling into the wind.

On the doorstep of the Manor sat a cat. A tiny, velvety-black one with very short hair and a bell around its neck to scare off the birds before they could be eaten. It could have been a kitten, although its quizzical expression added a few years. It was awfully cold for any sort of animal to be outside, let alone such a delicate one. I was sure it didn't belong to the Greengrasses, but there's no way I was going to leave those pleading eyes on the doorstep. I scooped it up, its body trembling as I opened the front door. The main hall was dark and I couldn't hear anyone. The cat began to purr loudly.

'Diana,' I called out, to no response.

Immediately there was a shattering clatter from the kitchen, just off to the left, and Mary came out into the hall looking a bit shaken. The poor cat leapt for its life and was cowering under the hall table.

'Morning, Madam. Sorry, I dropped a saucepan lid when I heard you shout. Are you looking for Lady Greengrass?'

I was down on all fours under the hall table.

'Yes,' I said over my shoulder. 'I found a cat on the doorstep.' I stood up and held it close.

'Oh Madam! Oh Madam!' said Mary, as if she was standing on hot stones.

'What is it?'

Mary was very anxious. 'Get it out, quick, before anyone sees. It'll be all right. I know the cat, belongs to a couple in the village. Quick, quick shoo it away.'

She seemed so frantic that I put the poor black bundle out of the front door, hoping it would find its own way home.

'What was that all about?' I asked Mary.

'Shh, don't let Lady Greengrass hear. Lady Cornfield's allergic to cats, which means no one else can have one. Makes Lady Greengrass cross to talk about it.'

Now that I thought about it, in all the many ancestral portraits hanging on the walls or the family photographs grouped on every side table, I'd never seen a cat. I'd never heard Diana talk about cats either. Dogs, yes, but cats, no.

'Did you say you were looking for Lady Greengrass?' asked Mary.

'Yes, but I don't want to disturb her if she's busy.'

'She's alone upstairs in the family sitting room and has been for a while. I was just going to take coffee up. Would you like some?'

'Yes please, but I'll wait and take it up for you.'

'No, no, you shouldn't be the one having to carry it.'

'Oh Mary, please let me. I'm going that way anyway.'

'If you're sure. It's almost ready.'

Mary shuffled back into the kitchen, leaving me gazing at a full-length portrait visible halfway up the imposing oaken staircase. It was of Alexander's father, James, at the age of about forty. He was dressed in the estate tweed, holding a shotgun and there was, of course, a loyal, black cocker spaniel sitting attentively at his feet. As is often the case, it was rather a better portrait of the dog than the man.

'Good morning, Madam,' said a male voice behind me.

I turned. 'Oh, Shepherd, hello. Have you been away?' I asked, as this was the first time I had seen him since Lord Greengrass's death.

'No, not me, Madam. The house has been quiet and I didn't want a man's presence to upset Lady Greengrass. I knew my Mary would fetch me if she couldn't cope…' Shepherd grinned over my shoulder. 'Talk of the devil,' he said quietly and I realised Mary was coming up behind me. When she was close enough to hear he joked, 'Doesn't stop me hovering in the kitchen for tit bits, mind you. Perks of the marriage.'

Having relieved Mary of a tray of coffee for Diana, I climbed the stairs, cups rattling in their saucers all the way up to the first floor, then along the landing and into the family sitting room.

'Good morning, Diana,' I said as my right foot pushed the door open.

She didn't even attempt to get up to help me but I suppose this was forgivable in her circumstance.

'Morning, Susie, I was hoping you would come.' She sounded strained.

'I have brought coffee. Would you like me to pour you some?'

'Yes please,' she replied, her voice carrying much better now she could stage-manage my arrival. 'Why not put the tray down on the pouffe between the sofas? It's steady enough.'

I squeezed between side table and sofa to get to it. There was in fact a round, Baroque walnut table against the wall but its entire surface was covered with large hardback books of country houses, garden designs and catalogues from the latest exhibitions at the Royal Academy. The penny dropped and I made sense of the phrase 'coffee-table books'.

'Milk and sugar?' I offered, pretty sure the answer was yes to both.

'Yes please. Two lumps of sugar. I have a real need for it at the minute.'

Diana was sitting in one of two elegant armchairs in the bow window.

'Mind if I turn the lights on?' I asked wanting to brighten the place up as the morning light was so gloomy.

'Do, Susie. The switch for the chandelier is to the left of the fireplace and the wall lamps go on at the door.'

With only one, albeit large, window in the room,

turning the lights on made a great difference. I picked up the coffee cups and joined Diana in the free armchair next to her.

'Are you warm enough Susie? I could get Mary to come and light the fire.'

'No, no, it's lovely and warm in here.'

What should you talk about if you were sitting in a posh sitting room with a woman whose husband has just died? I didn't have a clue. Like everyone else, I wanted to know the cause of death but I didn't feel that I could ask. Diana didn't initiate conversation either. Instead she stared down the room at the elegant fireplace, deep in thought, apparently oblivious to me sitting next to her. When my coffee cup was empty I had an excuse to break the silence.

'Would you like any more coffee?'

Without moving her head, Diana ignored my question and said, 'Susie, I hate to ask you but I wonder if you'd mind drafting a death notice for the paper? If you wrote it now I can send it to *The Times* and the *Telegraph* as soon as we have a funeral date.'

'Of course, but are you sure I am the person to do it?'

'Yes.' She briefly glanced in my direction, then returned to gazing across the room. 'I'd rather not ask Arthur until we have a draft for him to review, and I know that Asquintha would use all the wrong sorts of words and phrases.'

I didn't have the heart to point out that I am too young to have paid particular attention to death notices, and so I hoped Diana had an example I could follow.

'Do you have an old newspaper I could consult?'

'There's a *Debrett's* on the hall table which will help you with the wording and layout.'

I knew that *Debrett's* – famous for being 'the trusted source on British social skills, etiquette and style' – would keep me on the right track, and so I replied, 'Oh perfect. I'll do it straight away.'

But Diana wasn't ready for me to leave just yet. I got up and refilled both cups. Then it was as if the sugar in Diana's coffee had given her a burst of chatty energy.

'Are you comfortable in Nanny's bungalow?'

'Very,' I said, about to elaborate, but Diana's mind was darting about and she started talking as I was answering.

'I suddenly remembered last night that my car is still in the village.'

'I'll go and fetch it, if you like?'

'Well, I asked Arthur, but he's meeting with the servants this morning to reassure them all that things will continue as normal. Helpfully, Asquintha is going to put aside time before lunch to pick it up, but thank you for the offer.'

Diana was implicitly suggesting that the report I'd picked up from the mortuary yesterday had stated the reason for Alexander's death. But she was not forthcoming on the matter. I placed my empty coffee cup back in the saucer and carried it to the tray. Diana still had plenty to drink in hers.

'I'll go and draft the notice now and bring it back up for you to read,' I told her.

'Thank you Susie, you'll find a pen and pad of paper all ready on the hall table next to the book.'

I hadn't ever opened a copy of *Debrett's*. There it was on the hall table, sitting on top of *Debrett's Peerage & Baronetage*; the essential reference book for the British aristocracy. It really is quite something to have a bible for your social class.

I flicked through the index of the handbook and found

what I was after. On the Death Notices page it said:

> *'The public announcement of the bereavement and details of the funeral and/or memorial service are usually published in a death notice placed by the family in local or national newspapers. They vary in length, but should be kept simple and to the point. Essential details include the name of the deceased, residence (town or village), date of death, where and when services will be held and whether to send flowers.'*

I couldn't help thinking that most people would have worked this out without looking it up in this aristocratic handbook. However, reading between the lines, what Diana really wanted me to consult the book for was the wording.

The upper-classes have vehement rules when it comes to language, and anything 'ungentrified', as they put it, is met with scathing judgment. Silly little sayings such as, 'the only thing which has a jacket is a potato' are repeated by parents to remind their children, in this case, that a blazer must never be referred to as a jacket.

Language is an easy way for the aristocracy to single out the wannabes, I knew. Terms such as *train station*[1], *countryside*[2], *horse riding*[3], *drive way*[4], *gamekeeper*[5], *salad dressing*[6], *perfume*[7], *wealthy*[8], *passed away*[9] and many, many

---

1 *Railway Station*
2 *Country*
3 *Riding*
4 *Drive*
5 *Keeper*
6 *Vinaigrette*
7 *Scent*
8 *Rich*
9 *Died*

more if used in grand company, will expose your lowly place in the social pecking order. These subtleties, not to mention being in the know when it comes to pronunciation – 'Belvoir', for example, is incomprehensibly pronounced 'Beaver' – are inherited with birth.

I copied the example notice, changing names, dates and places accordingly so that it read,

GREENGRASS – *Alexander Michael, 9th Earl of Greengrass. Beloved husband of Diana, Countess of Greengrass; father of Arthur and the late Amelia. At home on 26th November. A funeral service will be held on xxth November x o'clock at Spire Church, Spire, Dorset BH203PC. Family flowers only.*

Although Lord Greengrass had died in the graveyard as the church was in the grounds of the estate, technically this was a 'home' death, I thought.

Once done I tore the sheet of paper from the pad and turned to go back up to the family sitting room. As my foot was about to land on the first step of the staircase, the loud shrill of the telephone sounded. I went back to the hall table and picked it up.

'Hello?'

'Detective Inspector Grey here.'

'Inspector, it's Susie Mahl. Can I help?'

'Susie? Oh yes, Vicky…I must remember to call you Susie. I was hoping for Lady Greengrass.'

'I can transfer you Inspector, but would you mind me asking if you've found a cause for death?' I knew it was presumptuous of me to ask but I was desperate to know.

'Not exactly and that's why I am ringing. It's a far

more complicated case than any of us anticipated, Susie. You can expect a call from Officer Moss in the next hour or so. As for now, if you could please get me Lady Greengrass on the line.'

'Give me a second and I'll pass you on.'

I raced upstairs and found Diana sitting in the same armchair, vacantly looking out of the window.

'Inspector Grey on the telephone,' I said as I handed her the receiver.

She cleared her throat before putting it to her good ear. 'Inspector?'

At that moment I realised I'd left the draft death notice downstairs. I went out of the room and hovered in the corridor ashamedly listening in to Diana's half of the conversation.

'Murder?'

'My husband?'

'In Spire.'

'Never.'

'No one.'

'I couldn't possibly.'

'What do you mean, you can't confirm?'

'If it's murder you have to be absolutely certain before you start such accusations.'

The conversation ended abruptly and I started tip-toeing down the corridor on the way back to the hall, but before I'd even reached the staircase I heard Diana call out, 'Susie! Susie!'

I retraced my steps to find her looking puffed up and on the edge of her seat.

'My dear, they say he may have been *murdered*!'

'Murdered?' I tried to sound shocked.

'Yes.'

It was bad news for the Greengrass family undoubtedly, and I tried to tell myself that no one could know for sure until the inquest had delivered its verdict, and the inquest hadn't even been opened yet, and might not be for a while, let alone deliver a verdict as the inquest would probably be adjourned on opening.

Still, undeniably, a thrill sparked inside me.

Murder…

How many people find themselves in the centre of a murder case without either, a) committing it, or b) being a member of the jury or the legal profession?

Hardly anybody, that's who. Other than me! I felt transfixed.

I waited for Diana to go on but she kept silent as she looked at me, with her chest heaving and a furious expression on her face. She was clearly unaccepting of the likely cause of Alexander's death.

I gently moved into the room and sat down on the firm, estate-tweed sofa. It itched the backs of my calves through my tights, and as a distraction I picked up the cushion beside me and placed it on my lap as if in some innate way this would give me comfort. It had large curly white numbers embroidered on it. The year of Amelia's birth. I looked up and caught Diana's eyes on it.

'Darling Amelia, and now my husband. Why me, Susie? Why me?'

I didn't have an answer, and I don't think she expected one. Life can be so incredibly sad at times and particularly when there is no explanation for its pattern. My heart went out to her and Arthur. I silently recited a Hail

Mary for them to find the strength to get through another death in the family.

Diana continued. 'Alexander and I grew apart physically with age, but we remained very fond of each other. I did love him Susie, however much he irritated me at times.'

She wiped her eyes with a corner of her handkerchief and turned to look once more out of the bay window, softly murmuring, 'How am I meant to rattle around this big house with no company?'

I didn't think this was the moment to draw her attention to the fact that the house now belonged to Arthur, which would mean, as had been discussed yesterday, that soon enough Diana would have to move out. In the interim, Lord and Lady Greengrass's ostracism of Asquintha could now work in her favour, if she wanted it to. She'd certainly be best equipped for keeping spirits high day to day while everyone got themselves sorted, and Diana's vulnerability might just give Asquintha the opportunity to show how capable she could be in time at running the estate. Arthur had shadowed his father for the past nine years and I'd be happy to bet that during this period she would have picked up lots of information regarding the ins and outs of Beckenstale Manor.

'What did Inspector Grey say exactly?' I asked. I felt immensely curious.

'Murder! Alexander didn't have many friends but nor did he have many enemies, and so to suggest he could have been murdered is absurd.' Diana shook her head.

'Did the inspector say why he thought so?'

'His reasoning was that as the medical report was inconclusive, the ongoing investigation would include suspected murder, as there were several things that weren't adding up. I simply can't believe this is the next step. As for leaping to this conclusion, just who do the ruddy police think they are? Common people, they never forgive us. But no one in their right mind would murder a man for a dog he ran over years ago.'

'Sorry?' I said.

'Oh nothing. My silly mind's rushing back to a few things from the past. But minor things they are.' Diana looked cross rather than upset. 'Let's get the mortuary report from downstairs and see if we can make head or tail of what on earth is going on.'

'Where is it? I'll go.' I willingly got up from the itchy sofa; I wasn't going to sit there again if I could help it.

'Face down on my side of the desk in the study. The door's open and you'll find the light switch at waist height on the left as you go in.' Diana spoke with the clarity that only someone who's been giving out orders for years could muster.

I hadn't seen the report, despite being the one who had collected it yesterday. I'd gone to the back entrance of the large county hospital to find Dr Cropper, who caused a bit of a fuss when I turned up with no identification, although soon enough he relinquished it to my flirtatious wangling with a, 'Do call me Toby'. And, after a call to Arthur, he handed me a sealed envelope. 'Here you go Susie, all yours, such as it is, to deliver to Lady Greengrass. Unusual case, this one,' he said, and with impeccable manners he stood up from his desk to see me off.

Downstairs I picked up the draft death notice from the hall table, and as I swung round to go to the study I very nearly sent Mary flying. 'Crumbs, I didn't see you there. I'm so sorry.'

'Don't worry Madam, it's my fault for not turning the lights on. I was just going to go upstairs and ask Lady Greengrass if she would like lunch in the conservatory or the dining room.'

I wanted to keep the servants as far away from the family sitting room as I could. If anyone overheard us, the gossip would fly faster than the speed of sound round Spire.

'Don't trouble to go upstairs,' I said. 'I'm sure the conservatory would suit, and I'll listen out for the gong if you wouldn't mind sounding it when lunch is ready.'

Mary shuffled back to the kitchen and I crossed the hall into the study. The mortuary report was easy to locate on Diana's side of the partners' desk. I reached across to pick it up and in doing so knocked over a Charbonnel and Walker tin full of pens that scattered over Alexander's desk. Damn. I tidied them up and then found a Post-it note that had presumably been hidden beneath the tin and was now stuck to the sleeve of my blouse. I pulled it off. It said:

25th Nov.
Dorset Horn, 6pm
077845974210
Cash

My heart jumped. Assuming it meant this year, this was the Saturday that had just passed, the day before Alexander had died. I'd even glimpsed Alexander in that very pub, when Antonia and I had gone to pick up Ben and Henry. How on earth did it not cross my mind at the time to wonder what he was doing? I knew that Alexander was an alcoholic, although he had been tee-total for years. In all the time I had known him he had never once so much as mentioned a public house.

I stuffed the note into my skirt pocket, not wanting Diana to see it. Then, with the death notice and mortuary report in hand I headed back to the family sitting room.

'Arthur! Hello,' I said, seeing him sitting in the place I had vacated on the sofa.

Diana was glued to her same armchair.

'Good morning Susie.' He sounded dreadful. 'Ma has told me the latest.'

Diana interjected, 'Is that the report in your hand?'

'Yes, and here's the draft death notice.'

I made my way towards her, but she raised her hand to stop me. 'Just put your draft down on the table and hand the report to Arthur, please.'

I did as she said and, not quite knowing whether to stay in the room or not, I hovered by the pouffe.

'Arthur dear, will you take a look again and see if there is any possible reason you can find for death,' said Diana.

'Ma, I very much doubt there will be anything that the medical officer failed to identify.'

'There may be. No one has asked me about long-term illnesses.'

I felt like a lemon, but I couldn't quite persuade myself to leave the room.

Diana added, 'It was a lengthy commemoration ser-vice, Arthur. Your father could have easily forgotten to put Lucozade tablets in his pocket. Simple as that. And you know how his prostate means he always leaves a service at least once to go and spend a penny...' She sighed and her attention reverted to me. 'Susie, I do hope you are not minding being in the centre of all this. It is a great comfort to me having you around, and for us all to have a stoic non-family member. Sit down and let's listen to what Arthur has to say.'

I didn't need asking twice although it meant perching on the itchy tweed sofa once again.

Arthur began stiffly. 'No severe abrasions – airways clear – arteries and veins clear – no evidence of heart damage – low sugar level – void of disease or infection, other than enlarged prostate – small cut of two centimetres angled forty-five degrees from left ear lobe: razor-blade cut, traces of shaving gel – slight redness of skin on wrists: probable irritation from rough cuffs of tweed suit – severe bruising on front lobe of the skull and small bone fracture – small cluster of deep bruising on chest – traces of green moss found in forehead abrasion. No obvious cause of death. Awaiting reports on toxicity.'

'How frightfully unsatisfactory,' said Diana.

'Ma, what was Inspector Grey's explanation for thinking it possible murder?'

'He suggested that having seen the level of bruising develop on your father's chest overnight, it could be that he was struck there by a perpetrator, the injury to his head being caused by him hitting it on the church wall as he fell.'

'So they're not certain it's murder yet?'

'Of course it's not murder, Arthur. The police are

making an error of judgment.' Diana's voice was emphatic.

'What are we to do?'

'Nothing, for the time being. Unfortunately for us the investigation is now a potential murder inquiry, but I'm sure they'll see it's all a big mistake soon enough. Inspector Grey is going to come at nine o'clock tomorrow morning to give us more details, but he said that we are to ring him directly if we remember something we have forgotten. Until then, I think we shouldn't dwell on this nonsense.' Diana looked much more convinced by her declaration than Arthur did, judging by his concerned expression.

There was a lengthy silence, broken by the sound of the gong.

'Diana,' I said. 'I suggested to Mary that she lay out lunch in the conservatory. I hope that's all right?'

'Yes, let's go down and take our minds off all this.'

Arthur paused by the telephone. 'I'll buzz Asquintha and the boys, they must be back from collecting your car by now.'

'Arthur, did you tell Mary that they would be joining us?'

'Yes, Ma.'

It was only midday. I was still full from Nanny's large bowl of porridge but more importantly I wanted time alone to gather my thoughts. Diana and I were walking down the corridor when (bravely, I thought) I made my excuses. 'If you wouldn't mind, I'm going to go back to Rose Cottage, as I have some work I need to do.'

'Oh, what a shame,' said Diana. 'I do understand, and you mustn't let us stop you from working. Will you dine with us this evening?'

'That's very kind, but I have already committed to cooking for Nanny.'

'How generous of you, Susie. We'd better catch you earlier tomorrow.'

I turned and smiled at Arthur who had caught us up. Diana's joviality seemed slightly misplaced, but maybe it was her way of coping with the situation.

'Thank you for sitting with me this morning,' she said. 'And please don't feel obliged to stay until we resolve Alexander's death, although it would be an enormous comfort to me if you did feel able to.'

Little did they know how much I now genuinely wanted to be here.

'Of course I will stay.'

'Thank you,' Arthur said enthusiastically. I suspected he had worked out that my companionship with Diana shielded Asquintha from at least some criticism.

'One last thing, Susie,' said Diana. 'I think you should be present at the meeting with Inspector Grey tomorrow. Would that be possible? And, Arthur, you must get all the servants together and make them promise not to breathe a word outside this house of any murder.'

'I'll see you both tomorrow at 9am,' I said, and left the landing ahead of them.

Crossing the gravel yard back to Rose Cottage, I was filled with a feeling of helplessness. The Greengrasses clearly needed an answer to Alexander's death, and the sooner the better.

Wondering if there was anything further that I could do, I decided to go to the county hospital and revisit

Toby, on the off-chance that I might be able to sneak in a few questions about the medical report.

I grabbed my handbag and car keys from the porch of Rose Cottage without bothering to go in. It began to drizzle so I ran to my car.

I touched my pocket to make sure my mobile phone was in there just at the moment that it began to vibrate. 'Unknown number' flashed on the screen, and having been told to expect a call from Officer Moss I answered.

'Susie Mahl? PC Moss here. We met at Spire village graveyard if you remember. I'm calling on behalf of Detective Inspector Grey regarding Lord Greengrass's death.'

'Okay,' I said.

And then the constable told me that DI Grey wanted to speak to me again, and could I go to the police station that afternoon?

I knew where the police station was already. Much like a racing pigeon, a good sense of direction was something I had always had. Ever since the first orienteering trip at school my friends had nicknamed me Maggy, which was short for Magnet. It's a great relief to me that they've all dropped it now.

I ended the call and sat holding my telephone as I pondered who else might have given a statement – surely I wasn't the first?

I wanted to talk to the Codringtons and discuss whether to mention burying the bone or not but thought perhaps that wouldn't be a very good idea. Covering things up rarely works in your favour, I couldn't help but feel.

Boldly, I decided to ring the number on the Post-it

note I'd stuffed in my pocket. I had various theories running around my head and wanted to set them straight.

It didn't even connect. Number not recognised. I counted the digits. There were twelve, one too many. Now I felt relieved, realising anyway that I hadn't thought through how I was going to conduct the conversation if the call had been answered.

I adjusted my seat and drove off to see Toby.

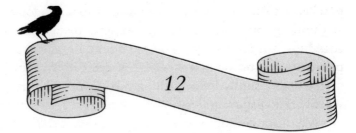

12

I'd only just walked in through the back door of the enormous, sterile white hospital when I came face to face with Toby.

'Susie!' he said, surprised.

'Hi…Toby,' I replied, and then to my discomfort I felt my cheeks go slightly red.

'Are you looking for someone?'

'I was looking for you, actually,' I said in what I hoped was a chatty way. 'But don't worry if it's not a good time.'

'I was just going out for lunch but that can wait – let's go to my office.'

This backwater of the hospital had a complete lack of atmosphere, but thank goodness it didn't advertise its function too heavily. The door I had come through was green and had a small, white plaque on it with black letters that read MORTUARY. There was a long and narrow white corridor, and off this was Toby's office.

The office was small, and other than a desk and several chairs, the only other furniture was a sofa. I sat down on the arm of it and Toby, having closed the door, perched on the front edge of his desk. I looked closely at the desk, but there were no personal belongings I could see, just an in-tray, a computer and a mug with a picture of our prime minister on it. I decided that Toby might have a similar sense of humour to mine – surely a deliberate play on the notion of 'mug'.

'What is it, Susie?' he asked.

I was slow to answer as I had now seen a small but chaotic glass-fronted cupboard behind him. Envelopes were stacked in disarray and a stream of white condolence slips looked jammed in the sliding door.

'It was a great shock for all of us to hear from the police that Lord Greengrass may have been murdered, and so I am hoping you wouldn't mind me asking you a few questions.' I thought I might as well be honest as to why I was there.

'Hmm.' There was a pause and then Toby worded his reply carefully. 'When you were here, Susie, I gave you the report despite the fact you had no identification. However, to discuss anything further, when a family member is not present, or without express written permission, goes against professional ethics, I'm afraid. I am sorry.'

I could tell by his apology that he knew I was trying to help rather than interfere, and so I didn't remind him that he had spoken to Arthur to verify who I was and why I was there.

'I understand, of course. I do know that I shouldn't be here asking for your help.' I looked at him in what I hoped was a winsome way. 'But now that we have read the report, the Greengrass family and I feel it doesn't give any real indication that there was anything on Lord

Greengrass's body to suggest a third-party attack. I wonder, then, why the police have concluded he's very likely been murdered?'

At that moment the door of the office was flung open, annoyingly obstructing my view both of Toby and whomever it was standing behind it.

A male voice spoke, 'I thought you were on your lunchbreak? I was just going to leave this on your desk. Update on Body 214, the suspected murder case.'

The timing could not have been better.

And Toby took the piece of paper from the owner of the voice, without for a split second acknowledging my presence. 'Thanks Joey, you just caught me. I'm about to head off for lunch now.'

The door swung shut and closed with a click, and Toby and I could see each other. Or, more precisely, I could see him, but he was looking down at the piece of paper in his hand.

It was hard to tell what he was making of whatever was written down. His expression gave nothing away, although ever so gently his left foot began to tap the floor.

I stared at him with eyebrows raised questioningly.

'Not here,' he said as he looked at me. Then he added, 'If you have time, do you want to grab a sandwich?'

Bingo. I found myself giving him a huge smile.

'Come,' he said, standing up and holding his office door open. 'There's a little café five minutes' walk away that no one from here ever goes to.'

I picked up my handbag and off we went, down a side street parallel to the hospital.

Charlotte's Café was out of place amongst the mews houses but it was more pleasant than I had expected. We sat in the corner at almost the only free two-person table.

Toby smiled at me as if I was an old friend. 'Do you live near by?'

'No, East Sussex.'

'Oh, I love Sussex. The Downs are so beautiful, especially those long shadows they cast in the evening light.'

'You know Sussex?' I asked, enjoying the romanticism of his description.

'I like to walk and the South Downs Way is one of my favourites.'

'I live just west of Ditchling Beacon and go up there almost every day when I'm at home.'

Plucking the menu from between the salt and pepper grinders he passed it to me. 'Here's a list of hot food, but over there,' he pointed to a blackboard behind the counter, 'is a list of sandwiches. I always have the streaky bacon and brie.'

I chose the rocket, emmental and honey-roast Dorset ham sandwich, and Toby went to the counter to order, shrugging off my offer to pay.

I noticed how a young waitress tried to catch his eye, but ignoring her Toby returned to me.

'Thank you very much, Toby.'

'That's okay, and in fact it's nice to have the company. How long are you in the area?'

'Possibly until the end of the week. It depends.'

'Depends on what?' he asked, emphasising the 'what' at the end of his question. He was teasing me, I thought, and knew very well what the 'what' was.

I played along. 'Finding a conclusion for Lord Greengrass's death.'

'Ah, of course.'

'Do you think he's been murdered?' I asked.

Toby looked over my shoulder, probably hoping the sandwiches would arrive. When they didn't, he gave me a succinctly honest answer, 'Yes.'

'What makes you say this?'

'A natural cause of death is relatively easy to diagnose once you have the body. If there is no evidence for this then forensics evaluations elevate the investigation to a Level 3.'

'What happens at Level 3?' I asked, as if it were a floor in an office block.

'I know the language sounds a little odd but it's a serious term, Susie.'

A hint of sharpness in his tone instantly made me regret making fun of what Toby did for a living. I realised I wouldn't like it either if somebody joshed me about my art.

'Level 3 is where my team carry out a full body X-ray,' he said. 'In Lord Greengrass's case this stage, which began this morning, has thrown up some interesting results.'

'And?' I asked.

'Joey, who came in to my office, was delivering the latest update and this shows that by the end of today we should have a confirmed cause of death.'

'Will Lady Greengrass receive a report tonight?' I asked.

'What is likely to happen is that Detective Inspector Grey and I present it to the family connected with the case in the privacy of their own home. This will be tomorrow morning at the earliest. By then we'll have a conclusive report and more information on any bruising as some bruises aren't detectable immediately after death.'

Our sandwiches arrived and we tucked in. Toby looked at me and smiled after his first mouthful and I noticed a fleck of black pepper had lodged itself between his front teeth.

I used to wonder whether to tell someone when they had food stuck in their teeth. However, about a year ago I was in church, standing in line for communion, and the woman in front of me had a clean piece of loo paper flapping out the back of her trousers. I thought long and hard about whether to tell her or not. Just as she was about to get to the front of the queue she reached her hands behind her and tucked in her already tucked-in shirt. Much to my relief the loo paper disappeared somewhere inside her waistband. Maybe it was because this happened to me in church, but I took it as a lesson in not speaking out when someone has something where it shouldn't be. The fleck of pepper in Toby's teeth was a mild distraction during our conversation but I left it for him to dislodge later.

'Delicious sandwich,' I said.

'They're good, aren't they?' agreed Toby, who was much further ahead with his.

I wanted to get back on to the subject of Alexander's death and decided that if I volunteered some details Toby might just give me something back in return. 'I'm not sure you know, but I was in the graveyard when Lord Greengrass's body was found. In fact, he might just have still been alive when I first saw him. It all looked normal, and so it seems strange that there was not more evidence at the scene if he was murdered?'

'If there is anything you have to say that would help with the case…' Toby sounded official again. 'You must, Susie, it's very important.'

'I'm only saying that I am a little puzzled by it all.'

'Go on,' he urged.

'Lord Greengrass was well known among his family and house guests for frequently using the expression, "I'm just going to water the flowerbeds" – and then he would go off to relieve himself outside, even when he was at his own home. I think that is exactly what he was doing in the graveyard, most probably having sneaked out during a hymn.'

'Yes,' said Toby. 'That makes sense.'

'While peeing, he could have taken his mind off his surroundings and been brought down by someone, I admit. But he was diabetic, and so he could also have fainted, which would tie in nicely with the fact he had low blood sugar.'

'Yes,' said Toby waiting for me to come to a conclusion.

'The bash on his forehead did not break the skin and therefore how could falling on a boulder possibly have killed him?'

'It couldn't have.'

'Well, what did then?'

Toby didn't say anything.

'But you're so sure he was murdered?' I said after a pause.

'Susie, you're not giving me much slack.'

I smiled a broad smile. I wasn't going to back down just yet, and I think Toby could tell.

In a slightly weary sounding voice, he said, 'In no particular order, Lord Greengrass was struck on the chest by something, fainted, hit his head and died. What I can assure you is that the clustered bruising on his chest was fresh at death and arranged in a place that it couldn't have come about any other way than someone else inflicting it. This is the missing information we were looking for in the Level 3 autopsy. Detective Inspector Grey's job is to find the evidence that will lead him to the murderer.'

Toby took in a deep breath and looked down at the table.

'Thank you for telling me.' I took Toby's indiscretion as a huge compliment.

'I shouldn't have, although it's nothing the police won't be explaining to the family.'

'I'm sorry for pushing you, but I can't bear to see Lady Greengrass torn apart as she is now. She may be grand in manner but she's always been generous to me and if there is any way I can reduce her pain and suffering I will.'

We had a moment of silence before Toby joked, 'I wouldn't be surprised if you cracked this case before anyone else got a whiff of who done it.'

I smiled at him, and pushed my luck again. 'Can you give me one clue from the paperwork that Joey brought to you?'

'No! You're not going to get any more out of me.' The fleck of pepper disappeared as Toby pulled his forefinger and thumb across his lips, miming the closing of a zip.

I didn't want lunch to come to an end, and not just

because I was so immersed in the murder case. I hadn't been out with a man for a very long time. Not that this was a date but I was enjoying the fact it felt as if it almost could be.

We chatted for a few moments about other things, and then I confided in a low voice, 'There's something I found recently I've not revealed to anyone.'

Toby looked at me seriously, and I couldn't help but notice how nice his blue eyes were.

I pulled the yellow Post-it note out of my skirt pocket and laid it on the table.

'This was on Lord Greengrass's desk. I have tried calling the number but it doesn't connect.'

As quick as a flash Toby said, 'That's because there are too many digits.'

I nodded in agreement. 'If it's unconnected with his death I didn't think Diana needed to see it. Alexander was a recovering alcoholic.'

'I'm sure you'll work it out. Would you like some coffee?'

'Let me get it,' I said, standing up, but Toby shook his head.

'I insist,' he said. 'Your shout next time.'

As Toby organised our espressos I thought that his lack of reaction to the Post-it note meant he didn't like to speculate. Not unusual for a man, I decided; us women are far more prone to having a good gossip and inventing theories that are founded on nothing much.

I stared at the number; the 07 was definitely how it began, they all do…Come on Susie, think…How could Alexander have possibly written it down wrong?

My thoughts churned. The one letter in the alphabet

which, when spoken, could be misinterpreted as a number is 'O.' And then I realised that I might have cracked the problem, just like that.

The person on the end of the telephone could easily have reeled off 07784 597 421, and flowed straight into their next sentence with 'Oh, by the way bring cash' – thus giving the extra number.

I was so thrilled with my theory that immediately I punched the numbers into my mobile and pressed the green button. It connected, and rang for ages.

I didn't take my eyes off Toby as he sat down with our coffees and returned my stare.

The rings stopped and a voicemail greeting said, 'Hello, you've rung Sarah Hember, I'm not available to take your call right now but please leave a message and I'll get back to you as soon as I can.'

I hung up and told Toby what I'd done.

'The voice on the answering machine suggested a privately educated woman, but linguistically not one from the Greengrasses' social circle,' I explained. 'This Sarah Hember had used the word "take", rather than "receive", which suggests to me that, if anything, she was only an acquaintance of Alexander and not a friend of his.'

Toby looked a bit taken aback at my lengthy explanation, and so I tried to make clear that these were the sort of minuscule details we had to pay attention to in order to narrow down the suspects.

He glanced at his watch, and then said hurriedly, 'I have to go, Susie. I'm sorry to rush off.' And he sprang up.

'You go. Don't worry about me.'

'Good luck with tracking down Sarah Hember.' Toby

drew a business card from his pocket and laid it on the table. 'If you're around all week and up for another sandwich, just let me know.'

A zing of arousal went through me as the door chimed and he dashed out.

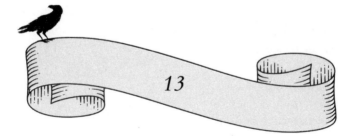

13

The door to the police station was unusually small for such an enormous building but it was the only obvious entrance. Heavy and sprung, I pulled it back, only to be confronted by a solid and inevitably locked inner door. I'd stopped off at the supermarket to get food for me and Nanny, but I was still fifteen minutes early for my 3pm appointment.

A bored female voice boomed through the intercom: 'First name, surname and who you visiting?'

I smiled just in case I was on camera. 'Susie Mahl for Detective Inspector Grey.'

'Thank you,' came the monotone reply.

Following this, nothing happened. I looked down at my feet and waited for what seemed like a very long time. The uninviting voice on the end of the intercom had put me off pressing it again. Finally I was buzzed in, and came face to face with the stumpy Detective Inspector Grey.

'Good of you to come in with such short notice. It's non-stop this afternoon: getting statements, tracing alibis and calling for witnesses. Shouldn't take long now you've arrived.'

And before I had time to so much as nod at the receptionist, Inspector Grey had marched me through one of five doors in the foyer. I was told to take a seat at an empty desk in the centre of a spotlight-hot interview room. The chair was warm and the stale air smelt as if there had been several people in here today. Straight ahead of me was a poster stuck on the wall which stated something about how evidence given by witnesses could be used in court.

Detective Inspector Grey stood by the door and regarded me very earnestly, almost as if he thought I might try and escape.

I felt mildly intimidated by the surroundings and jumped with surprise at the cry of 'Moss!' being shouted down the corridor. Within a moment the police constable arrived with a folder under his arm.

'It's just a few simple questions, Susie,' said Inspector Grey. 'Can I ask you to describe how you spent the morning of Sunday the 26th of November?'

'I had spent the weekend with Antonia and Ben Codrington and their friend Henry Dunstan-Sherbet,' I began. 'Ben and I were in the graveyard of the church, putting a lead on his dog Situp, when we heard a strange sound and went around the corner of the church to where it was coming from. There in a nook of the wall was Lord Greengrass lying on the ground with Henry trying to save his life. Ben rushed back to the house and telephoned the police and we all waited until the ambulance and then you two arrived.' I thought I had neatly swerved the issue of the piece of skull bone being replaced in the grave.

'Right, stop there, Susie. There are a few specific

details within all you have said which we will have to go over.'

'Okay,' I said nonchalantly.

'Firstly, did you enter the graveyard with anyone?'

'No.'

'Why were you in the graveyard?'

'I was following Ben, who was following Henry.'

'Why were you following each other?' Inspector Grey's manner was distinctly peevish.

'Henry had gone to bury a bone that Situp, Ben's dog, had dug up the night before. Ben followed after Henry and I followed Ben.'

'Why Susie? Why exactly did you follow Ben?'

'I felt guilty not helping them.' Feeling a bit hot, I took off my coat and slung it over the back of my chair.

'Tell me again how you, Henry and Ben came together in the graveyard?'

I couldn't see why this was important but I gave the best answer I could. 'Ben and I bumped into each other coming in opposite ways around the north porch, with me walking anti-clockwise and Ben clockwise. As we were about to go around the north transept Henry appeared from under an old yew tree in the north-east corner of the graveyard. He rushed towards us and we all congregated at the back wall of the north transept.'

'Good Susie, good. Every single detail like this is what we are after,' said Inspector Grey, condescendingly.

He pushed a piece of paper and a pen towards me. 'Here is a plan diagram of Spire church and graveyard. We need you to mark a few things on it. Dots for your footsteps, a T where the yew tree is, a B where you bumped into Ben, a C where you all congregated, and an X where you saw Lord Greengrass's body.'

I did as he said and then pushed the piece of paper back to him. He lined it up next to two similar sheets, both of which had the same plan diagram on them. The policemen ummed and ahhed as they compared the marks made on each.

Inspector Grey asked, 'Were you the first to see Lord Greengrass's body?'

'No, Henry saw him first, then Ben and Situp, and then me.'

'Forget the blasted dog.'

'Okay,' I said meekly.

I was asked to give as good a description of Lord Greengrass as I could.

I was a bit pink as I told them he was wearing a Beckenstale-estate tweed suit and a pair of brogues, and we'd noticed a mark on his forehead and that it was apparent that he had been answering a call of nature.

'Do you mean to say his penis was out?'

'Yes, Inspector.'

'Was anyone carrying a walking stick or baton of any kind?' Inspector Grey stared hard at me.

'No, Inspector.'

'How would you describe your relationship with the Greengrasses?'

'It began as a working relationship. I was commissioned by a friend of Lady Greengrass to draw Alexander's spaniel, Harriet, for his seventieth-birthday present. And ever since then I have been to stay at Beckenstale Manor once a year, almost always over the August Bank Holiday weekend. So I think it is fair to say we have a reasonably close relationship.'

'How long have you known the Codringtons?'

'I've only met them twice.'

'And Henry Dunstan-Sherbet?'

'I hadn't met him before last weekend, when I stayed with the Codringtons.'

'When did you last see Lord Greengrass alive?'

'Saturday night at the Dorset Horn.'

'Did you have a conversation?'

'No.'

'Can you think of any reason why Lord Greengrass may have been murdered?'

'No, Inspector.'

Just when I thought the interview was never going to end, it was over. We all stood up at the same time.

Inspector Grey accompanied me to the station foyer, where I told him that I'd be seeing him tomorrow morning, as Diana had asked me to attend the meeting with her.

'Has she now? Well that may just get you off our list of suspects. One can never be too sure though.' I couldn't decide if he was frowning or trying to smile at me.

As I drove back to Beckenstale Manor I replayed the interview in my head. Somehow I seriously doubted that either Inspector Grey or his sidekick had the nous to solve this case. Poor Diana, if my suspicions proved correct.

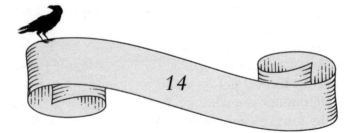

14

The daylight was dwindling by the time I left the county police headquarters, but I was eager to visit Spire graveyard.

In the shadow of the church it seemed much darker. I parked where I'd pulled up to let Antonia out on Saturday night.

Thankfully I couldn't see anyone about and so I headed to the exact spot round the back of the church where Ben, Henry and I had found Alexander on the ground. It was a small place, but well hidden enough for someone to conduct a quick murder. Alexander had done a lot of shooting in his life and like most country gents of his age he was a little deaf, and so maybe he hadn't been able to sense someone creeping up behind him. Or perhaps he'd knocked himself out well before any murderer appeared on the scene.

The nook was still cordoned off with jaunty blue-and-white chevroned plastic police tape. It was concealed by two tall supporting walls, both running at a forty-five degree angle away from the main body of the building. In the narrow gap between them, just above head height, was a plinth holding a two-foot-tall statue of a seated Christ.

I decided I would not be breaching the law by very much if I were to duck under the tape. Longing to find some evidence, I got down on my hands and knees to comb through the winter grass in the dusk by the light of the torch on my mobile phone. Of course, I didn't find a thing.

The only obstruction was a mossy boulder sunk in the ground right where Alexander had been lying. I remembered the mortuary report's 'severe bruising on front lobe of the skull...traces of green moss found in braised skin of forehead'. This must be what he had knocked his head on. I tried to budge it but it wouldn't even loosen a little.

I stood up and studied the nearby brickwork for blood but once again there was nothing I could see. I reached up to the stone Christ, whose right hand was raised while the left hand was in his lap, and tried to shift him. He weighed a ton and was firmly attached to the plinth with no prominent bits that were of the right height for Alexander to hurt himself on.

I slipped back under the tape and crossed over to the yew tree from where Henry had appeared. I crouched under its sagging branches to look for the disturbed grave where he would have replaced the piece of skull bone. There was disturbed earth but not much, and so I thought Situp had dug in just the one spot. Hardly any grass had grown under the canopy of branches and so I couldn't see that anything else of interest was here.

Defeated, I walked across the cold-hearted graves towards my car wondering whether Alexander had knocked himself out and had then been murdered. Or had he been murdered, fallen to the ground and knocked his head on the way down; or been pushed to the ground when he knocked his head on the boulder and died as a consequence?

Suggestions of something dark shivered down my spine and, although I'd been fond of Alexander and didn't want to believe he'd done anything wrong, I was uneasy. I thought about him being in the pub the night before he died; it didn't feel right.

As I put the car into reverse, the combined facts of him at the pub, the curiously generous charitable donation, and Diana's throwaway mention of the dog he had run over, made me doubt that Lord Greengrass was as squeaky clean as I had once believed.

As my car meandered up Beckenstale Manor drive there was one of those memorable winter sunsets where the deceitful golden light makes it seem as if there is warmth in the air. It was spectacular, and I felt quite overcome. In the dying light, the handsome house glistened at its reflection in the lake, making me think about its rich contents which others would like to get their hands on.

I parked and made my way to Rose Cottage, and as I was turning the corner of the red brick garden wall and about to go through the pretty cast-iron gate, my attention was grasped by a flick of raw sienna glowing on top of a green tuft of grass. Bending down I realised it was an autumnal leaf that had blown far from its tree, and was now all curled and crinkled into a delicate sculptural form. The detail of the leaf was amazing, and every bit of me wanted to preserve it on canvas forever. I carefully laid the leaf on the palm of my hand and took it to the safety of my bedroom.

Many people probably think it is easy to find something to paint, and of course having ideas is relatively easy. But finding something that ignites that flame inside and convinces you of the value of your subject is something much rarer, and it cannot be contrived. There is no logical pattern to this process and at barren times I can get myself into a fearful panic that never again will a subject present itself. So when, like now, something grasps my attention by chance it is the best feeling ever, and fuels inside me a strong desire to paint forever.

Still, the leaf could wait.

I was worn out. I lay down on top of the eiderdown on my single bed and gazed at the ceiling as my mind went over the events of the last few days. Suddenly it struck me that the feeling I'd experienced when Diana had turned to me and exclaimed, 'My dear they say he may have been murdered,' was very similar to the one I had just had looking at the leaf.

I began to see parallels between investigating a murder and painting a picture; the two things share far more in common than at first is obvious. Both are about getting to the absolute truth: weeding out all the distracting details, getting rid of the periphery and paring down to nothing other than the simple facts. It seemed to me that uncovering a murderer could follow a very similar process to painting a leaf or drawing a pet. Careful observation and allowing my hand-eye co-ordination, or my mind, in the case of a murder, to be led by visible facts rather than previous knowledge.

What I mean is that when I come to paint or draw

something familiar, such as a leaf or the nose of a horse, I have to block out the image my memory has conjured up already, and instead study whatever it is in front of me, as if it is an abstract shape that I am seeing for the very first time. I have to explore it with my eyes and senses alone, without processing my thought into words. If I abide by this I get to the absolute essence of the subject when I paint. Therefore, if I can put truth on canvas in my art, should there be any barrier to get to the bottom of the truths in our own flesh-and-blood lives? I couldn't see why there should be.

All of a sudden I had the unshakeable conviction that I would be the one to solve this case. And if I combined my obsessive observation with my nosy-parker instincts then surely I had a good chance of uncovering the murderer. A highly charged feeling rushed straight through me. I punched the air and flung myself back into my pillow.

Too fired up to sleep, even though I had felt shattered only minutes earlier, I flicked on the telly.

Local news reporter Mark Foster's middle-aged, deadpan face stared at me. The volume was on mute and the strap line along the bottom of the screen read: '*Breaking News: Landed Gentry parishioner found dead in Spire Graveyard...*' As the words ticker-taped across the bottom of the screen the sentence grew in length: '*... murder investigation led by Detective Inspector Grey: 0800 4617 2323, the number to call with any information relating to this death.*'

The rumour mill would be in overdrive. I was in for a late night of gossip with Nanny, that was for sure.

As it was, Nanny was home earlier than she thought

and by 7pm we were in her front room sitting in the two armchairs, staring straight at the permanently on but rarely audible television.

I'd cooked us spicy meatballs on a bed of rice.

'Fancy food this, Susie, and nicely laid out,' Nanny said, and then returned to what she really wanted to talk about. 'A shocking day. I knew there was something funny going on but I can't for the life of me believe it was murder. That's one hell of a grudge someone must've had…' Nanny's eyes were bright with excitement as she continued to talk about the scandal, rarely pausing for breath.

I was very hungry. In that way sleepiness can make you, I was no longer concentrating on conversation and only noticed Nanny was half a bowl behind me when I looked up to listen to her question, 'Do you think the murderer's still in the village?'

'Diana doesn't actually think he's been murdered, so we'd better not jump too far ahead,' I reminded Nanny.

'Of course he was murdered, Susie. The news wouldn't say what wasn't true. And Mary and me were thinking that Lord Greengrass upset a fair few people in his time. For what it's worth I reckon that Ronnie from the Horn had something to do with it – he's a sly dog if there ever were one, and he's always had it in for posh people.'

Nanny pushed a meatball into her mouth.

'Ronnie?' I asked. 'You can't be serious.'

'Dunno. But he's a temper on him and it's been worse since he lost his friend at the beginning of the year.'

'But why would he want to kill Lord Greengrass?'

Another meatball disappeared into Nanny's mouth.

'Lord Greengrass talked gruff to people, like us servants, and he built a troop of enemies.'

'In that case, why have the same servants been here for so many years?'

'Truth is that servants like this place. The Greengrasses give more perks than most big houses and it's not as if they are a large family, so it's easy work with plenty of free time.'

Nanny had seen two generations through Beckenstale Manor. Bridging the gap between servants and family gave her an insight into the goings-on here the likes of which no one else had. I found it quite difficult to tell where her loyalties lay and never more so than right now.

'Mary reminded me this afternoon of Phil and Iona Yard. I'd almost forgotten that they used to live on the estate.'

'Who were they?'

'Years ago they farmed the bit where all the new houses are, as well as the land now covered in those planted trees. Shame Susie, I liked it with sheep and cows. Much prettier.'

'When did they leave?'

'Let me think – it was after Arthur left school and I'm pretty sure he'd finished at university too. Eighteen years ago would be right. We thought Arthur would come back and help run the estate immediately, but Lord Greengrass pushed him to go and work in London first.'

I'd heard Diana say exactly the same. 'It's his father's fault he ever married that woman. He made him go to the City. Had Arthur come here straight after university then Asquintha never would have crossed his path.'

'Tell me more about the Yards,' I urged Nanny.

'Can't remember exactly. I liked them alright, but it

didn't end well, I can tell you that.'

'So they fell out with the Greengrasses?'

'Don't quote me on this but I think Lord Greengrass told the Yards to leave, just like that, with no matter that it meant losing their job and their home. Shepherd said they got paid a packet, enough to buy themselves a nice house but it weren't the same. Their old farm was everything to them.'

In Nanny's words I hardly recognised the Alexander I knew. What a cruel man if this was even half true. And it could well be completely true. Farmers employed by an estate were, I knew, unlike contract or tenant farmers who have individual written agreements, liable to be sacked at any time for no good reason.

It wasn't pretty, but contract law almost always has a loophole where employers can wriggle out of a relationship with their employees. Well-known in farming speak as 'the three waves goodbye', a compulsory chain of meetings between employer and employee to discuss declining profits of the farm. These meetings are the necessary hoops an employer has to jump through before they can sack their employee, under the premise that together they have failed to come up with a viable business plan. Every farmer in the country knows that a fourth meeting will ensue with a lawyer present and the bad news will be broken to the farmer that his job is being taken away.

'So you reckon the Yards had the three waves then?' I asked Nanny.

'They did. And so Mary says the Yards'll have a big grudge.'

Nanny popped the final meatball in her mouth, and

announced to me with a wink, 'And Butler Shepherd weren't too keen on Lord Greengrass neither.'

Nanny's suggestion made me feel very awkward. It was disloyal and highly unlikely.

I ignored it, and changed the subject. 'Where were Arthur, Asquintha and the boys on Sunday morning?'

Nanny, in her excitement, got the wrong end of the stick. 'Now you're on to something, Susie. Asquintha'd have more motivation than the rest of us to get rid of Lord Greengrass. She's a tough time being accepted.'

I didn't want to provoke Nanny's suspicions of Asquintha so reverted to my initial question. 'But Nanny, I was wanting to know where were Arthur, Asquintha and the boys on Sunday morning?'

'Arthur took the children to church in St Catherine's, a bit of a way from the Manor.'

'Why there?'

'There's a Sunday school that's popular locally, and Asquintha believes that their children should go to church where there's a bit of entertainment for them.'

'And Asquintha?'

'Enjoying a lie-in.'

I asked Nanny if she fancied a cup of tea.

'I nearly forgot to say, Susie. I saw Antonia Codrington in the village today and she wants you to drop in tomorrow. That doctor chap left a bag and she wonders if you'd mind taking it back to Sussex when you go.'

I said I would, but then I wondered if Antonia was trying to set me up with Henry. If so, I could see the logic behind me taking his bag to my home for him to collect. But I could also see that being married for a long time meant they must have forgotten how loaded arranging for a single man to call on me alone at home would be.

I drank my tea in bed, then popped to the loo one more time and curled up under the duvet, all ready to drift off. But annoyingly I couldn't slide into sleep.

My mind was all abuzz.

To distract myself I flicked through the photographs of Situp I'd taken on my camera. Most of them were taken outside and in all but one Situp was alert and full of playfulness. Strangely though, in every single picture taken inside Situp had his head dipped low and his tail between his legs. I hadn't noticed it when I was staying – so much for me being super-observant at all times! – but now it was perfectly clear that there had been something inside the Glebe House that upset Situp.

I placed my camera on the side table, turned off the bedroom light, lay flat on my back, eyes closed and eventually drifted off thinking about the little black cat and how the wonderful velvety quality of its short-haired coat would be a challenge to paint accurately.

Zzzzz.

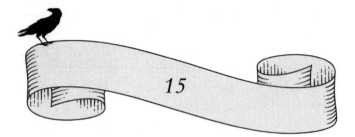

15

Unbeknown to me, although I mustn't get above myself and think that it is my right to be kept up to date with the investigation, both Arthur and Asquintha had been called into the county police headquarters for questioning yesterday evening. This all became apparent at this morning's meeting, which had just begun. Detective Inspector Grey, mortuary clerk Dr Toby Cropper, Diana, Arthur, Asquintha and me were sitting down the two long sides of the marble-top table in the conservatory. Mary had just been in and placed a tray of hot coffee and a plate of biscuits on the table.

'Shall I pour the coffee, Ma?' asked Arthur.

'Yes please, dear.'

'Not for me, thank you,' said Inspector Grey, obviously itching to get on with delivering his news. He and Toby were sitting opposite the rest of us and there was a slim folder on the table in front of them.

I was momentarily distracted, trying to decide if it was insensitive to be having a murder investigation meeting in a conservatory. It was far less gloomy than the library, but all these condolence flowers stuffed into vases and placed round the edges of this glass Victorian extension emphasised the sad subject of death and funerals. Fortunately no one else seemed affected by the poignancy of our surroundings.

Arthur sat down between his mother and his wife, moving the Phalaenopsis orchid out the way as he placed the plate of biscuits in the centre of the table. None of us reached for one. Asquintha, who was sitting next to me, hugged her mug with both hands, looking as if she hadn't slept a wink last night.

'Right,' said Inspector Grey, flipping open the folder. 'Let's continue.'

Firmly and rather too loudly he went on. 'With no explanation or evidence of natural cause of death, a subsequent in-depth autopsy has revealed that unlawful killing is almost certainly the unfortunate outcome. I will be overseeing and carrying out the full investigation into this. I can assure you, My Lady, that the case will not be dropped until we have found and convicted the perpetrator.'

After a pause, during which time we all shot quick looks at each other, Inspector Grey went on. 'Under my instruction the forensics team has carried out further examinations and we now have clear evidence of murder. Dr Cropper will now continue.'

Dressed in a respectable corduroy blazer, if a little dishevelled, Toby cut a handsome dash alongside portly Inspector Grey. With a well-educated accent his soft voice carried an academic lilt as he explained: 'An X-ray revealed a patch of internal bleeding around Lord Greengrass's precordium, which is the area immediately above the heart. From this we can tell that the cause of death is *commotion cordis*.'

Inspector Grey nodded in a way that implied this is

exactly the outcome he had predicted. I, on the other hand, very much doubted if any of us other than Toby knew what '*commotion cordis*' meant.

Saving us from our ignorance, Toby elaborated. '*Commotion cordis* is Latin for agitation of the heart, which in its simplest form would be explained as cardiac concussion. This symptom is seen in patients whose chest has been struck directly over the heart during the cardiac cycle, that is the cycle of the heart beat, thus causing cardiac arrest.'

Toby looked towards Inspector Grey, who then said, 'Our investigation report states that between the hours of 11.15am and 11.25am, during the Spire Commemoration service on Sunday the 26th of November Lord Greengrass, whilst relieving himself in the graveyard, fainted due to low blood sugar, and as he fell to his feet he unintentionally knocked himself out on a mossy boulder, firmly secured in the ground...'

Diana drew in a heavy breath. We all took our eyes off Inspector Grey and looked towards her.

'...And from the depth of the abrasion on Lord Greengrass's forehead we can measure the blow at point 0.725 on the unconscious scale. This tells us that he would not have regained consciousness for at least 180 seconds. It was during these three minutes that the murder was carried out.'

Arthur stuck up his hand. I thought it an extraordinary action for a man in his thirties, and in whose home we were all sitting. Then again, who knows how anyone would act in a similar situation?

'Could it be that Father died of a heart attack?' said Arthur.

'I am sorry to say that I can be absolutely sure that could not be the case,' Toby said gently. 'Your father's family has no trace of predisposing cardiac abnormalities, and although a heart attack can lead to cardiac arrest, they are not the same thing.'

No longer raising his hand Arthur desperately asked, 'But how do you know it wasn't a heart attack which led to the cardiac arrest?'

Toby explained that he had worked for some years as a heart surgeon. 'A heart attack is a sudden interruption to the blood supply to part of the heart muscle. This can cause immense chest pain but the heart is still sending blood around the body, and the person remains conscious and continues to breathe. However, when a cardiac arrest occurs, the heart suddenly stops pumping blood around the body, resulting in instant loss of consciousness and inability to breathe, and without specialised resuscitation death will occur in a matter of a very few minutes. The evidence from the autopsy shows that Lord Greengrass had a cardiac arrest after a blow to the chest.'

Arthur accepted the explanation and turned to his mother, whose expression didn't flicker. There looked to be a silent battle going on between her thoughts and the news being delivered.

Clearly refusing to believe that her husband had been murdered, Diana spoke with an accusatory tone. 'Wasn't that man Henry Dunstan-Sherbet a doctor? Couldn't he have done anything?'

'I'm afraid not, My Lady,' said Toby patiently. 'As I said, a cardiac arrest leads to death within minutes and requires immediate cardiopulmonary resuscitation to halt it. His statement is that Lord Greengrass had already died when he found him.'

'Didn't he know how to do the resuscitation?' asked Diana, ignorant to the fact it required necessary medical equipment.

'Without a defibrillator there was very likely nothing that anyone could have done,' said Toby patiently.

So, that was it. Now we all knew that the bruising on Alexander's chest was evidence that with one blow someone had ended his life.

By the looks of her, Diana was still struggling with the facts of her husband's death. She stared stonily out of the conservatory, and then took a long, slow sip from her mug of coffee.

I noticed that Asquintha was still grasping her mug with both hands. I wanted to reassure her but she was too preoccupied to catch my glance.

Inspector Grey cleared his throat. 'I think I could add some useful detail.

'We are searching for the murder weapon which, in accordance with the area of bruising, is approximately three and a half inches in diameter, blunt-ended and upwards of half a kilo in weight. We are proceeding with the investigation as quickly and as thoroughly as we can, and have conducted several interviews.'

'I think it would be useful for you to give us an update on this,' said Arthur, turning to give Asquintha a nod. Diana agreed.

Inspector Grey put on his reading glasses and unclipped the top piece of paper from the folder in front of him. 'Henry Dunstan-Sherbet, Ben Codrington and Susie Mahl, who were with Lord Greengrass in the graveyard, have all been interviewed.' My heart gave a heavy beat at the sound of my name, but the inspector continued without so much as a glance in my direction. 'On the evidence we have gathered, they were the first people to come upon Lord Greengrass, having been alerted to his whereabouts by a deep gurgling sound.'

Inspector Grey looked to Toby, who nodded in agreement, before continuing. 'This gurgling sound is produced by a mixture of air and saliva travelling up the oesophagus. The lack of live muscle to set it free gives it its distinctive lowness of pitch. This sound confirms Lord Greengrass's final breath before death, and is evidence proved by those who heard it.'

Asquintha turned to me, raised her eyebrows, subtly nodded her head and smiled a little as if to say, 'I wish I was in your lifeboat.'

It's a cruelness that during a police investigation – although the precise opposite is supposed to be true – it feels very much as if all connected with the deceased are potentially guilty until they are proven innocent. While of course I was happy that I was apparently off the list of suspects, I wasn't entirely convinced that any lay person could with certainty swear that something heard was indeed the sound of a last breath, as opposed to merely a distressed breath. But I decided to keep this scepticism to myself, and contented myself with what I hoped was a supportive smile in Asquintha's direction.

Inspector Grey continued with his long-winded way of saying something startlingly obvious. 'In our experience, we have found narrowing down the list of suspects works best if we begin investigating family members first, followed by those most closely connected to the family.'

Fortunately for Arthur, taking his children to Sunday school had provided him with Reverend Roger as an alibi.

Unfortunately for Asquintha, at this point the rest of us twigged that she had been home alone, having a lie-in, at the exact time of Alexander's murder. She didn't have anyone to vouch for her whereabouts.

Asquintha saw what we were thinking and added quickly, 'I had just risen and showered when Arthur and the boys returned home.'

Arthur agreed immediately that his wife's hair was still wet at 12.30pm, when he returned home, but the look on Inspector Grey's face made it perfectly clear to all of us that this claim wouldn't stand up in court as evidence of innocence.

Diana was of a similar opinion. 'Wet hair doesn't prove anything,' she said, which seemed a sharp and uncalled for disloyalty to poor Asquintha.

And inevitably Inspector Grey twisted the knife. 'It is uncollaborated where Lady Cornfield was between 11.15am and 11.25am.'

That was it. Asquintha was guilty until proven innocent, and the rest of us who'd given statements were off the hook.

Asquintha looked worn down and distressed. It was difficult to tell whether her slumped shoulders and cowed attitude were because of an unfair accusation, or a guilty conscience that was defeating her.

Whatever, I wanted to offer her comfort but knew as a (self-appointed) detective I must remain impartial in order to see the truth.

Toby's head dipped towards the table, giving away his unease of the finger-pointing at Asquintha. He struck me as a man who had an effortless way with women. A combination of good looks and charm doubtlessly attracted all, and right now it was difficult for him to watch Asquintha suffer.

Couldn't he just focus on me? I thought, shamefully. After all, I was the youngest, and also the only single woman at the table.

'Shall we move on?' said Arthur in a glum voice as he strove to deflect our attention away from his wife.

Inspector Grey skim-read another document in his file.

'Turning our attention to the household, Miss Jenny has confirmed her absence with an international call to Mary on Sunday morning that the telephone company has verified. And groundsman Sid was returning a broken rake to the garden centre fifteen miles north of Spire village.' Using his finger to find his place in the statement Inspector Grey continued, 'We have evidence of his refund receipt with 11.17am printed on it, confirmed by checkout sales assistant, a Miss Daisy Lorne.'

There was a pause, and we waited for more names to be crossed off the list of suspects, but none came. Instead Inspector Grey finished up with, 'That's all for now.'

'No more?' said Diana querulously. 'How can we possibly muddle along together when there may be a murderer amongst us?'

'My Lady, I can assure you that your safety is paramount and our investigation into your husband's death of primary importance,' the inspector tried to reassure her.

'How do you proceed from here, Inspector?' asked Arthur, trying to introduce some logical order.

'Today will be spent gathering statements from Antonia Codrington, her nanny May, publican Ronnie Riggs, his daughter Katy, Butler Shepherd, Housekeeper Mary and your nanny, Angela Child.'

I hadn't ever thought to ask Nanny's real name. A. Child. It amused me. Particularly as I've always joked that a book of nominative determinism would make a good Christmas bestseller. The sprinter, Usain Bolt and Belgian theologian, Monsieur Crucifix would be the best in it so far.

'What would you like us to do?' asked Diana.

'Remain calm and carry on with your routine as best you can, My Lady. I suggest we pencil in a similar meeting to this one for tomorrow morning.'

'Susie, will you make a note of that please?' Diana said.

I gave Toby a quizzical look and made a mental note of tomorrow morning's meeting.

Finally letting go of her coffee cup, Asquintha stood up. First to leave the room she hardly even whispered goodbye. Toby's eyes followed her path out the door and reverted when Arthur came into his sight.

'Thank you Inspector, thank you Dr Cropper. I'll see you in the morning,' he said.

'Before you go, Lord Cornfield,' said Inspector Grey, 'I will need you to show me to your family gun safe, please.'

'Of course.'

'And what will you be doing in the gun safe, Inspector?' asked Diana as if she was trying to catch him out.

'I'll be measuring the butt plates for the record, My Lady. The area of clustered bruising on your husband's chest, combined with his previous occupation, and passion for country pursuits, has suggested, unlikely as it may be for a Sunday morning in a country graveyard, that the butt of a shotgun could have acted as a murder weapon.'

'Good God!' sighed Diana. 'If that's the case, why on earth did the killer use that end?'

Inspector Grey sounded patient, 'To ensure he or indeed she was not heard, we presume.' He then stood up. 'Before we go, with your permission My Lady, I would like to have a look in your husband's study please.'

'Susie will accompany you.' And without a further word Diana swept from the room in a manner that suggested she'd like to be moving faster than her ample figure allowed.

'I'll take you to the gun safe now,' said Arthur.

Inspector Grey turned to Toby, 'I'll be back in a moment or two.'

This was my cue to remain here, and that I could show him Alexander's study afterwards.

I knew the rules of guns in houses. Although my father didn't shoot, I was aware that, by law, all guns had to be kept in a gun safe. It is illegal for anyone, living under the same roof, without a shotgun or firearm certificate, to know where the keys are kept.

'Would you like a biscuit?' I said, pushing the plate towards Toby. My tummy turned with that nervous feeling of being left alone with someone you were desperate to impress but didn't know how to. I realised I fancied Toby.

'Seems you're quite the favourite round here,' he said.

I smiled, but felt completely unable to discuss the family in their own house.

Toby whispered, 'Don't worry, Susie, there's nothing I couldn't see for myself. That poor daughter-in-law.'

I nodded, pleased that he wasn't overly quick to assume Asquintha had anything to do with Alexander's death.

'Lovely house, isn't it? You're lucky to get to stay in a place like this,' Toby went on.

'I suppose your job only takes you to dead ends.'

My joke was pretty feeble, but Toby laughed none-theless, and I started to wonder if perhaps he had noticed me noticing him.

'In my view, Inspector Grey is barking up the wrong tree in the gun cupboard. But I suppose it's good to cover all bases.'

Thank goodness we'd been conversing in hushed voices. No sooner had I spoken than Inspector Grey's voice sounded nearby.

We both looked towards the door and there he was. 'Come on then Susie, lead me to the study.'

He seemed in an inappropriately good mood, saying to Toby before we left the room, 'Dr Cropper, I can report there is one gun with a butt of precisely three and a half inches, which is a child's single-barrel .410 shotgun, and all the other gun butts are far larger at five inches. The .410 is coming with me to the police station for tests, and I've locked it up in the safe in my car.'

Toby didn't comment on the gun, but he did say to the inspector, 'I don't have to be in the office until 10am, and so if you'd like assistance in the study then I'm happy to stick around.'

Wanting to keep Toby nearby for as long as possible, I willed Inspector Grey to say yes. And amazingly he did. 'An extra pair of eyes is always a help so come on then,' he said.

I took them both to the study. In fact I was really pleased as it let me be closely involved in the hunt for evidence, even if only for a short while.

Diana had been treating me more and more as a lady-in-waiting, rather than a friend, which was what I really hoped I was to her: collecting the mortuary report, writing the draft death notice, passing on messages to Mary, making notes, and now overseeing these two men.

I couldn't say that I'd take all these orders on the chin under normal circumstances, but right now it was precisely these little jobs that were facilitating my personal investigation of her husband's murder in a fittingly discreet way.

Once inside the study, I closed the door and in doing so revealed a case of books that attracted Toby's attention.

Meanwhile Inspector Grey chaotically riffled through neat piles of paperwork on Lord Greengrass's desk.

'Look Inspector, here's a shelf of daily diaries. Go all the way back to…now let's see…' Toby licked his fore-finger and ran it along the bindings revealing gold leaf embossed dates, '…er, going back at least forty years. Imagine having recorded your life for that long?'

Inspector Grey gave Toby a stern look.

'Might as well bag up the most recent one. I suppose it could be useful in place of an absent witness.'

Toby handed me a diary from the bottom shelf and I slipped it under my arm as Inspector Grey handed me a marker pen and a bunch of sealed plastic bags, saying,

'Make yourself useful and pop today's date on these and remember to write "Personal Journal, study bookcase" on the one you're holding.'

I did as requested, pleased I'd gained his trust; something I needed if I was going to get involved in the case.

Meanwhile Inspector Grey – clearly much more used to this sort of thing than I was – had already bagged up various items, including a wall calendar, an alarm clock, a knife-shaped letter opener, a worn leather address book and a packet of diabetic energy tablets.

I knelt on the floor and arranged these plastic bags in a row, then reached for the diary to do my bagging, and out fluttered a loose photograph that landed gently on its front.

Calmly but quickly I grabbed it and slipped it into the top of my tights before the others could see. I was then quite shocked at what I'd just done, but not shocked enough to put the photograph back.

Guiltily I jumped at the sound of the study door opening.

Arthur walked in. 'Are you all okay to let yourselves out when you're done? I must go and brief the servants and Ma would like to be left alone for a while.'

'Of course,' said Inspector Grey. He didn't seem to think it worth spending much further time looking for evidence at Beckenstale Manor as he then said, 'We'll be out of here in the next five minutes.'

Arthur asked if I'd like to join his mother for lunch. 'One-fifteen if that's okay for you?'

I accepted, and then realised Inspector Grey was looking down at me. 'Right, hop up Susie, and give me those evidence bags.'

I handed them over.

'And that one,' he said, with his hand indicating the bag with the diary in it beside me.

'Ah. Of course, here you go.'

Within two minutes of Arthur leaving the study, Inspector Grey, Toby and I had all left the Manor and gone our separate ways.

In the secrecy of my bedroom at Nanny's, with the door closed for privacy despite there being no one around, I slid out the photograph.

It was a recent picture of Alexander and there was a man stood next to him who carried a shotgun under each arm. The first thing to strike me was the awkward amount of space between them. Alexander had a half smile but his companion looked positively grumpy.

I knew that I really should hand it in to the police station but right then I didn't want to. I felt bad but I told myself that it wasn't as if the butt of a shotgun was a remotely likely murder weapon.

I laid the picture on the desk and studied it; both men were dressed in full tweed. The stranger had on a deer-stalker, one of those tweed hats with earflaps tied at its crown. Other than the ironic association with Sherlock Holmes, this distinctive model, only worn by rural workers and never landowners, identified the man as Lord Greengrass's loader. Behind the pair was a distinctive stocky, round stone tower, and on the back of the photograph was scribbled in blue-black ink: 'That Day' in Alexander's unmistakable spidery handwriting.

I slipped it into my sketchbook to think about and perhaps revisit later. Right now I wanted to ring Sarah Hember again.

No one was around. I knew Nanny had taken the boys on an outing to the local deep-sea world down at the coast. Personally I hated this sort of attraction as I always felt sorry for the poor ocean creatures captured in a tank, and even worse that they were so close to their natural habitat.

I retrieved the Post-it note from the pocket of the skirt I had been wearing the day before and read it again.

25th Nov.
Dorset Horn, 6pm
077845974210
Cash

There was something peculiar about it, I thought, and I was frustrated that I couldn't see or guess at what this might be. I found the last dialled number on my mobile and pressed the green button.

BANG! BANG! BANG! came pounding through Rose Cottage.

In a split second I had cancelled the call. My heart jumped into my throat as images of murderers with baseball bats in their hands flashed through my mind. I heard the front door fly open and crash against the wall of the porch.

'MISS MAHL, you in there?' boomed a male voice.

Spooked, my imagination ran riot and didn't allow me to think who it might be who wanted to know where I was so urgently.

With an effort I pulled myself together, slipped the Post-it note under my pillow, straightened my skirt, punched 999 into my mobile and hovered a shaking thumb over the call button.

'Who is it!' I shouted from behind the bedroom door.

'MISS MAHL, where the heck are you? It's Shepherd.'

He looked cross as he stood on the step with the door wide open, letting a chill of cold air into the house.

'Hello Shepherd,' I said, a bit surprised by quite how composed I sounded.

'Ah Madam.' His voice was much calmer. 'Sorry about the crash of the door. Didn't want to barge in on you.'

Other than stepping over the threshold, he had all but barged in, I thought.

I walked very slowly down the corridor towards him, holding my mobile hidden behind my back with my finger poised above the call button still, I could feel the bolt of adrenalin and I couldn't help but notice that Shepherd was a big man.

'I won't come in, Madam, as I've got my boots on.' He wiggled one foot at me. 'But I wanted to tell you about something I saw the other night. Mary's been keeping me quiet but that's not sitting right with me.'

'Go on,' I said cautiously.

'I was in the pub on Saturday night. Lord Greengrass was there and it's not like him to be at the boozer. I was alone, just drinking up at the bar and so I kept an eye on him. He didn't drink no alcohol all the time he was there.'

'Why are you telling me this, Shepherd?' I turned off my phone and put it in my pocket.

'I saw you have the ear of the inspector and I didn't want to go to Lady Greengrass. And there's no way I'm speaking to the police until asked.'

'Go on then.'

Now I'd given him permission to speak, he struggled to get the words out.

I tried to help by asking, 'Did Lord Greengrass see you?'

'I was pulled up to the bar very obvious.'

'Well, if we assume for the moment that he didn't see you, was there anything he was doing that meant he didn't see you?'

'You lost me there, Madam.' Shepherd looked confused.

'Just say what you came to tell me.'

Shepherd looked at the floor. 'A lady came in the pub, and I don't know who she was. Neither of them were dressed up. You know what I'm saying. She joined him at his table but didn't take a drink. Lord Greengrass handed over an envelope, shook her hand and then she left. It was all very quick.'

'What?' I said, a bit more loudly than I meant to.

'That's all there is to it, Madam. It's something and nothing I daresay, but I just had to get it off my chest. What if that lady had something to do with what went on the next morning? What if Lord Greengrass was involved in something he shouldn't have been?'

I asked Shepherd for the exact details, and we went through it again.

'He definitely saw me,' Shepherd finished up. 'Tapped me on the shoulder as he left and said, "No telling Lady Greengrass about this, it's my little secret, okay?"'

Although some people might have taken it to the contrary, this snippet of information calmed my concerns about the secret meeting.

Despite what Nanny says about the gruff manner with which Alexander treated his staff, I knew from personal experience that he was invariably kind and thoughtful towards his wife. In my experience, Diana was the one who rarely showed signs of affection and, as some firmly-rooted wives do, she consistently pecked at him.

She would lose her rag at petty things; birthday presents and Christmas presents being a particularly favourite reason for a flush of ungratefulness and belittling of her husband.

An exquisite ruby evening-watch: 'What a bore to have to wind it up every time I want to wear it, you simply must return it.' A magnifying glass with mother-of-pearl handle: 'Am I expected to remove my perfectly adequate spectacles to use this relic?' And that's only the gripes that I had heard.

In fact, Diana was routinely so ungrateful that Alexander's persistence in the face of such an unenthusiastic response sometimes felt like his rather imaginative way of getting her to vent her anger on a thing, rather than with him. But, as charming as Alexander was (or at least I thought he was), now that I considered what I had seen of their marriage more deeply, I didn't think he'd physically loved Diana for quite some time. Both had their own room, each down their own landing and on different floors of the house.

Predictably, Shepherd was now regretting what he'd said to me. 'He wasn't doing something wrong, I am sure of that. Don't tell Mary I told you, Madam. Please don't.'

I tried to mollify him. 'Of course, Shepherd. I'll keep it to myself. Thank you for telling me. I'm sure there's a simple explanation that has no relevance to his murder.'

As I pushed the front door closed I thought that this detective business was hard to get my head around.

So many things that didn't quite make sense, hardly any clues of substance, a string of suspects and very probably a few dead ends.

Suddenly I felt drained and tired. I knew if I hung around in Rose Cottage much longer I'd be tempted to curl up in bed and have a nap.

I had to get out and as there was time before lunch I decided to go and collect Henry's bag from Antonia. It would clear my head to have a change of scene.

I opened the door to leave Rose Cottage and a man in red jacket and shorts practically fell in on top of me.

'I'm so sorry,' I said. 'What timing!'

He handed me an envelope, and I realised he was the postman.

'I think you might be able to help me,' I said. 'I'm wondering if you've worked in this area a long time, and whether you might be able to tell me where Phil and Iona Yard moved to?'

The postman looked at me.

'I have a letter for them,' I said, with such conviction that he didn't question why, eighteen years after they had moved on, I wanted to send a letter to people I did not have the address of.

'The Yards, of course I remember them. Out of my area now but only just. Little farm in Farby.'

'What's the address please?'

'Little Farm, Farby.'

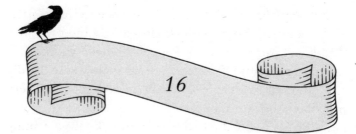

16

It was cold, and I drove to Spire wrapped up in my coat and wearing gloves. I parked on the high street so I could walk directly through the graveyard.

The area of Alexander's death was still cordoned off with the blue and white police tape, and as I headed for the lych-gate in the yew hedge an empty fizzy drink can shoved into the corner caught my eye. I stubbed my toe as I leant down to pick it up and put it in my pocket, later to put in a bin; one of my pet hates is litter and I'm always retrieving it.

I looked down at the ground and saw what at first I thought was a perfectly round and not particularly big stone. Picking it up, it was far heavier than it looked, and when I'd wrestled it from under the hedge I saw it was a stone orb topped with a cross, a *Globus Cruciger*.

My goodness! At that moment I might have the very murder weapon in my hands. Certainly, in my admittedly somewhat limited opinion, it was heavy enough to deliver a fatal blow, and given the shape it might well not even break the skin.

I trotted over to the nook where Alexander had died,

slipped under the two-tier cordon and held up the orb to the stone Christ's cupped left hand. It looked as if it would fit perfectly; my artist's eye has made me very good with measurements.

I quickly ducked back under the tape and stood staring at Christ, almost believing he might talk to me.

I needed to get rid of the orb so hurriedly I chose a fresh spot in the hedge (I didn't want the murderer coming back to remove his weapon) and pushed the orb far into it, making sure it was well hidden amongst the branches. Thank goodness I'd been wearing gloves. I walked away, relieved that no one could trace it back to me.

Ding dong went the Codringtons' front-doorbell and almost immediately I could hear Antonia's long legs striding towards the other side of it.

'Susie, how nice to see you, come in. Do you have time for a cup of tea?'

'Yes please, that would be great.' Holding up the Coke can I asked, 'Mind if I put this in your bin?'

'Sure.' Antonia took it from me and I followed her in to the now familiar kitchen. The wood-burner was glowing and Situp, recognising me, got out of his basket and wagged his tail as he came to say hello.

'That's better, Situp,' said Antonia looking at her dog with more fondness than I'd seen her look at her little girl Bella. 'We were worried he was out of sorts when you were staying, but like an only child I just think he gets jealous when we have visitors and our attention is taken away.'

'I can completely understand that.' I was pleased to hear there was a reason for his behaviour as I'd thought too that he'd been a bit more subdued than I had expected for a youngish dog. Situp seemed to appreciate my thoughts, as he sat in front of me and solemnly offered me a front paw.

'I think he likes you.'

'He's such a lovely dog.' I patted his tummy as he sat as close as he could beside me and then leaned against my legs.

'Yes, aren't you a good boy?' cooed Antonia to her enormous hound. Situp looked at her as if to say he was a very good boy indeed.

'Home alone?' I asked in the hope that we could have an open discussion.

'Yes. May's taken Bella to stay with my parents in Herefordshire to give us a break for a few days. Ben has a manuscript deadline at the end of the week and so he needs to have total peace and quiet.'

'Is Ben here?' I asked.

'Yes, but not really… if you know what I mean? He's locked himself out there in the office as he tends to do.'

Antonia stood at the kitchen counter, spooning loose tea-leaves into her spotted teapot while the kettle boiled.

I pulled a chair out from the table, took off my gloves and coat and sat down. Before I even had to prod, she started telling me the things I had wanted to hear.

'Inspector Grey was round here this morning hoping to find more evidence. Not that we had any to give him. He's sure Alexander was murdered in the graveyard. Ben thinks the murder malarkey is a false accusation, and that Alexander must have fainted and knocked himself out on a rock, but I'm not sure that would be enough to kill him. What do you think?'

'I know he was a diabetic and at the time he fell his

sugar levels were low,' I replied. 'But I agree with you. It seems unlikely that a pretty light bash to the forehead would have been enough to kill him.'

I was selective regarding how much I told Antonia of what I knew. I'd been included by Diana in this morning's meeting as a trusted friend, and it would be entirely wrong to share any of the information that I'd heard in the conservatory, however tempting now.

Antonia brought the tea and a biscuit tin to the table. 'You have to have a bit of shortbread as it's my alibi,' she said in a conspiratorial way, as she sat down and pulled the lid off.

I smiled as that seemed to be what she was wanting me to do.

She pushed the tin towards me. 'It's quite funny really, considering I hardly ever do the cooking.'

'How does it work then?'

'Hear me out Susie!' she said, and then launched into a lengthy explanation. 'I started making shortbread when I got up on Sunday morning, but when the conversation of burying the bone aggravated me I put the dough in the fridge and went with Bella to let Minty out of her stable. By the time we returned you'd all left the house so I got the dough out the fridge and continued making the biscuits. It takes eight minutes to bake shortbread. I cut the shapes, put them on a tray and popped them in the oven. Six minutes later I heard a knock on the back door. I picked up Bella, put her on my hip and went to open it. Ronnie was standing on the porch step asking if he could speak to Ben.'

'And you asked him in?' I said, and then remembered that she wasn't overly fond of Ronnie.

'I couldn't exactly say no. I didn't want him to go looking for Ben and find him burying the bone.'

'Yes, of course.'

'But at the very same time that I was at the back door, Ben must have entered the front door to shut Situp in the kitchen.'

'Didn't you wonder why Situp was in the kitchen?' I interrupted again, unable to stop myself asking questions.

'Not at all. I assumed he'd been a nuisance and Ben must have brought him back. It's quite usual. And then the cooker alarm went off, almost as soon as Ronnie was in the house. I rushed through to the kitchen, put Bella down, took the shortbread out of the oven, with Situp doing his best to get between my legs, and laid the shortbread out on cooling racks. Then we came to look for you in the graveyard, taking Bella and Situp along for the walk.'

I saw that the eight minutes of shortbread-baking, and then the walk to the graveyard, covered enough time between 11.15am and 11.25am for Antonia not to have committed the murder. Not that I had ever really considered her to be a viable suspect; I couldn't think of any possible motive.

I couldn't help myself blurting out enthusiastically, as I liked Antonia, 'How brilliant to have such exact timings as to your whereabouts!'

'Isn't it just?' she agreed.

I reached into the biscuit tin and pulled out what was trying to be a duck but had lost its beak, one foot and the tip of its stumpy tail.

'What did Ronnie want to ask Ben?'

'Do you know, I never got round to asking him and now I wouldn't dare. Ronnie is clearly the most obvious suspect. I can't believe that only moments after the murder I invited him into our house.'

'What makes you so suspicious?'

'No one can vouch for his whereabouts before he rang our back-doorbell, so I hear,' replied Antonia. I detected a slightly triumphant note in her tone.

I was cross that I hadn't worked this out myself.

Indeed, it brought home to me that in future I must listen very carefully to every single detail of what someone is saying while they are saying it. I should treat people's comments just like I do when painting a bird in the sky. One moment the bird is there ready for me to capture in my memory, whereupon I lock it there immediately, knowing that if I don't, the next moment it will be gone for good.

Antonia looked at me straight on. It was a look I assumed she held in board meetings with chief executives she was advising. One of such seriousness I knew what she was about to say was worth listening to.

'Ronnie was wearing a scruffy, wax jacket when he came to the door and his hands were stuffed into the enormous pockets...' She paused for a split second. 'I remember, because he nearly went flying when he tripped on the step.' Antonia took in a deep breath and finished her sentence with a sense of drama, 'He could have been hiding a weapon.'

I tried to keep my expression calm. Antonia had just given away what was very probably the hiding place for the *Globus Cruciger*, on its way to the hedge.

'Seriously, do you really think Ronnie might have

done it? Remind me again why you don't take to him.'

'Well, I don't really know, if I'm honest, other than we've never really clicked. It isn't as if we've lived here long, although we have been to the pub pretty regularly, or at least Ben has. Neither of us can believe Ronnie would really commit murder. But it feels a strange coincidence, him turning up at our back door for the first time ever, mere moments after Lord Greengrass's death.'

'What was he like when you saw him?'

'Oh you know, just as he always is, flirting and smelling of booze.'

'Do you know how long Ronnie has been running the Dorset Horn?'

'Oh years. He could tell you anything about anyone in this village, that's for sure.'

'Where did he come from?'

'No one knows, so I hear. I suppose he's a bit of a dark horse in that respect.'

'No one knows?' I asked.

'Someone – I can't remember who – said that he doesn't like to talk about it. He trots out this mantra: ask no questions, tell no lies; my past is past and future to come.'

Antonia refreshed the teapot and we continued chatting, darting from one theory to another.

I knew that if any of us were certain who had murdered Alexander, then we wouldn't be idly conjecturing in this manner. But we didn't, and so the thrill of speculating had got the better of all of us. It is characteristic of that unattractive trait that affects most people when circumstances are horrible and unexpected. It's like driving past a car accident and being unable to stop yourself having a look. We all get a guilty kick out of it, but it's human nature at its worst.

I didn't think it was wise for Antonia, a relatively new resident in Spire, to start accusing her neighbours of any wrong-doing, and so I changed the conversation before she could say something she might regret. 'Nanny passed on to me your message about Henry's bag.'

'Oh good. I hope you don't mind taking it back to Sussex.'

'Not at all.'

'I don't think it's urgent. He said there was nothing much in it.'

Antonia pointed to a faded, canvas satchel sitting on the other end of the transparent table. 'That's the bag over there; it's only small.'

The prospect of being in touch with the handsome Henry had been for a little while mildly attractive. But now that I'd met Toby, I realised I hadn't actually thought about Henry very much at all.

After a lengthy dearth of attractive, single men in my life, who would have thought that two prime specimens would cross my path in the space of just a few days? According to my dear but not always very wise mother, this is how husbands appear.

'More tea?' Antonia broke my thoughts, holding up the spotted teapot.

'Yes please.' I pushed my mug towards her.

'Have *you* been questioned, Susie?'

'I have. I was called in to the station yesterday afternoon.'

'So was Ben!' exclaimed Antonia.

'I know he was. I shouldn't really say but at Beckenstale

Manor this morning, Inspector Grey told the family that Henry, Ben and me are no longer suspects.'

Antonia flung apart her long, thin arms, took in a deep breath and let out a large sigh. 'Thank goodness. What a huge relief.'

'Isn't it?' I said, nodding agreement.

'Ridiculously, we both began to feel guilty when we thought it was going to be difficult to prove our innocence. Oh, Ben will be so much more relaxed now. And as for Henry, I have been feeling terrible that we got him involved. Although Ben reminds me every time I say this that Henry did ask himself to stay.'

I helped myself to another bit of shortbread. It was even better than Geoffrey's mother's, despite the fact she was Scottish.

Antonia wanted to know more. 'Naturally I never doubted any of you for a moment, but how did the police come to the conclusion that all three of you are innocent?'

'From what I can make out, it was all to do with the noise that Lord Greengrass was making when we first heard it. I can only describe it as a very deep gurgle, which at the time sounded almost inhuman. But apparently Inspector Grey has a doctor's confirmation that what we heard was in fact Lord Greengrass's last breath, and that's why it sounded so unusual as actually that strange sound is what it does sound like. And by the time we had heard it there was nothing any of us could have done to save him.'

'Yes, they're right,' said Antonia, as if she were convincing herself. 'I read somewhere that it can take up to twenty minutes, from the time of death to when the system packs up, for a body to stop twitching and making disturbing sounds. I know, as I was once on a plane to America when a man had a heart attack and there was nothing anyone could do. We all sat there watching as his life left his poor body. It was a dreadful thing to see, Susie, absolutely dreadful.'

I didn't doubt it for a moment.

Antonia continued, 'I am so sorry that Situp ever dug up that damned bone.'

'It's not his fault,' I reminded her. 'Any dog could have done the same. And I'm sure it's nothing to do with anything that caused Alexander's death.'

'I know. But all the same, I feel bad about you three being first on the scene.'

'Don't worry, we're all grown up.'

She smiled at me, pleased that I did not bear a grudge.

'Isn't it surprising,' said Antonia, 'how easily the police passed over that business with the bone. They didn't seem to be bothered about it at all.'

'Thank goodness.'

I took a sip of tea. 'I must go in a minute or else I'll be late for lunch with Diana, but I was just wondering if you asked Ronnie about where he was before he came to your back door?'

'I didn't need to as he was complaining that he'd spent all morning clearing up the bar from the night before.'

'Do you think he always clears up the next day?'

'I wouldn't think so. I've heard that most landlords like to get the bulk of the work done the night before as they have to stock up and get the lunches and so forth the next morning. But the Greengrasses' butler, according to Ronnie, had been in the pub boozing heavily on Saturday night and it had been a struggle to get him to leave. By the time he managed it was very late, and so Ronnie went straight home and left the mess to deal with on Sunday morning.'

'Is he a drinker?'

'Is Ronnie a drinker?' Antonia repeated ironically. 'He keeps a glass of whisky behind the bar. I'm sure the ice in it is the only way any water passes his lips. He's one of those old-time soaks who holds it together well.'

'My Great Uncle Stephen was like that, although the large red crustacean in the centre of his face gave it away. His nose was consumed by booze years before I was born.'

It was time for me to go, and Antonia held the kitchen door open for me as I went through into the cold porch and tiptoed my way around the boots and scattered shoes.

'Sorry about the mess,' she said. 'We are always in a rush when we come through this little part of the house, either taking kit off and longing to get warm in the kitchen, or putting kit on desperate to be out in the fresh air. Let me open the door, it gets so stiff at this time of year with the wet weather.'

Antonia pulled hard on the handle and the whole thing almost toppled her over as it flung open. I patted Situp who was following us out.

'Bye, Susie, keep in touch, and do let me know if there's anything at all I can do for Diana.' Antonia waved with one hand as she held Situp's collar with the other.

I disappeared through the hedge, hurrying to the car in the hopes of having enough time to telephone Sarah Hember before Diana expected me for lunch.

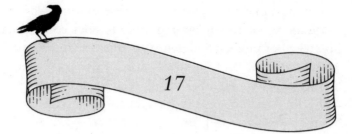

17

A fog was building on the windscreen as I held the telephone to my ear, nervously waiting for an answer.

'Hello,' said a meek-sounding voice.

'Good morning, Mrs Hember. My name's Susie Mahl. I am a friend of the Greengrasses and wanted to get in touch with you.'

The voice at the other end of the telephone took on a high-pitched panicky timbre. 'Oh Miss Mahl, I haven't known what to do. I saw the news and have been feeling so incredibly guilty that Lord Greengrass and I had our secret.'

She'd started crying, I could tell by the muffling sound of her putting a hand against the mouthpiece. Knowing how useless I am on the telephone I decided to chance my luck in the hope she lived near by.

'I'm in Spire village and wondered if I could come and see you?' My fingers on both hands were tightly crossed.

'Yes, I'm at home.' She snuffled down the line. 'I live in a farm cottage not far out of the village, past the church. Second turning on the left, Pinclanty Cottage.'

'Great. I'll be with you in five minutes.'

I hung up, hardly believing Mrs Hember could possibly live so close. Then I hoped my nosying around wasn't about to land me in any sort of trouble. Judging by the tears Mrs Hember wasn't feeling at all happy.

Could Alexander really have been having an affair? Surely he was too old for that? But then again, I really hope the zest of life doesn't leave us just because we're in our seventies. And Alexander did have a glint in his eye. Even Diana had said so, when she'd recognised a similar look in Henry; and Alexander had kept his financial affairs private from his family.

I knew deep down that Diana was someone who preferred to be on her own, and that she didn't really like other people's company. It wasn't inconceivable that in response to this Lord Greengrass could have been keeping two women at the same time without anyone knowing. I had liked him too much to believe he'd strayed, but I reminded myself that I shouldn't be too idealistic or naïve.

Given the close proximity of Sarah Hember's home, Diana may well never have noticed if her husband had disappeared for an hour or two in the day.

Pinclanty Cottage came into view, its sign swinging in the breeze. I turned into the drive and before I even got out of the car I could hear a pack of howling dogs crying out. The door to the pebble-dashed, rather ugly house opened and there stood a short woman who looked like she'd just returned from the hairdresser.

'Hello, Mrs Hember, I'm Susie,' I said as I walked up the path between two lawns trimmed like a doily round the edges.

She had gone back inside and I trailed along behind, closing the door after me. The house was hot and full of china animal figurines. Three cats prowled around the landing, but the overriding smell was one of dog.

'Please, call me Sarah,' she said as I followed her into the kitchen.

'Thank you for letting me turn up out of the blue.'

Without a word, Sarah turned towards me, and her watery eyes looked fearful as she shoved a crumpled envelope in my direction. I had no option but to take it.

'Is this for me?'

'It's the cash,' she mumbled, lips quivering. 'I wasn't going to keep it, honest I wasn't.'

'Don't worry, Sarah.' I looked at her in what I hoped was a sympathetic manner. 'I'm not here for this.' I flapped the envelope in my hand as if I knew what it was for. 'I just wanted to make sure you are okay, and to get to the bottom of your meeting with Lord Greengrass. If you can tell me why it was that you met him on Saturday night, then I promise I won't breathe a word to the family if you don't want me to.'

My conscience was clear in making such a pledge as I knew that I could tell whatever I was about to discover to the police if needs be.

'Lord Greengrass was buying one of my purebred cocker spaniel puppies. It was going to be a surprise for his wife.'

I hadn't expected this, and I wanted to believe her. 'Why did you meet in the Dorset Horn?'

'It was a secret. He didn't want Lady Greengrass to know and he knew she'd never look for him in the pub.'

'I see. This all makes sense now.'

It then upset me how unfair it was that the one present from Alexander Diana would likely have loved was now never going to reach her.

Sarah's voice was still wobbly as she explained. 'He paid cash in advance. The puppies are ready to leave their mother this week, but I'll find it another home.'

'May I see it?'

I wanted to confirm that she was telling the truth. Sarah was just a little bit younger than Diana, and definitely more attractive, and so I still felt slightly sceptical.

'Of course,' she said, seemingly very happy that I'd asked. 'They're out the back.'

We went through the kitchen and out to a small patio housing kennels.

'My goodness, you have a lot of dogs.'

'I love dogs, Susie. Always have. They're my companions.'

She unbolted a stable door and we both stepped in onto a bed of straw. Lying curved into the corner was an exhausted-looking bitch with four sweet puppies suckling.

'I've nicknamed him Secondo,' said Sarah. 'He's the one with the wagging tail. Pick him up if you like.'

I bent down and took the hungry puppy away from his mother. 'He's adorable.' I'm not normally a huge one for baby animals, but he was very cute.

'Lord Greengrass chose him.'

The puppies all looked identical to me, but the fact Alexander had chosen one especially for Diana made me wish I could give it to her.

'Would you mind if I did a drawing of him? I'm a

pet-portraitist and don't often get the chance to draw such little bundles.'

Even I was surprised at what I'd just said.

Sarah looked a little nervous again. 'I've got someone coming at one o'clock, but if you're quick then yes, of course.'

'Thank you so much. I won't take a second.'

I put Secondo down on the straw and took my sketchbook out of my bag. He started hopping around like a bucking bronco, which made us both laugh.

It's fun drawing something that moves as there is never a long enough period of calm to struggle over the detail. You just have to get it down on paper as quickly as you possibly can. Secondo's behind was bopping in the air and I exaggerated his movement with several poses drawn one on top of the other, producing a messy though decipherable animation of the scene.

'My goodness that was quick,' said Sarah, even though she was curiously – I thought – uninterested in the actual finished picture.

Lickety-split we were back in the kitchen, Sarah convincing me I should take the money.

'I'll give it to Lady Greengrass as soon as I get back to the Manor, but do you think there's any chance you can hold off finding Secondo another home until next week?'

'Why?' asked Sarah, surprisingly abruptly.

'I think Lady Greengrass might still like to buy him, once things have settled.'

Sarah sounded dubious. 'Well, we'll have to see. I don't like my babies going to a broken home. They need love, comfort and stability. Dogs are very intuitive and a recent death in the family could be upsetting for them.'

'I completely understand. But I know Lady Greengrass would make an adoring owner, and of course she would have all the more time for her puppy now her husband is no longer with her.'

I promised to ring her either way within the week, and so without even touching on the fact that Alexander had actually been murdered, we were on the doorstep saying goodbye and as my keys turned in the ignition the dogs on cue started to howl.

As I drove away I wondered about Shepherd's version of events. Surely he must have recognised Sarah Hember and known about her dog breeding. If so, he should have been able to work it out for himself that Alexander was most likely buying a puppy.

I headed up Beckenstale Manor's drive which winds itself through the park before getting to the grand house.

It was only once I'd reached the yard and was parking my car that I realised I'd forgotten to take Henry's blasted bag from Antonia's kitchen table. Drat. But there was no time to turn around as it was only three minutes before one o'clock.

Now that I'd conquered the Post-it note, Toby was on my mind. The puppy revelation seemed a perfect excuse to be in touch. Even though I risked being late for lunch, and upsetting Diana, I reached for my mobile, and typed:

> Sarah Hember innocent. Selling
> Lord Greengrass a puppy. Thanks for
> lunch.

I paused as I wondered how to sign off. Sigh.

Then I typed Susie and pressed send before I could change it to anything else.

It's very difficult in the casual spirit of modern communication to know how to end a correspondence. None of us truthfully like to use the expression 'Best wishes', but it – or 'Best' – fits the gap when 'Yours sincerely' is too formal, 'From' too childish, 'Love' too much and 'x', or even 'X', can't be sent before the other person has sent you one first.

I have a Russian friend who tells a story of when she first came to work in London. At the top of her profession in conglomerate social marketing, she's a feisty, level-headed woman who travels the world to give seminars to vast audiences of hungry venture capitalists. All this capability is hidden behind a beautiful, elegant, urbane girl who mistook the 'x' at the end of an email as a British symbol for signing off. After a week in her new London job with 300 emails sent to the great and the good, Julia was called into the Chief Executive's office where, without her being offered a seat, her boss boomed, 'How you converse out of work, madam, is entirely up to you, but never again in your senior role within this company let me or any client receive an email from you with kisses at the end. It's unprofessional and downright disrespectful.'

Gulp. My poor friend! There are few things worse than being misunderstood to such an extent you are left without the slightest bit of hope of explaining yourself.

My phone buzzed with a message.

Good work Pet Detective. Toby x

I liked 'Pet Detective'.

Very clever, Toby.

I didn't allow myself to think the kiss meant anything special, but it did put a spring in my step as I hurried from my car in search of Diana.

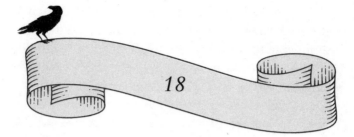

18

'Lady Greengrass is waiting for you in the conservatory,' Mary called down to me. She was perched high up on a steep set of folding steps as she dusted the enormous chandelier hanging above the hall.

'Thanks Mary.'

I found Diana standing in front of an electric blow-heater.

'Hello Susie. I am so pleased you've come back for lunch. I don't fancy a crowd but it's nice having you for company.'

Good, she seemed pleased to see me, and willing to overlook my being just a little late.

I was glad that I'd put on a cardigan over my polo neck. It was polar cold in the conservatory, a room I previously thought reserved for summer dining, but alas it was now clear that the Greengrasses liked to use theirs all the year round, no matter what the weather. I tried to be positive, reminding myself that the conservatory had a lovely view out over the lake and into the park beyond, and as it was a sunny, clear day it was nice to be in such a light room.

'Sorry about the chill,' Diana said as she rubbed her hands together. 'Shepherd obviously turned off the heating in here after this morning's meeting. It shouldn't take too long to warm up, though. Here, let's sit together at this end of the table as it's close to the heater.'

Diana sat down on her chair as if it were a throne. There was a sense of pride surrounding her and for a moment I felt irritated. But I tried not to let my emotions show as I re-laid our places using the cutlery that had been put at the opposite end of the table, and then placed the bowl of disappointingly cold food between us.

'Aren't Arthur, Asquintha and the boys joining us?' I asked as I sat down.

'No. They were going to, but after this morning's discussion they changed their minds. Arthur said they wanted to spend the day with just the two of them and so he's arranged for Nanny to take the boys out.' Diana sounded put out.

'Sounds like a good idea. Asquintha looked worn out this morning,' I said mildly.

Diana's voice didn't soften. 'That's no excuse. If you ask me why neither of them are joining us, I'd say it's Arthur not standing up to his wife who, reading between the lines, was overly sensitive to the scrutiny in this morning's meeting.'

'Hmm,' I mumbled, not wanting to add anything to the conversation.

Unfortunately for me, Diana was not willing to let the subject of Asquintha drop. 'As she doesn't have an alibi that blasted woman has got us all in the awkward position of having to take her word for it.'

Diana put a fork mounted with goats' cheese, red

onion and lentil salad into her mouth and with hardly any time to swallow, she asked, 'What sort of mother leaves her husband to dress and take the children to Sunday school, Susie?'

I came up with a pathetically diplomatic answer. 'If Arthur wants to spend time with his children, then I think that's nice.'

It upsets me when childcare is so obviously an onerous duty as far as their parents are concerned. It's confusing why couples choose to have children if without them is the only time they feel they have 'their life back'.

It wasn't for me to judge as I don't have children, but like Diana, I had wondered why Asquintha would stay at home and leave Arthur to take their boys to her choice of church, which for someone like me is an institution right at the centre of what it means to be a family.

But I could see that Diana's negative opinion of Asquintha stemmed more from her constant struggle in accepting a middle-class daughter-in-law. As far as I could see, she never let an opportunity to criticise Asquintha slip by.

On cue, Diana added, 'I just don't understand why husbands have to take an equal share in bringing up children these days. Alexander never once changed a nappy or dressed the children, and he was all the more of a gentleman for it. I despise this contemporary drive for equality of the sexes. Susie, we must celebrate the differences, that's what I say.'

Not being a wife I wasn't overly keen to voice my opinion on the issue as I knew that Diana only wanted me to agree with her. But I knew that I certainly wouldn't mind marrying a man in touch with his feminine side. Changing nappies, bathing children, being able to sew and iron were all perfectly acceptable in a man, as far as I was concerned.

Diana wasn't really paying me much attention. 'Cross-class marriage is when it all goes wrong, as Arthur and Asquintha show. In come common values and a desire to be one of the people. If I could give you a sound piece of advice on the matter, Susie, it would be stick with your own sort.'

I had a sudden naughty urge to ask her who 'my own sort' might be, but I kept quiet. I knew that Diana frequently speaks without thinking, and it might seem rude to probe further.

I felt sorry for Asquintha, and I wished that Diana respected her more. It would make anyone unhappy if they felt they could never please a forceful mother-in-law when they had to live together, cheek by jowl. My fingers were crossed that Asquintha really was innocent.

There were second helpings and it was clear Diana had her appetite back.

At last there was a change of tack in the conversation. 'Did Inspector Grey find anything particular in the study?'

'Nothing he made a noise about although he did package up a few things.'

'Did he really? Well, he jolly well should have asked me first. What liberties,' Diana huffed, 'What did he take?'

I listed the various bits and bobs, which sounded much like I was playing the party game of who can remember the most objects placed on the tray.

I've never liked party games. I have always driven myself to be good at things rather than to be good at winning, unless of course one led to the other. From a very young age the pleasure others got in coming first in trivial activities would very often make me not want to join in. My parents had been very puzzled as they didn't understand why I would feel so strongly.

Diana was surprising nonchalant about the items that Inspector Grey had taken, until she cried, 'His diary?' as if that had been an absurd choice to remove.

'Yes, the latest one.'

'They're welcome to it. He wrote it in the study every evening before bed. Dull as ditchwater I would imagine.'

'He let you read it?' I asked, surprised at such unusual openness on the part of Diana.

'I wouldn't have wanted to, even if he let me. Poor Alexander wasn't the most engaging writer. You should have seen some of his early letters to me. He used to go off on a tangent about birds in his garden or the smell of the morning air. Waffling on like a dilettante.'

To me this sounded very romantic; Diana simply did not know how lucky she had been to have found a husband not afraid to open his heart to her. The possibility that you could form a relationship through letters, rather than dreaded telephone calls or text messages, felt to me a perfect way to fall in love.

As for reading a husband's diary, I told Diana that I doubted I'd be able to resist, nosy as I am.

'Just you wait, Susie. Marriage isn't all sweetness and light. Sometimes things are best buried under the carpet. Or, in my husband's case, written down for no one to read.'

Was this really the only way to have a lasting marriage? Maybe for Alexander and Diana it had been so. I preferred the example set by my parents: get it all out on the table before it goes bad, work through it, and love each other regardless.

For me, being a Catholic, I will adhere to the rule, more popular in previous generations, that once married in the eyes of God it is a sin to break your vows. I don't doubt that in a large part this is why I'm still single, and still searching for the man I can imagine spending the rest of my life with. It's a tall order, and sometimes I feel I'm looking for unattainable perfection. If only I were a little more easy-going and capable of revelling in the thrill of the here and now. The noveau riche and famous are particularly good at this. Marriage for them seems to be a whirlwind romance and a huge party with the bride at the centre, all in the knowledge that it can be dissolved if commitment becomes too much; shrugging off the insincerity of ceremonial vows when a higher profile or better-looking option comes along. The fortunate outcome in most cases is that it raises the individual's public profile, no matter what.

I've seen this first-hand. When I was a recent graduate, I moved to London and by chance landed a job as a roving house-sitter among a rich vein of celebrities. Whilst they were residing in their Californian condo or Ibiza party pad I was effectively personal assistant back in the UK, looking after their homes. My efficiency at getting things done within a specified time frame, however short that may have been, combined with an unexpected ability to foresee and dispel a problem before it materialised, led me to the homes of rich pop stars and successful actors. I limited myself to London and I was never out of work. For six years I lived in the lap of impersonal luxury within Zone 1, and watched marriages end, and the newspapers eagerly report who had wronged whom. By the seventh year I had found the merry-go-round of my employers' bed-hopping and philandering too depressing to be around any longer.

'Susie,' said Diana in a warm voice, noticing I was lost in thought. 'Are you okay? I do hope this whole business isn't getting too much for you. You must say if it is.'

This was the kind and caring Diana I liked.

'I'm sorry. I was just thinking about marriage and how many pitfalls there are.'

'Oh, don't you worry about that. With your pretty face, you shouldn't be left on the shelf much longer.'

I think this was supposed to be a compliment.

I ate up the small bit of salad left in my bowl. Diana rang the hand bell and in came Mary.

Without a word she laid down a tray of coffee and dark chocolate truffles and removed our empty plates. She'd hardly left the room when Diana told me, 'Poor Mary has got herself into a ridiculous state about the staff interviews with Inspector Grey this afternoon. Servants are not equipped for such interrogations; they're simple souls.'

'I was nervous when I went to give a statement yesterday. It's not a nice feeling being interrogated, and you feel as if you are having to prove yourself innocent,' I said, with empathy.

Diana gave a disgruntled sigh. 'It was abhorrent that Arthur needed an alibi. That anyone could think he could have murdered his own father is absolutely absurd.'

Diana reached for the chocolate.

'We must have one of those delicious truffles. They arrived with a bunch of flowers last night from our Lord-Lieutenant.'

'That was kind of him,' I said, taking one and putting it straight in my mouth.

'*He's* a she, and it would have been me representing the Queen in our county this year if they hadn't thought it unfair to hand over an almost full-time job during Alexander's first year of retirement.'

'What a great honour in a county so full of respectable people,' I said.

I passed Diana her cup of coffee with two lumps of sugar and took a sip from mine.

'Well, it won't come my way now that Mrs Fishbone's got it.'

I'd never heard of Mrs Fishbone.

'She's just like her name, a bloody irritation when you come across one; and thanks to her taking a stand against Alexander's planning application for the land he sold we have not spoken in years. It's not that I like all those common people living on what used to be part of our estate, but it really was unpleasant of her to put up such a protest. What's more, in losing the battle, she had the audacity to spread a rumour that Alexander was a dishonest man.'

It amused me that although Diana was cross with Mrs Fishbone, she was happy to enjoy the chocolate truffles the Lord-Lieutenant had sent over.

Generally, I thought, Diana seemed surprisingly unfazed by the fact a murder investigation into the death of her husband was busy going on all around her. And now that Alexander was gone, it seemed that she would carry on more or less as she had done before.

Diana said she would be dining with Arthur, and so maybe Nanny and I could eat together again.

Just before I got up to go, knowing Diana would be wanting her afternoon rest soon, I remembered Mrs Hember and the puppy.

I wasn't sure what Diana's reaction would be, and so I said cautiously, 'I forgot to mention earlier, but I found out this morning that Alexander had bought a cocker spaniel puppy to give you as an early Christmas present.'

'Oh my darling husband! Has Sarah Hember had another litter? We have been waiting an awfully long time. What a tremendous surprise, but how could you possibly know?'

I explained all about the note in Alexander's study, with Mrs Hember's number scribbled down, and that I'd decided to call in case it was connected to Alexander's death.

Diana sounded thrilled. 'Is the puppy coming today?'

'No, not yet. Alexander had already paid for him, but Mrs Hember insisted I gave the cash back to you.' I put the envelope from my bag on the table. 'She understands you might not want to take him, if you'd rather she found another buyer then I have to let her know within the week.'

I brought my sketchbook out. 'Here you go, this is vaguely what he looks like.'

'You are clever, Susie. What a little character, and so full of beans. Tremendous.'

'If you want, you can keep the drawing. In fact, please do; it's just a quick sketch I did when I met him.'

'I'd love to have him, Susie. Thank you.' She instantly tore it out of the pad without an ounce of care. I tried to keep smiling, which was a bit of a tussle considering I treat all my work with the utmost respect.

'Can you let Sarah know as soon as possible that I shall be keeping the little darling? You could tell her that Sid will be in touch to collect him once we've buried Alexander.' Diana smiled as she looked at my sketch. 'What a dear, dear man my husband was. I've wanted a replacement ever since Harriet went.'

I stood up to go but then noticed she was pulling a handkerchief out of her sleeve and wiping away what I am sure was a tear. Then I heard her say in a small voice, 'I mind very much that he's not in the ground, Susie.'

My heart went out to her; maybe Diana had been affected more than I'd thought. 'I am so sorry for you that the process is taking time.'

The embroidered handkerchief went back up her sleeve with a final sniff and I patted her arm in that reserved English way, knowing a good old blub always makes you feel better.

'We all need to find peace,' concluded Diana, 'and this will only come once we've laid him to rest.' Back out came the hanky. 'We could only begin to come to terms with Amelia's death once the funeral had been.'

I was pleased to see that buried beneath Diana's remarkable stoicism was some emotion. I had so wanted to believe it was in there, and now I knew.

'I am sure that very soon there will be an explanation.'

'I hope you're right Susie,' she said, pushing her hand-kerchief up her sleeve once more.

'Would you like me to spend the afternoon with you?' I asked, knowing the answer.

'No thank you. I am going to go for a rest.'

We were back to routine as usual.

I left the Manor feeling determined to get to the bottom of what had happened by the end of the week. My personal investigation needed to step up a gear, I thought. It was time to narrow down the suspects and get my hands on some firm evidence.

Back at Rose Cottage I swapped my loafers for walking boots, put on a Puffa jacket over my winter clothes, stuffed a pencil and sketchbook in my pocket and strode out through the park in the direction of Spire village.

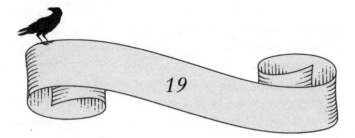

19

'Hi Antonia. I'm so sorry I left Henry's bag behind.'
'Come in, come in. Aren't you cold?'

I stepped into the porch and shoved the front door closed behind me. 'I'm not too bad, thank you. I'm a fast walker, which keeps me nice and warm.'

'Come into the kitchen, at least for a bit.'

She was still alone.

'There it is on the table,' she said, pointing at the bag, and going to stand in front of the wood-burner on her never-ending slim legs. 'I hadn't even noticed you'd forgotten it.'

I took my scarf and gloves off.

'We know,' said Antonia, 'that Henry has found it hard to meet like-minded people around Brighton, and so Ben thought returning the bag would be a good opportunity for you two to be in touch. Henry's a good friend of Ben's.' Antonia paused, a blank expression on her face, as if weighing whether to continue: 'Henry's possibly not someone to get romantically involved with, if you were thinking along those lines.' She smiled at me. 'He is very good-looking but I don't want you to be hurt.'

Antonia's warning made me nervous. Had she picked up on the frisson of excitement when I was first introduced to Henry, or was she just helping him make friends in a new place?

'Doesn't Henry live in London?' I asked, giving her an opportunity to clarify her intentions.

'Yes, but he's lecturing in Brighton for some time and you might be a good companion for him, for a month or two.'

'Ah, yes,' I said, realising there was no way out. Why is it that when you're single you long for your friends to get a grip and introduce you to an array of suitable men, but as soon as they do, like right now, the whole idea makes you want to paddle away as fast as you can?

It was hot in the kitchen so I removed my coat and perched on the back of the sofa.

Antonia had a confiding look on her face, and I raised my eyebrows slightly in the hope that she would carry on. 'He married Olivia, an old girlfriend of mine. Ben and I introduced them, and although they seemed happy enough at the start they divorced after eighteen months.'

'That was swift. I never realised. He didn't give the impression he'd been married.'

This was a black mark against Henry, though I wasn't sure at what point he could have dropped in to conversation the fact he'd been married, and actually why should he anyway?

Antonia seemed to intuit how I felt. 'You never can tell these days, Susie. If you are talking to a single man who has turned forty, you need to be careful as they've almost always had a past. And if they haven't, then that is just as worrying, although for a whole other set of reasons.'

'Henry's not forty, is he?'

'No, he's not. All I'm saying is that you need to think very hard before you marry someone. I daresay Henry is no worse than other men of his age, when his looks could have allowed him all sorts of high jinks.'

'Does he have children?' I asked.

'No, but you've hit the nail on the head as to the weak point of his and Olivia's union. They never discussed having children, and it came as a shock to Olivia when Henry announced on their honeymoon that he categorically didn't want any. Poor girl. I completely understand why she left him, although it wasn't easy for her as she really did love him. In the end, though, I think she loved the idea of having children more.'

I couldn't believe couples didn't discuss having children prior to getting married, particularly in this day and age where women have their own careers. Surely it'd be one of the major things you had to agree on before going in to it?

'And there was also the fact that Olivia thought Henry was deeply complicated, and very needy,' Antonia added.

I knew it. Henry was a troubled soul.

'How did Henry cope after they'd separated?'

'On the surface he returned to the single-and-up-for-anything Henry we'd always known. I do think men are so much better than women at blocking things out. But I take a peep at him sometimes when he doesn't know I'm looking, and I can't help thinking his *bonhomie* and his suaveness is all a bit forced.'

'What happened to Olivia?'

'Oh, she married another Harley Street surgeon and

popped out two little ones almost immediately. I'm happy for her but Bradley isn't really our type, and so we see far more of Henry these days. He never mentions Olivia.'

This reference to Bradley was the first snobby comment I'd heard from Antonia, and I felt disappointed in her. It's such an unattractive trait in upper-class people when they are incapable of, as they would put it, 'making allowances', for the middle-class partners of their friends. I liked Antonia and wished she hadn't said it.

'Why didn't Henry want children?' I asked and immediately regretted joining the ranks of people who think it odd when they meet a childless couple.

'Some people just don't, Susie,' said Antonia, a trifle world-wearily. 'But in this case Olivia was sure it was because Henry had issues over who his father is. We've never heard Henry talk about it, but she told me he thinks he's not his father's son.'

'What does Ben think?'

'Ben and Henry have known each other all their lives and Henry has never said anything to him. But then, as we all know, men rarely talk about feelings.'

'I have a friend who is adopted and his parents never told him,' I said. 'He only found out by rooting around his medical files once he was eighteen. I think he would've been better off not knowing as it's thrown him a bit off-kilter since and his birth mother doesn't want to know.'

'Ben says we mustn't judge, and that if Henry doesn't want to talk about it, then neither should we.'

I thought Ben was right and that I'd learnt a bit too much about Henry for the amount of time I'd spent in his company. It's never healthy knowing too much about someone you've only just met, and particularly for someone like me, who has it in my nature to want to get to the bottom of things. I couldn't make up my mind if my new knowledge made him seem more or less attractive, although it was certainly making me think about him.

I put on my coat and scarf, and remembered to pick up my gloves and the bag, which felt very light.

'You may bump into Ben,' said Antonia. 'He took off with Situp. I think he's struggling with his writing today as his brow looked crinkled, and so he may have gone far. It's what he does to get through writer's block.'

I had a final question. 'You haven't come across a Mrs Fishbone round here, have you?'

'Oh god, *that* woman. She's frightful.'

'Diana would agree with you. She was telling me about Alexander's disagreement with her. I think they fell out years ago over a planning application.'

'That doesn't surprise me. When we were landscaping the garden, we marked out an area to put up a Wendy house for Bella, and you wouldn't believe it but we had to apply for planning permission.'

'Planning permission for a Wendy house?' I repeated. This seemed silly.

'Yes, isn't it unbelievable? Mrs Fishbone is the one who got in the way. She came down on our application like a ton of bricks, saying it was the wrong height and it was too close to our boundary and it overlooked someone's property and took their light away, and goodness knows what else. We were going to put in revised plans, but then Ben and I decided that she'd got it in for us and so we were never going to win as she's our Lord-Lieutenant and carries a lot more clout round here than we do. The local builders we used told us we should slip the planners a golden handshake, but Ben's far too honest for anything like that. I would have happily done it but I couldn't go behind his back.'

'You can get inflatable Wendy houses now,' I said, not missing an opportunity to solve a problem. 'I'm sure that would be allowed.'

'Maybe it would be but as you can see out of the window,' she pointed towards the garden, 'we've put a sandpit in the place it was going to be. Bella loves building castles, and so I've told her that I'm hoping she marries someone with a castle one day.'

I laughed with Antonia at the honesty of what she wanted for her daughter.

'I must go,' I said. 'If we don't see each other again this week, I'll be back to deliver the drawing before Christmas.'

'Don't worry Susie, Christmas is almost upon us. I'd hate for you to think you had to get it to us beforehand, particularly with all that's been going on.'

I let myself out. There was plenty of daylight left so I didn't need to head to Beckenstale Manor quite yet.

I had far more information than I could hold in my head and wanted somewhere to gather my thoughts and put it down on paper.

The Dorset Horn beckoned, and if there's one place primed for eavesdropping then surely a public house is it.

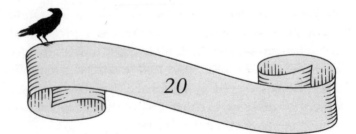

20

It was looking to me as if I had got both Alexander's and Henry's characters only half right. I didn't want to think sceptically about my friend Lord Greengrass, but it was hard not to with recent revelations.

The thing about murder is that the motivation does not necessarily have to be rooted in something of deep significance. I was fast beginning to think that sometimes something tiny but nonetheless significant to the murderer can spark the desire to kill. Or, just being in the right place at the right time could have led to a spur of the moment action. It's unpleasant to think about but it's true.

I was sitting next to a woman at dinner not that long ago and she was telling me about a recent Glaswegian court case where her father was the judge. A husband had murdered his wife with a pair of fire tongs for buying the wrong colour of budgerigar. Absolute truth, I promise.

These thoughts filled my head as I walked to the pub, which sits at the furthest end of Spire village from the church. I paused outside, looking up at the swinging iron ram above, thinking that the noise from inside sounded unusually busy for a Wednesday afternoon.

In the bar there were far fewer people than I expected. The woo-ha was coming from a table of Lycra-clad cyclists toasting each other. I didn't envy them being out and about in this crisp weather in such thin sports gear. All but one had very red noses, and rather than lager or soft drinks they were drinking steaming hot toddies. A cooing couple sat in an alcove by the coal fire.

The only others were two old codgers perched on stools pulled up to the bar, who each had half-drunk pints of ale in front of them. They were listening to what sounded like a rambling tale that Ronnie was telling, but then his eye caught mine.

'What can I get for you, my love?'

I was up at the bar and could feel the eyes of the men on stools straining to get a look at me without moving their heads.

'Half a shandy, please.'

'You visiting?' Ronnie pulled down on the beer tap in front of me.

'I'm staying at Beckenstale Manor.'

Ronnie's eyes flicked up at me, and his hand slipped on the tap. 'Whoops, took me by surprise, you sayin' you stayin' at the Manor.'

'I'm an old friend of the family.'

'Young old friend,' Ronnie joked, thankfully distracting us both from the underlying topic.

I paid for my drink and went to sit at a small table with my face to the door and my back to the bar. It's much easier to listen subtly to other conversations if you are facing in the opposite direction, I find.

I brought my sketchbook out of my pocket and with my eyes and thoughts in one direction, and my ears, intent on the conversation up at the bar, in another, I set to noting down what I'd learnt today. It was surprisingly easy to do both at once. Thanks to their age, these men were all a little deaf and that meant they didn't whisper.

'It's been so long since we've seen you, Ron. We woke up this morning and just decided to jump in the car.'

'Afraid I can't offer you a bed. I'm living now with Katy and she ain't lettin' me bring anyone in, male or female.'

'Wise that daughter of yours. Must take after her mother.'

There was a pause, in which I thought Ronnie might well be grimacing at these patrons he clearly knew of old. Antonia had told me his divorce had been messy. Then he said in a conspiratorial way, 'There's been a murder in Spire.'

'Gossip we want Ronald then, not entertainment,' chuckled one of the old-timers.

In my sketchbook I was mapping out what looked like a family tree but was in fact a mock family, each person representing a suspect. I used initials rather than names, and as I worked I looped connections between people. It sounds complicated but was the clearest way of seeing who was most closely connected to Alexander and who was least. I find that a visual aide-memoire helps me more than a simple list, although I know others think the opposite.

'That posh idiot from the big house got what was

coming to him in the graveyard on Sunday. I'm amazed it took someone so long to give him his due, and donk him on the head,' Ronnie went on.

'Ocht.'

I smiled when I heard the response of his audience. I didn't for a moment believe that they hadn't already heard of the murder. Then I thought that Ronnie may well be in for a windfall, as the notoriety of the village and this Agatha Christie-esque crime would likely bring in extra trade from those coming to gawp.

'There was a murder in this village?'

The elderly chaps were playing at being slow to cotton on. To my mind, there were elements of panto-mime to this scene. Although unrehearsed, they were feeding Ronnie the lines, and he was allowing them to do so.

'Yup.'

'Anyone fingered?'

I guessed that at least one of them had been watching 1970s crime drama reruns on BBC Encore. *The Sweeney* had a lot to answer for.

'Nah, not that I've heard.' Ronnie paused. 'It weren't me, before you go leaping to conclusions. Top-up, anyone?'

I was halfway through my shandy. The warmth of Antonia's house had made me thirsty but I was aware I shouldn't drink too quickly.

Ronnie continued, 'It's certain he was murdered, so I hear, as there's evidence…'

Drat. He'd been silenced by an extra-thin cyclist who was making his way from the far table to the bar. Why is it that when bicycling became cycling even the most amateur of Sunday sportsmen starting dressing as if they were professionals? The man passing my table had on skin-tight Lycra clothing, which left very little to the imagination. Those flaccid bulges really are too much to bring out in public, and I didn't much care either for the padded seat in his sports tights; it gave an unsightly impression of a baby's nappy. I gave an involuntary shudder as I averted my eyes.

I focused on my Tree of Suspects, while another round of hot toddies was ordered. I knew that at some point I would have to start putting red crosses through initials on my diagram, but it was going to be tough. I hadn't quite worked out yet what would happen on my system should one of these people have not actually committed the murder but instead been part of a conspiracy.

Painting trees sprung into my mind. Initially, you think how on earth am I going to represent all those leaves, the multiple grooves of the bark, the branches of all different shades and thicknesses? For a while it seems an overwhelming task. And then you see that if you let your hand and eye lead the way without conscious thought you find yourself portraying the simplest impression of the subject. Painting on top of this impression, and showing how the light falls on each separate element, soon gives definition to the tree. Almost before you know it, all that detail which made you apprehensive before you started has suddenly appeared in front of you.

I thought that if I could apply a similar method to my investigation, keeping the logic simple and not allowing myself to get caught up in or distracted by the in-between details (and right now this included dwelling on whether anyone was involved in a conspiracy), then hopefully all would have become clear by the time I had reached my conclusion. I remembered something an old boyfriend had once shown me written down: 'It deosn't mttaer in what oredr the ltteers in a wrod are, the olny iprmoetnt tihng is taht the frist and lsat ltteer be at the rghit pclae. The rset can be a toatl mses and you can sitll raed it wouthit a porbelm.'

So, I told myself, all I have to do is to get to the bottom of the beginning and the end of Alexander's murder; and find out what sparked it and who committed it. And to have any chance of saving Greengrass family relations, I must work it all out as quickly as I possibly can.

I took a large gulp of my shandy.

Turning back to my Tree of Suspects, I had A.G. (Alexander, Earl of Greengrass) at the crown, then, suspended and dangling from various branches depending on how closely connected they were to him, the initials of everyone whose name had come up in the last few days: D.G. (Diana, Countess of Greengrass), Lr.C. (Arthur, Lord Cornfield), La.C. (Asquintha, Lady Cornfield), G.S. (Groundsman Sid), N.A. (Nanny Angela), B.S. (Butler Shepherd), H.M. (Housekeeper Mary), M.F. (Mrs Fishbone), S.H. (Sarah Hember), A.C. (Antonia Codrington), B.C. (Ben Codrington), N.M. (Nanny May), H.D-S. (Henry Dunstan-Sherbet), R.R. (Republican Ronnie – I liked these initials), R.dK. (Ronnie's daughter, Katy), P.Y. (Phil Yard), I.Y. (Iona Yard), S.L. (Strange Loader). And finally I added S.M. (Susie Mahl) for the sake of thoroughness.

The cyclist returned to his table followed by Ronnie and a tray of hot toddies. As soon as he was back behind the bar he struck up the conversation with his friends again.

'If I were yous,' said Ronnie to his audience. 'I'd keep your visit short and sharp. People are sniffing around and everyone has their own theory. If you're seen talking to me I daresay the coppers'll have you in for questioning.'

'Murder happened in the graveyard on Sunday morning?' said one of the men on the stools.

'Thoughtful place to do it,' said the other.

I smiled to myself as I remembered my favourite sign, which is in Whitby, North Yorkshire: a large sign on a metal pole instructs 'No Overnight Camping' right beside the entrance to the graveyard.

'Who do you think done it, Ron?'

'Don't know and couldn't care. Never liked him. I'm sure it was him who ran over my dog all those years ago.'

'Mabel, your Staffy?'

'Yes. It still pains me to think about it.'

If there's one thing I've learned from people with pets, it's that when their beloved animal dies the owner suffers greatly.

Murdering someone ten years later in retribution for causing the death of a dog seemed a bit extreme, but I wondered if long-harboured grudges were perhaps the most potent. Mabel must have been the dog Diana briefly referred to under her breath on Tuesday morning.

Maybe on Sunday morning Ronnie was on his way to visit Antonia at the Glebe House, when he saw Alexander faint and with it an opportunity to give him a once-over.

Could what everyone assumed was murder in fact have been the disastrous unintentional result of a bit of rough-housing, which was never intended to cause death? Could Alexander's age and weakening health have led to a much worse outcome than had been meant?

I finished my drink and, as I went to leave, a pinboard by the door with newspaper cuttings caught my eye. There, right in the middle of the various stories, was the headline '*Egerton Goughs Sell Listed Building to Landmark Trust*'. Underneath a black and white picture of the very same round and fat stone tower that was in my photograph of Alexander and his loader.

Egerton Gough, Egerton Gough, I chanted to myself as I went out of the door and promptly scribbled it in my book. I was desperate to get back to Nanny's house and look them up.

The sun was beginning to go down and now the air had a really bitter bite to it. I took the road back to Beckenstale Manor's drive, fearing being alone on the now dark wooded footpath to the park.

The door of Rose Cottage was unlocked although Nanny didn't call out as I entered.

The noise of company in the front room travelled down the corridor. Tiptoeing to my room as I didn't want to announce my arrival just yet, I shut myself in the quiet of my bedroom, kicked off my shoes, plonked Henry's bag on my bed and wriggled off my coat. Slumping on the chair at my desk, telephone in hand, I typed 'Egerton Gough' into Google. A list of results appeared. My eyes raced over them looking for relevant information.

Their large pile of a house turned out to be barely twenty miles from here. It was a 10,000 acre estate, according to Wikipedia, and one of the best shoots in the country. Then I spied the information I was really after: Mr Egerton Gough, chairman of the Game Conservancy succeeded by the Earl of Greengrass.

It seemed ironic that anyone could chair the Game Conservancy while also being a keen fan of shooting pheasants.

I wanted to telephone but I knew I couldn't possibly visit at five o'clock in the afternoon, which would actually be more like six by the time I could get there.

I felt a bit restless. What to do? Then I looked down at Henry's bag and it wasn't long before I had convinced myself that, now it was in my possession, I had the right to look inside it.

Sadly there was nothing interesting. It was all very disappointing, being a comb, a half-eaten pack of chewing gum, a *Spectator* magazine, a blue biro that had been chewed at one end and an A5 notebook. I flipped through it quickly, but it didn't seem to have anything in it.

Damn. Antonia was right, there was nothing here that Henry couldn't do without or that yielded any new information. I put everything back in the bag and stuffed it under my desk.

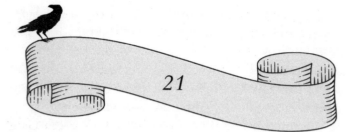

21

Lying on the single bed, faced with another evening spent alone and churning theories over in my mind, I asked myself, why not call Toby? I had nothing to lose, and he was the soundest person around to bounce ideas off.

I got up and pulled the curtains shut. It was only five o'clock but almost dark outside. My mobile was on the bedside table winking at me. Calling Toby was open to misinterpretation, I knew, but there was no time to hesitate on the next step in the plan. I dialled his work number, which I'd saved as soon as I had received his business card.

'Toby,' I said, suddenly feeling strangely short of breath. 'It's Susie.'

There was a dreadful din coming down the line and I could only just make out his 'Hang on a sec'.

'Shall I call you back?' I said, probably too softly as there was no answer. 'Toby?'

The background noise disappeared and I could now hear him clearly. 'So Susie, what's up?' he said. 'Great news on the puppy.'

'Yeah, I cleared that up thanks to your help…Um, I was wondering if you're free to meet for a drink this evening?'

'That would be great.'

My heart fluttered with his enthusiasm as he'd agreed instantly, although I then slightly deflated when he added, 'I could do with a drink. Been a long day and the damn photocopier's just let out a horrendous noise before – kaput! – it's given up on me.'

'How annoying,' I commiserated. I hate photocopiers, and they hate me. 'Technology's all very well until it goes wrong. Shall I come to you?'

'No need to do that. I'll be done here soon and we can meet halfway. Do you know the Pig's Trotter in Farby village, just beyond Spire?'

'No, but I'm sure I can find it.'

'It's about four miles on the main road, heading west out of Spire. No village as such, more a pub and red telephone box on a bend in the road. Would six-thirty work for you?'

'That would be ideal. See you then.'

I hung up as soon as I could. The thought of further telephone chit-chat with Toby made me so nervous that I'd rather be presumed rude than get into it. I wanted to have a bath but I had to say hello to Nanny first.

The door of the front room eased open over the fluffy carpet. The room was too warm, the curtains were closed and the television was silent although switched on. Shepherd and Mary were here.

'Hello everyone, I hope I'm not interrupting.'

'Not at all, Susie,' said Nanny, just as I caught Mary shooting Shepherd a hard-to-read glance. 'You're welcome to join us.'

Shepherd tapped an armchair next to him. 'Come and sit here.'

'Don't start treating this house as if it's yours, Shepherd. Susie has more right than you to pull up a chair in my front room.' Nanny sounded a bit piqued.

Mary tut-tutted at her husband, who ignored both of them.

All three of them had clearly come straight from work; Mary and Nanny were in their blue pinnies and Shepherd was so tightly stuffed into his three-piece suit I was surprised his hanky hadn't shot out of his top pocket the moment he'd sat down.

Nanny said, 'Susie, we've hardly seen you today, where've you been?'

'I think Diana wanted me out of the house while Inspector Grey was getting statements, but that's fine. I'm here to give her comfort and don't mind at all. It suits me that she doesn't want me all the time.'

Nanny was in high spirits. 'You'll be pleased to hear we're all off the hook following our interviews. You can sleep soundly tonight.'

'I never thought it was any of you,' I reassured the room just in case I needed to. 'I thought it must have gone well as you all sounded very jolly when I came in.'

'These women,' said Shepherd, 'have a bit of a routine.'

And with that Nanny said, 'Come on Mary, let's do a repeat for Susie.' And I saw an uninhibited side of her I'd never suspected. Both women stood side by side, holding their right hands up to their mouths as if they were grasping a microphone.

Nanny went first with 'I Just Called to Say I Love You'.

Mary followed with 'Killing Me Softly With His Song'. I found her swinging hips distracting.

I smiled and said they were great, and I was off for a bath. I was clearly not necessary to their fun, and as I relaxed for fifteen minutes in the hot water I could hear them going from strength to strength.

'Ain't No Mountain High Enough'. Nanny.

'You're the One That I Want'. Mary.

'The Look of Love'. Nanny.

'Lay Lady Lay' and 'When A Man Loves A Woman'. The Nanny and Mary duo.

And with that I reached for my towel. There are few things I enjoy more than a hot bath. It would definitely be my luxury on a desert island. I like it absolutely piping hot, don't stay in it long and look like Sir Lancelot's just rescued me for at least ten minutes afterwards.

I exchanged my thermal underwear from the day for a midnight-blue twinset, and thankfully I had a whole outfit Toby hadn't seen me in yet. It was about time the jazz tights had a second outing.

Just before I left the house Nanny said, 'That's how we did it Susie, we sang our hearts out to Inspector Grey, reeling off the Sunday morning love songs we'd listened to on Radio 2. Didn't miss one out of the order.'

'How fantastic, good on you!' I turned to Shepherd. 'Did you sing too?'

'Course not! But mine were like a white rabbit out a hat. I bunched my wife on Sunday morning. It was the silver lining, I tell you. Did myself in with the drink on

Saturday night and apologised to my Mary,' he smiled across at his sweet ageing wife, 'on Sunday, with a fist full of chrysanthemums.' He couldn't quite pronounce the word but gave it a jolly good try. 'And for once in my life I kept the receipt. So I had 100% proof that I'd visited Tommy's garage at 11.18am. And it's backed up with his word to prove it.'

I picked up my car keys, wished them a pleasant evening and dashed off before Nanny could remember that she hadn't grilled me on who I was meeting.

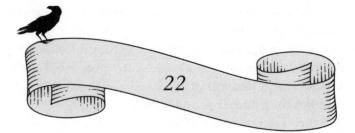

22

'I can't wait to hear what you've been up to since the puppy visit,' were Toby's first words to me.

'Oh good,' I smiled at him as he stood waiting for me outside the pub, under the glow of the porch light. He was looking particularly dashing in an open shirt and faded blue chinos.

The pub was quaint. A burrow of low-beamed tunnels and nooks and crannies. Green-baize tables harkened back to the home of card games. It looked like the sort of old-fashioned place that might still have a skittles alley out at the back.

Toby nodded at a few locals as we made our way towards the bar. Wednesday night had broken the back of the working week and so it was quite busy.

'Hiya Toby,' said a busty bar lady. 'We've not seen you for a while.'

'Been busy,' said Toby.

'I bet you have,' she tried to lean closer towards us and whispered in a hushed voice, 'We thought you were probably working on the murder...'

Toby didn't acknowledge her invitation to gossip, and

instead he looked at me to ask, 'Drink?'

'Vodka and tonic please.'

'Coming up,' said the bar lady as she turned to the shelf of spirits and exposed a tattoo of angel wings beneath the straps of her top.

'I'll have a pint of the ale please,' said Toby.

I thrust a note towards her. 'They're on me.'

Toby didn't protest, which I liked.

My father doesn't think a woman should ever pay their way. He says, 'If any man's lucky enough to take my daughter out they should treat her like a lady.' But he doesn't know what it's like out in the dating jungle nowadays. If a man pays for everything, as a woman it's all too possible to feel you owe him something in return. Consequently you find yourself going much further than you want to to avoid any accusations of 'taking advantage'.

I thought that by paying for these drinks it would keep me and Toby on an even keel. Our drink had been, after all, my suggestion.

'You take the bench Susie, as it has a nice comfy cushion on it.'

We'd come to a discreet table through the back and Toby sat in a lovely Orkney armchair.

My father likes a pub. His local drinking hole is a den of ageing men whiling away a Friday night. Going there at the end of the week is a routine he's followed all my life. Mum remains at home, being of the dated opinion that pubs aren't places for ladies. Cleaver Square has two pubs but Dad only ever goes to one, declaring the other 'full of young fillies'; apparently young fillies change the atmosphere.

'Nice place this, don't you think?' said Toby.

'Yes, it's very cosy. Reminds me of a place in Oxford where the ceiling was so low almost everyone had to sit down.'

'What about the bar staff?' Toby smiled.

'The floor was sunken behind the bar. Not sure if it was always like that or whether people were just shorter in the olden days.'

'I'm sure people were shorter. Haven't you ever noticed how low the doorway is on an original red telephone box?'

'That's a good point, I'd never thought about it.'

'Well next time you're in London go to the entrance of the Royal Academy and there under the arch you'll find a Grade I listed original Giles Gilbert Scott red telephone box and you'll see what I mean.'

I then thought I wouldn't point out to him that there is now a whole generation of younger people who barely even know what a telephone box is, low door height or not.

'So Pet Detective, what's the latest?'

Pet Detective! I had been repeating this catchy term to myself ever since I got Toby's text message, and was finding it increasingly endearing. Still, it was a bit embarrassing hearing him say it out loud, though Toby himself didn't reveal an ounce of awkwardness in doing so.

'Afraid not much. I actually wanted to pick your brains about local footpaths.'

'Ah, you've chosen the right person as I'm chairman of the local ramblers' club.'

I laughed. 'You are *so* the type. I can picture you in a

pair of zip-off trousers, carrying your map in a water-proof case.'

There was a pause, and then Toby said in a more serious tone, 'Go on, Susie, I could tell at our second meeting that you have the bit between your teeth for solving this case. How's it going?'

'Slowly,' I said, slowly. 'Although I bet I can get there quicker than Inspector Grey.'

'That means you've got something?'

'I might do but I'm hoping I can tell you in confidence. It is mainly details of certain people's private lives, which under normal circumstances I wouldn't be bandying about.'

'I don't think you would have rung me up if you didn't think you could trust me. Let's talk in confidence.'

I was hoping Toby would say this. I needed him to act as a sounding board, and he could help me weed out dead-ends and highlight important leads. And of course to have him as a confidant would allow me to contact him without, I hoped, seeming as if I was chasing him.

Although I enjoy working through my thoughts independently, I like very much to have a sounding board.

I'd discovered this the moment I met my first tutor at the Ruskin, and since then my working relationship with him, and our sifting through together of my ideas, has been essential to my artistic practice. Every so often I invite him into my studio to give an honest and truthful opinion of some art I've created. It's so valuable as I find I become so intricately involved and close to my painting that at some point I am no longer able to stand back and see it for what it is. In the case of something as deeply personal as a painting, I have then to put on a suit of armour, metaphorically speaking, to shield me from the sharp stab of his comments. But even when I don't like what I hear, I always think about it carefully; constructive criticism and feedback really can make a difference.

I knew that I needed someone like Toby to point out the mistakes I'd got too close to see. There was something honest and trustworthy about him, and I sensed I would value his opinions.

I showed him my tree of suspects and explained how it worked.

'Such a neat diagram, Susie,' he said, pulling the picture towards him and studying it carefully as I talked him through the initials. 'This is good and clear but surely you can cross some people off it?'

'I wanted to run my thoughts past you before I did.'

'Give me what you've got.' Toby pulled a large notepad out of his bag. 'Let's write down everything first.'

His systematic approach suggested he liked a less visual way of compiling information. But I knew it was time for a list, as there were various details not connected to any one person that needed to be set down.

To get things going I began to explain my theory behind not being waylaid by conspiracy to murder.

Toby understood what I was driving at. 'I think you're right in assuming that if you uncover the motive by looking at the details, the rest will become clear.'

With that I outlined my suspicions and theories and Toby wrote them down.

I wanted to hear his ideas before I mentioned the *Globus Cruciger*, which I felt was my biggest clue so far.

'Been hard at work, haven't you?' he said, with the suggestion that he was slightly surprised by the thoroughness of my investigation. 'What about S.L.? You haven't talked much about him?'

'I don't think Strange Loader's important for now.'

'You said his work involves guns, which, bearing in mind the shape of the bruising, could bump him up the list.'

I frowned.

'Okay, whatever's best for you.' Toby backed down quickly. 'I'm just here to help, I don't want any of the responsibility.'

What a perfect answer. I needed an accomplice, but one who let me take charge. My reason for not talking more about S.L. is that I did not want to put Toby off me. In fact I wanted him to like me a lot and if I immediately told him about another piece of evidence I'd been concealing he'd have reason enough never to trust me.

'Let's start with the first thing on the list, the Codringtons' dog,' he said.

'It was just an observation from my photographs that there might have been something going on inside the Glebe House.'

'Any idea what?'

'None at all, and he seemed perfectly happy when I saw him today. Antonia thinks it was jealousy of visitors staying.'

'That probably explains it. After all a dog's tail is a tenuous clue. Let's leave it for now.'

'Let sleeping dogs lie.'

'Exactly!' said Toby smiling. 'Moving on, Lord Greengrass's behaviour.'

'I always liked him, but from what Nanny's told me he doesn't sound as kind and caring as I thought he was. Taking this into account, there is reason to think he might have upset people in his lifetime, and what happened to him could be their revenge.'

'We'll put down unfair dismissal, dishonesty and unpopular with the working classes as accusations against him. Is there anything you want to add?'

I flicked through the photographs on my mobile and showed Toby the one I'd taken of the charitable trust document.

'Sorry Susie, I'm not following.'

'Lord Greengrass, unbeknown to his family, gave a heck of a lot of money to his old Cambridge College's specialist medicine project. Don't you think there's something strange about that?'

'I think there's something strange about you taking the photograph.' Toby, although disapproving, sounded impressed by my daring behaviour.

'I think it's necessary information. Alexander didn't study medicine.'

'That is odd.'

'The thing is...'

I stopped as Toby interrupted. 'Before we go into any of this in more detail, would you like another drink?'

It was only then that I realised how quickly I'd drunk the first one. It had gone down a treat.

Toby headed to the bar and my eyes followed. He was polite, handsome and easy-going. Not to mention that

I could now see he had a delicious bottom.

I looked down and my eyes went towards a flimsy bit of paper, roughly cut round the edges, drooping out of the top of the wire condiment-carrier. I plucked it out. 'Organic Product's for Sale'. I know someone who'd be driven mad by this misuse of the plural, not to mention the apostrophe: my friend Sam. Last time I saw him, in London, we were walking past an awning and he halted, deeply depressed by the signage: 'Meat's and Veg's'. Bad grammar amuses rather than irritates me but dear Sam is a book editor by profession, and I think he has a point about apostrophes used in ignorance or to make a sentence more fancy. Here's hoping his mother sorts this out in the wider scheme of things, as she's devoted a large chunk of her life to fighting the battle to get better state education.

As I looked at the piece of paper in my hand I saw,

Eggs, Veg, Bread and more...
Farby Farm Shop, open 7 days a
week 7am – 4pm.

A simple map was scribbled on the back and underneath were the words,
See you soon, Phil & Iona Yard

'The Yards advertising again?' said Toby who was back with the drinks.

'Um?' I was deep in thought.

'They're always at it, those fliers are in every pub, café and tourist office across this county.'

Toby sat down and propped his head up with one elbow on the table and scrunched his auburn hair in the cusp of his hand. He looked tired. 'I was thinking about that charitable donation when I was up at the bar. What was the family's reaction?'

'Diana said she would have stopped it had she known.'

'There's your reason why he kept it quiet. It's not as unusual as you might think for an economics alumnus to endow the medical department of their old college. Late-onset morality among successful bankers and old aristocratic families is what keeps these faculties developing. Most medical graduates never earn enough to do the same. Good on Lord Greengrass, I say.'

Toby took his head out of his hand. 'Let's address P.Y. and I.Y. then.'

'All I know from Nanny is that the Yards were very happy farming at Beckenstale until Alexander effectively sacked them. Mary and Nanny think they may have had something to do with his death.' I took a quick sip from my vodka and tonic. 'Do you know them?'

'Everyone local knows the Yards. They've lived round here for years, although I only know them by name. I don't think I've ever actually met them. I don't shop that posh.'

I said that neither did I. Organic produce only makes its way into my cupboard if by mistake I fill my basket from the wrong vegetable boxes in the supermarket.

'Diana's never mentioned their farm shop,' I said as I slipped the flier into my handbag.

Toby looked at me, and then wrote:

1. Visit Farby Farm Shop.

A man in a blue and thin white-striped apron loomed above us and lowered a large meat platter down to our table.

'I was hungry and ordered this. I thought you might like some too.'

'Yum.'

I was pleased Toby had got us some food as it would help soak up the alcohol before I had to get back in my car. We both reached for a slice of bread from the basket; it was still warm and the butter melted as I spread it.

'Right, onwards,' said Toby with a half eaten gherkin in one hand and his pen in the other. 'One hundred percent I don't think Diana was involved or committed her husband's murder.'

'Neither do I, but what makes you say that?'

'Well, do you know how long ago Lord Greengrass stopped drinking?'

'Ages ago. From what Diana's told me, he's been dry for at least ten years. She often praised the day he took himself off to AA.'

'There we have it; if she was going to murder him she would have done it long ago.'

'I see. You think nothing he could have done would have been worse than when he was a drunk?'

'Pretty much. My uncle's an alcoholic. Our family have seen his wife put through hell all their married life. I can tell you for certain that if Diana didn't murder her husband when he was drinking then nothing he did after would tip her over the edge.'

I crossed out D.G. and felt sad at the thought that almost every family can dig up an alcoholic.

'Good, we're pacing ahead. Put a line through Lr.C. and all the Beckenstale staff. We know for sure it's not them,' said Toby.

I told him about Nanny and Mary singing their alibi

for Inspector Grey, and how funny it had been watching them recreate the scene, but then he took the wind from my sails by pointing out that they could have listened to the radio programme later, on catch-up or a podcast, and got the running order of the songs then.

I sighed, but it was this sort of comment that showed me how much I needed a sounding board.

I put a mini pickled-onion in my mouth and immediately the acid caught the back of my throat and it very nearly shot straight back out again. Toby, for the first time since I'd met him, looked sheepish and, with watery eyes, I tried to pretend nothing had happened as I took a piece of cold ham to eat with the crust of my bread.

'You can cross out S.H., A.C., B.C., N.M., H.D.S., R.dK. and S.M. of course,' said Toby.

'How do you know Katy's innocent?'

'She's dating a friend of mine, and as I've already told Inspector Grey, Katy was at his house, as was I, on Sunday morning.'

'I see,' I said, jumping to the disappointing conclusion that maybe Toby had a girlfriend afterall.

'La.C. What are we going to do about her?' he said with such a friendly smile that immediately I decided once again he was in fact single.

'I just don't know. I hate to think it was her.'

'You said she's been reticent and has more reason than most to dislike the Greengrasses but she is married to their son. If she truly loves Arthur, surely she wouldn't kill his father.'

'If I trust my instincts, I can't possibly believe it is her.'

'Let's leave her be and hope narrowing down the others will help us decide later if she really is a prime suspect.'

'Ronnie's basically my key suspect. He has no one to verify that he was in the pub and not the graveyard between 11.15am and 11.25am on Sunday morning.'

'Hmmm.Your visit to the Dorset Horn didn't give us anything did it?'

'No. I have absolutely no proof; but still I do think it might have been him.'

I told Toby about finding the *Globus Cruciger*. 'Ronnie could have been in the graveyard on his way to the Codringtons' house, perhaps he saw Lord Greengrass faint and took the opportunity to make mischief. If he'd grabbed the globe it would have come free, and the cross on top would have given him the purchase to use as a weapon.'

'My God Susie!'

I then confessed that I hadn't mentioned this theory to the police.

Toby was silent. 'Spire is a small village, Susie. It would be damaging to accuse Ronnie if he's innocent. For the sake of not completely ruining his trade I think we should bide our time. It would be too obvious if he made a run for it, so at least we know where to find him when we've narrowed down the other suspects.'

Then Toby wrote:

2. Keep an eye on R.R.

'As for withholding information from the police, this is a thin line you are treading Susie, and I would strongly advise you to own up to finding the *Globus Cruciger*.'

'But I re-hid it in the hedge.'

'Even so, you can't keep concealing information from

the police. It's dishonest and this is a piece of evidence which could aid the investigation.'

Toby was right.

'Okay,' I said in agreement. 'Thank you for being straight with me.'

'I trust you Susie, but don't want to see you getting into trouble. I'm sure you can finesse how you will tell Inspector Grey, so let's move on.'

I looked at my tree. La.C., R.R., P.Y., I.Y., M.F., S.L., were the only initials not crossed out.

'Mrs Fishbone, she's our Lord-Lieutenant. Surely you can cross her out,' said Toby.

'Okay, I know she couldn't possibly have done it her-self, but she is the one person I feel may well know who did it.'

'Surely she would have said?'

'I don't necessarily think so. From what I've learnt she sounds quite an unpleasant woman, who gets a kick out of having something on somebody else.'

'This Henry Dunstan-Sherbet, he a friend of yours?'

Did I detect the slightest of edges to Toby's voice?

'No,' I said, a little too defensively. 'He's an old friend of Ben Codrington's.'

'Were they at uni together?'

'No, Ben was at Oxford and Henry's a Cambridge medic, same college as Lord Greengrass coincidentally.'

'Do you think there's a link?'

'What between Henry and Alexander?'

'Yes, that charitable donation went to medicine, didn't it?'

'Yes, but Henry didn't know Alexander.'

'Are you sure?' Then Toby wrote on the pad:

3. Look into charitable donation.

'Yes.'

I asked Toby about last breaths.

'We, or my team in the mortuary, have to do their very best, as we are doing here, to narrow down the options of causes of death,' he said. 'A last breath has a very distinctive sound and according to all three of your statements we agreed that what you heard was Lord Greengrass's last breath…And I spoke to Inspector Grey this afternoon and he said that May, the Codringtons' nanny had spent her day off at the dog races with her sister June. They have handed in all their chits, which confirmed bets placed over the time of the murder. There's something to be said for the older generation who don't throw anything away.'

Toby looked at his watch and then tore the list out of his pad and gave it to me. 'There you go, Susie. Let's discuss again once you've looked into these.

'Now are you going to tell me about S.L?'

Damn it, he hadn't forgotten I'd kept something secret from him. Was a good memory a point in his favour, or against? I couldn't quite decide.

'Promise you won't judge?'

'I wouldn't worry – so far I like what I see.'

That was the most forward thing any man had said to me for a long time. I tried and failed to stop a loon-like smile racing across my cheeks, so I had to make a show of searching in my bag for my sketchbook with my face firmly pointing downwards. I pulled the photograph out of my sketchbook and placed it in front if him.

'Where did you get this from? It's the original.'

'I found it in Lord Greengrass's study. Do you know this man? It's S.L.'

'I'm sorry to say I do. It's a sad story, as he died at the beginning of the year. I recognise that picture as the one used in the paper when Lord Greengrass resigned as chairman of the Game Conservancy, and when S.L. died.'

'Lord Greengrass resigned? I thought he retired.'

Toby pointed at the stranger. 'That man is Kevin Hawker. He was loading for Lord Greengrass at the Egerton Gough shoot, and was shot by a neighbouring gun.'

'How absolutely terrible. He wasn't a friend of Ronnie's was he?'

'He may well have been. He was local and so he probably drank in the Horn.'

I remembered Ronnie's dead friend, whom Nanny had mentioned.

'How did it happen?'

'There was an American man who'd won a day's shooting at a charity auction; he had all the gear and no idea. He swung at a low bird and killed Kevin stone-dead. Lord Greengrass resigned from the Game Conservancy the very next day and this picture accompanied the newspaper story.'

I slipped the photograph back into my sketchbook together with Toby's list and crossed S.L. off my Tree of Suspects.

'Pudding? They've got good ice-cream here.'

'I'm okay, thanks.'

'Well, we should come back sometime. It's worth it for the ice-cream, although nothing over here is nearly as good as the Italians. I was in Verona earlier this year,' it hurt to hear he'd been somewhere so romantic, 'visiting my sister,' I smiled again, 'and I can't tell you how good the ice-cream is there.'

'Pistachio with salted caramel is my favourite. I can never resist going for two scoops.'

'You are posh! Salted caramel is fancy.'

I thought the opposite actually; these days salted caramel this and that is everywhere, but it made me realise that I hadn't considered our backgrounds until now. Toby spoke with only the occasional twang of a West Country accent. His clothes were clean and shabby, his shoes round-toed and wax jacket suitably worn – he definitely didn't fall into the money-driven, nondescript layer of the county classes; types I don't generally go for. If I had to, I'd probably pigeonhole him as intelligentsia.

My father has always wanted a son-in-law with brains. Several times over the years he has reminded me that looks don't last but intellect will challenge, interest and accompany a partner all their married life. He had a point, but luckily for me Toby had both brains and looks.

'I did go to private school.' I rose to his teasing.

'Did you?' Toby sounded surprised. 'I know you've got connections as you wouldn't be a friend of Lady Greengrass if you didn't. But you've got more about you than most horsey public school girls.'

'Well, I'm not horsey that's for sure.' I was mildly offended by his assumption. 'My south London background probably gives me the edge. I was very lucky and got fully-funded scholarships to school.'

'I knew it.' Toby congratulated himself. And I congratulated myself that he had been thinking about me.

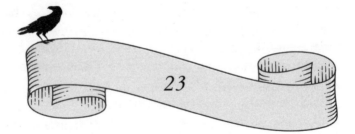

23

Nanny was still up when I got back, with the glow of orange light escaping from under the door. I knocked and pushed it open. The television was blaring.

'Susie!' her face lit up, although her colour was already high; she was a little tipsy as she fumbled with the channel changer to turn the volume down, and in fact turned the TV off entirely.

'Whoops, never mind. Did you ever hear the television up at the Manor? I could practically hear it down here. Shooting Susie, that's what does it, too many pheasants. Lord Greengrass could hardly hear at all.'

Nanny was exaggerating but only a little.

'Nice evening, Susie?'

'Yes, we went to the Pig's Trotter. It's a lovely pub.'

'Did you try their ice-cream?'

'No, but I did hear about it.'

'You eaten?'

'I have but have you? I could knock something up quickly if you want?' I offered, although I really didn't feel like doing this at all.

'I ate early with the boys. We had macaroni cheese.

When they move into the manor house I won't be doing any of the cooking any more so I'm making all the things I like making while I still can.'

'Will you miss cooking?' I couldn't tell from her roundabout sentence.

'Not an ounce. I don't mind cooking for the children, but Arthur and Asquintha are a different matter. She's gluten-free and that makes it difficult.'

'Is she really? Poor her.'

'Well Susie, I would never ask, but I bet Asquintha couldn't tell me what would happen if she did eat gluten.' Nanny stared into the room. 'Nothing. That's what, Susie. It's all about being able to afford specialist food and believing that eating it will make you super skinny.'

I agreed. You only have to look on a London menu and notice the price rise on gluten-free options to see that Nanny had a point. I would have thought that if an ingredient was taken out, it would make the end product less expensive but it always seems to have the opposite effect. You pay more for yeast-free, gluten-free, sugar-free, fat-free, whatever it may be that it does not have in it. Almost the worse something is for you – supersized, deep-fried, triple-layered, double-coated – then the cheaper it is. There is a balance in the middle somewhere and I thought of Antonia, who had said to me as I'd watched little Bella being fed half-fat wholewheat couscous, 'Here's hoping that celebrity chef that came up with this recipe can work out the balance some day soon, and then his poor wife can stop having babies to promote his latest book.'

I bent down to pull the Farby Farm Shop flier out of my bag and flapped it at Nanny. 'I picked this up in the pub. I bet they sell all sorts of faddy stuff.'

She took it from me and put it straight down to rest on the table between us, hardly glancing at it. 'I wouldn't know.'

I didn't let Nanny's reaction put me off. 'I never knew there was a farm shop so close by. It seems strange to me that no one's ever mentioned it.'

'I'll be in trouble if her Ladyship sees that flier. Neither she nor his Lordship liked us shopping there and so we stopped.'

'They are the same Yards who used to farm here, aren't they? The ones Mary mentioned?'

'Yes,' said Nanny quietly. 'They are.'

Was there a hint of guilt in her answer or perhaps she was just fading at the end of a long day? Either way I didn't think it was fair to point out that on Monday she had told me she had 'no idea' where the Yards lived. Nanny clearly feared the wrath of Diana and I wasn't unsympathetic.

'Who's this friend of yours that's put a rosy glow in your cheeks?' she asked.

How could Nanny tell? People often can, can't they? It's like when friends of the family say, 'Gosh, you look so well'. What they really mean is 'I am so pleased to see you're happy and have someone in your life'.

The longest relationship I'd ever had was eleven months. A year for me was a hurdle, and I hadn't yet found anyone special enough to get over it with. It's great fun having a boyfriend but I didn't think my life was unhappy without one. And then I thought of Toby, and I wondered if perhaps I was now ready to find someone to feel more serious about.

'Just someone I know locally,' I replied vaguely, and then asked Nanny about her evening.

Shepherd and Mary had stayed for some time and quite a lot of alcohol had been consumed, Nanny letting slip that Shepherd liked to tuck it away.

'Just like Ronnie,' I said, intentionally introducing his name.

'Ronnie! That's who we think did it.' Nanny gave a hiccup. 'I'll bet he was snooping round the graveyard on Sunday morning.' Two more hiccups followed. 'Pardon me, Susie, I thought I'd got rid of them before you arrived.'

'What makes you think Ronnie was in the graveyard?'

'Because that's where Lord Greengrass's body was found.'

'Yes of course. Any other reason?'

'Shepherd heard that the police were at Ronnie's house this afternoon for a long time.'

'Did they find anything?'

'None of us know.'

Nanny let out a yawn and so I picked up my bag and turned for the door. 'I'll see you in the morning. Thank you again for having me to stay. I'm getting quite used to living here.'

I didn't feel all that sleepy, sort of too tired to read a book but not tired enough to go to sleep. I'd scoured last week's *Week* cover to cover and wished I had another with me. Diana's coffee-table books would come in handy now but I wouldn't find anything similar in Nanny's house. There wasn't even a bookcase in my bedroom.

Nightie on, I went to brush my teeth. Looking in the mirror I remembered the *Spectator* in Henry's bag. That would do.

As I went back to my room I could hear Nanny's heavy breathing coming through the ajar sitting room door, clearly she'd failed to get up from the armchair.

Henry's bag was under the desk, just within reach without me having to get down on the floor. I stuffed my hand in the top of it and pulled at the magazine and out with it came his notebook.

I couldn't resist looking through it once again. This time I took care flicking the pages and found one thing written at the end, in small writing.

> 6:45pm
> 125 Devonshire Place
> 6 sessions
> £80

Curious, I sat on my bed and Googled 125 Devonshire Place. Up popped a martial-arts website registered to the address; no wonder Henry had such a strong athletic physique. I cast the notebook towards the open satchel and missed.

The *Spectator* provided an array of suitably drab, densely texted and unillustrated articles. I chose the longest and five minutes later it had sent me fast asleep, snuggled down cosily under the duvet.

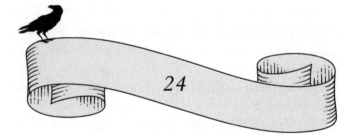

24

Other than the night before, I had been dressing, during my unexpectedly lengthy stay at Beckenstale Manor, in demure underwear, not feeling in the mood for anything fancy or remotely uplifting. It'd been mainly my thermal twinset, with me washing it at night, drying it on the bathroom pipes and slipping into it again the next day. But the morning after my drink with Toby, I was back in a push-up bra and skimpy panties.

It was early and still dark, but I was all fired up for a visit to the Farby Farm Shop. I didn't have a plan, and so I decided to strategise on my way there, or failing that, take in my stride anything thrown at me.

'Morning, Susie,' said Nanny's voice as soon as I opened my bedroom door. I wasn't expecting her to be up yet and, having flicked on the light in the corridor, I wasn't prepared for the shock of the salmon-pink Terylene vision before me. It was magnificent, although I couldn't help but think that poor Nanny would go up in a smoke if she stood anywhere near a naked flame in this particular nightie. The look of me shocked her too as she gave a visible jump.

'Sorry, Nanny.'

'Don't you worry a bit. It's me who should be sorry. Look at you all dressed already and back in that lovely, woollen skirt.'

'I woke early and thought I'd pop out to see the sunrise.'

'That's the artist in you, Susie.'

I smiled in agreement.

My headlights lit up the ornamental ewes grazing in the park. *I must try and find time to draw them before the winter sets in and their fleeces become dirty and raggedy,* I thought to myself. I love sheep and I'm always tickled by this rare breed of squat, docile bundles of wool with two ears poking out and an adorable pink nose with a grin beneath. Diana had told me that although once Beckenstale Manor had been a large producer of lamb, these days there was no need for the estate to employ a commercial farmer. A freelance shepherd kept this ornamental flock looking pretty and would have a few of the younger ones tupped from time to time to keep numbers even.

It was light by the time I turned into the yard before the farm shop, and I wasn't surprised to see mine was the only car. In my rear-view mirror I watched a thin-shouldered woman, Iona I guessed, flipping the sign on the door to 'open'.

'You're our first customer,' she said, as I unavoidably dinged the enormous bell on a string attached to the door.

I was left to stroll around and take a gander at their shelves. Squeezing between wooden boxes of vegetables and trying hard not to topple over the glass bottles of olive oil standing to attention on top of an old ale cask, I made my way to the prettily wrapped soaps and assortment of hand creams. There was an offer on gift boxes of three bars of guest soap – rose, sandalwood, and lime and bergamot. They smelt lovely so I thought they would do very nicely as a weekend present for my host on a future commission.

'Lovely gifts you sell,' I said on my way to the counter that doubled up as a barista bar. There was a delicious smell wafting from the coffee machine and some rather tempting Danish pastries that looked as if they had just come out of the oven.

'Thank you. We spend a lot of time sourcing our stock; my husband and I like to give the customer that extra bit more.' She took the soap from me and slipped it into a brown paper bag. 'Anything else for you today?'

'Please can I have a cup of black coffee?' I dithered over a pastry and then chose the largest.

'Sit-in or take away?'

'Sit-in please.'

'Pop yourself on one of those stools and I'll bring it over.'

The stools were two feet from the till and pulled up to the window, which looked out into the yard. Not a good view but enough to stare out at.

'Are you local? I don't think we've met before?' she said, as I turned around and took from her a steaming cup of coffee.

'I'm working for someone who lives nearby. I'm drawing their dog.'

'That sounds a lovely job. I'm Iona by the way.'

'Thank you.' I put the coffee down in front of me. 'I'm Susie.'

She headed back to the till with purpose, and then passed me a pastry. 'Just let me know if there's anything else I can get for you.'

I saw a noticeboard of local services near the door, and I thought it might be a good place to pin one of my business cards; having seen how much the coffee and pastry were, the people who could afford to shop here might very well be the sort of people who would think nothing of spending hundreds of pounds on having me immortalise their pet. But I decided to wait and see how the visit went before doing this, as if Iona realised I was staying at Beckenstale Manor she might not be keen.

'Thanks,' I said, picking up the local freesheet from the rack by my side. Its headline made my eyes open the widest they'd been all morning. '*Earl-ing Abuse At Murder Victim*' it said, and there was a strapline beneath: '*Lord-Lieutenant's Exclusive Interview*'.

As is often the case the headline was all bark and no bite. The manipulative editor was hinting that Lord Greengrass's murder could be linked to some sort of dodgy dealing that happened eighteen years ago. The gist of it was built around Mrs Fishbone's speculative accusation that Lord Greengrass had in some way bribed the planners to get permission for a housing development on the parcel of agricultural land that he had sold off.

To me the hard facts detailed in the story, along with the Lord-Lieutenant's comments, read as if they had been a tiny part of a much longer interview given in the past to the newspaper on something else, and were possibly libellous assertions that Mrs Fishbone should never have said. How could she possibly stand by these comments, if in the end her claims were proved to have nothing at all to do with his death?

Why don't more people employ the simple but effective 'no comment' if a journalist is asking a difficult question or two? By not doing so, Mrs Fishbone had revealed that she really did have a personal axe to grind, and now nobody had made that more obvious than this paper's editor. I decided not to take a copy of the freesheet to show Diana or Arthur as I thought it would only upset them, and pour salt into old wounds.

The coffee was very good and I sat staring out of the window, wondering how on earth I could discover whether Iona, who seemed to be very sweet, had anything to do with Alexander's death.

Life is unpredictable though, and sometimes fate steps in just when you least expect it.

A gruff-looking man burst through the door behind the counter. 'Iona! You seen the paper?' he shouted, furiously shaking a copy clutched in his fist. 'She's done it now, that Fishbone. Right on the nail.'

I tried to pretend I'd hardly registered he was there.

'Phil,' said Iona in a motherly tone as she indicated with her eyes that I was there.

He swivelled to look at me.

'Good god, I'm so sorry,' he apologised instantly, in a voice that made him seem as if he had become a completely different, much meeker person. 'I had no idea we had a customer.'

'Don't worry,' I said. Although I knew I could be staring a murderer in the face, there was something about Phil and his wife that I rather liked.

I shuffled around on my stool in the hope that it didn't look like I was paying them too much attention, and pretended to check messages on my mobile.

Phil put on an apron and began sharpening several large knives on the butcher's block.

Tiresomely they obviously weren't going to talk about the freesheet story in front of me, and so I slugged the last sip of coffee and counted out coins to the precise value of my bill, added a few more for a tip and put them in the saucer as I got up to leave.

Sometimes I wonder if I have traits of OCD as it gives me inordinate pleasure when I can pay for something with the exact change. Occasionally I feel shy of handing over, say, fifty pence in pennies and tuppences, but it is hugely satisfying and so I do it anyway.

When I reached the door I turned to say, 'Thank you very much.'

'Bye,' said Phil. 'Sorry for me outburst.'

We all laughed, me much more nervously than they (I had just noticed how very large the knives were that Phil was sharpening) when the loud bell on their door made me jump, and then I was in my car, soap in the glove box and driving out of the yard.

Thankfully Nanny's bedroom door was open when I got back into Rose Cottage and I saw no sign of her. I assumed she had gone across to the main house as the boys were off school this week because of their grandfather's death.

I was disappointed with my feeble behaviour. I'd wasted a trip to the farm shop and had got absolutely nothing out of meeting the Yards. A sad failure on the part of the Pet Detective.

I sat at the desk in my room mindlessly staring out of the window at the weathered rose garden. I don't like winter, I never have. The short days and unreliable sunshine get me down, but I'd still rather live in England than anywhere else. I often think if I were dropped in the landscape I would know exactly what time of year it is. There's no other country, where the seasons turn with such beauty.

Nanny's house was lovely and warm. I knew that all bills – electricity, oil and gas – were paid for by the Greengrasses as they paid the utilities for anyone on the Beckenstale Estate. Alexander had once explained to me that there was an element of self-interest in this seeming generosity – these running expenses were offset against the estate's profit and therefore helped reduce income tax. Owners of large houses with land are always keeping an eye out for legitimate expenses they can use in this way.

A home petrol pump has therefore been added to most country piles and comes under the account heading of 'farm vehicle expenses', despite being used to refuel all the family's private vehicles too.

Several times on pet portrait commissions, I have been instructed to top up my tank before I depart. I always say yes as petrol is so expensive these days.

After five minutes I still felt down in the dumps, and so I told myself that desperate times called for desperate measures. I called Toby.

'Susie!'

'Sorry to call so early, but I need to run something past you.'

Then I tried to draw him out on whether he felt the

Yards were likely suspects as murderers.

'It's not part of our plan that you ring me up and pursue whether I think someone did it, but for what it's worth, I say no, I don't think they murdered him. It seems too obvious as everyone knew they had a falling out. As Agatha Christie taught us the most likely suspect is never the culprit.'

Toby wasn't taking my question seriously, which annoyed me. Didn't he want to find out who did it?

Toby added, 'The Yards and Mrs Fishbone will have had to give a statement by now. Just wait for the meeting with Inspector Grey and the family this morning and then give me a call back. That way we won't be wasting time on false leads.'

Yes! Toby was keen for me to ring him again.

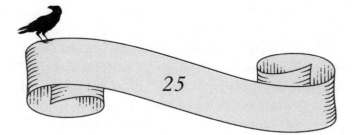

25

The Manor's front door was open when I trotted over a few minutes later, and I half expected Mary to be mopping the hall, but in fact it was Diana who greeted me.

'Don't shut the door Susie. I know it's chilly but there's a terrible smell in here that I'm trying to get rid of.'

I came into the hall and sniffed. 'I see what you mean. That's not nice is it.'

Actually it was pretty mild from where I was standing, but as I got further inside it was obvious that it was the smell of something dead.

'Very unpleasant indeed,' said Diana.

I was in no doubt about what had happened. 'You have a dead mouse under the floorboards.'

Diana looked livid.

'That stringent smell is definitely a dead mouse; it happened all the time at home,' I added.

As a child I'd always begged my parents to get a cat to sort out the mice, and thus the smell problem. But my father disliked cats, especially their penchant for killing his adored garden birds, and so he had come up with a ridiculous family motto: 'Mahls love cooking and hate cats'.

'Asquintha is to blame,' said Diana, her lips thin and angry. 'That woman and all her pretentious allergies. We wouldn't have this problem if Arthur would just stand up to her and get a blessed cat.'

I wasn't sure what to say that wouldn't excite Diana further.

'SHEPHERD!' she yelled.

Shepherd was in the hall within a millisecond.

'Yes, My lady,' he said, and gave a short bow to acknowledge me.

'Susie can explain the dreadful smell and you can do whatever needs doing.' Diana went to stomp away.

'Diana,' I said as calmly as I could. 'There's nothing Shepherd can do. Lifting up the floorboards would mean relaying the entire floor.'

'Nonsense,' said Diana. 'And when you've finished talking to Shepherd join me in the family sitting room.'

I knew about geometric floor patterns and chipped in quickly, 'This is a mahogany parquet floor of the highest spec. There just wouldn't be the craftsmanship out there today to lift it and re-lay it and even if there was I doubt very much you'd find someone who would want to bear the responsibility.'

'What shall we do?' Dejectedly, Diana sat herself down on the worn embroidery of one of the two Louis XVI chairs sitting on either side of the hall table.

'I think your only option is to buy an air-freshener and use it until the smell has gone. The best type are those plug-in ones they sell now. Luckily the smell won't be pungent for too long.'

'Oh no I couldn't possibly have that in the hall. It would be the equivalent of having fresheners dangling in the loo. Not here, Susie, not here.'

Why was it that even a bloody air-freshener could involve an element of snobbery?

I tried again, 'You could fill the hall with scented candles.'

'Much better idea, Susie.'

We left Shepherd pondering scented candles and who was going to go out and get them.

'My goodness, that's a beautiful bunch of lilies,' I said, as we went into the sitting room. There was a huge vase on a small wooden table.

'Aren't they? They came from Gonville and Caius, Cambridge with that card.' Diana was already sitting on the sofa and she pointed towards the mantelpiece.

The card had an abstract design on the front. Pleasant colours but not vibrant, and I thought it very suitable for condolence wishes.

'Read it to me again, Susie, they were such nice words.'

I stood between the pouffe and the glowing fire and read aloud:

'Dear Lady Greengrass, Although we have never had the good fortune of meeting I wanted to send you our deepest sympathies. Your husband, a most generous benefactor, will be remembered by us all, and future generations, for making possible the building of our advanced modern-medicine block. This comes with thoughts and prayers for you and your family from all the dons of Gonville and Caius College Cambridge.'

'I'm pleased they have marked Alexander's passing in this way.'

Diana had been won over by a bunch of lilies but I was still struggling to make sense of Alexander's extravagant endowment.

'The flowers are exquisite,' I said, putting the card back on the mantelpiece and sitting down on the sofa opposite Diana. As usual, the tweed itched me through my tights. 'Was Alexander always keen on medicine?'

'I would have thought so.'

This was a reply that didn't really go anywhere, but Diana didn't seem to be suspicious about the donation at that moment. Maybe I was the only one who still thought it odd.

I changed my mind about not telling Diana of the story I'd seen in the freesheet.

'The local paper has an interview with Mrs Fishbone on the front of it today, I believe.'

'The *Telegraph*! How on earth did she get in there?'

'No, no, I meant the local rag.'

'And what does she have to say for herself?'

'She expresses her speculation that Alexander had bribed the planners with cash when he applied for development rights on ten acres of the ninety he was selling.'

'And?' said Diana, taking me by surprise with her instant deflection of this news.

'That's all. The headline was trying to link it to his murder, I think.'

'Ridiculous. That was nearly twenty years ago,' fumed Diana. 'Just who does Mrs Fishbone think she is, bringing this up again when I'm in mourning?'

This mention of mourning was the first time Diana had used her own situation as ammunition to write someone or something off. I thought she was trying to distract me away from the truth.

In fact it was so out of character that in an instant I was convinced that the sale of this land and the subsequent redundancy of the Yards, the fury of Mrs Fishbone and the unexplainable charitable donation were absolutely all central to Alexander's death.

'Susie, anyone who can afford to do so uses cash to get their own way. Everyone knows this. It's the good fortune of having money. My husband was acting in the way any other person of our means would in the same situation.'

Diana's imperious tone was designed to make me believe I was being naïve to think otherwise.

'Why Alexander decided to sell that land I can't remember. But if he wanted to, I don't see why there is anything wrong with lining someone's pockets to get the job done.'

Diana's attitude was something I disagreed with vehemently; I thought it very wrong that the rich could get what they wanted with a backhander, while the rest of us have to play by the rules. Her comments shook the very foundations of how I had perceived the Greengrasses.

It's always disconcerting when you see a side of someone you never imagined. In a trice I found myself riddled with doubt over whether I really knew this family or not.

Diana hadn't noticed that I was in a quandary. 'If she wasn't our Lord-Lieutenant I'd think Mrs Fishbone might have murdered Alexander herself, from the way she is behaving.'

I asked, 'What happened to your tenant farmer when the land sold?'

'The Yards?'

'Yes.'

'They moved on long ago and we lost touch. I daresay they'll be having their say in the local paper too.'

'Do you think they might be connected to the murder too?' I tried to sound gullible.

'You are a dear girl, Susie, trying to see it from our behalf. I don't want you concerning yourself with all this nasty business. If it's getting too much you must go home. I've got quite used to it now and am sure I'll cope without you.'

'I'm sorry for bringing up the Yards, it was just a thought. I'm definitely going to stay a little longer if that's okay as I hate to think of you all alone.'

'Thank you Susie, and you can rest assured that the Yards have nothing to do with Alexander's death. Of that I am perfectly sure.'

I tried the trick of silence. It worked as Diana then said, 'Iona cried every year the lambs went to slaughter, while I very much doubt Phil could have walked the graveyard inconspicuously with his club foot.'

'Oh gosh, I never knew that was the case, of course he couldn't have.'

I was inclined to agree with Diana that the Yards were out of the frame. This left Mrs Fishbone, and if she were involved then she must have been in cahoots with somebody, otherwise she would have been missed from the commemoration service.

At this rate I wasn't going to have any suspects left. Toby would not be impressed.

Ding-dong went the front-doorbell, which was operated by pulling on a large handle attached to a chain.

'Is it that time already?'

We sat there waiting for Mary to come and tell us who had arrived.

'My Lady, Detective Inspector Grey is here and so would you like me to show him to the library?'

'Yes please, Mary. We will be down shortly.'

Diana picked up the telephone, dialled a number and put the receiver to her good ear. 'Arthur!'

I got up, gave the backs of my legs a jolly good scratch, and then followed Diana downstairs.

Inspector Grey jumped up from his seat as we entered the room.

'Morning My Lady,' he said.

'Good morning, Inspector. Arthur will be here shortly and Susie is still with us.'

'Morning, Inspector,' I said.

'Miss Mahl,' he acknowledged.

'Inspector, yesterday I was walking through the graveyard and noticed that the stone sculpture of Christ at the back of the church, where Lord Greengrass died, was missing its *Globus Cruciger*.'

'Its what?'

Diana stopped in her tracks and both she and Inspector Grey looked at me as I explained there might be a stone ball and cross hidden in the graveyard.

'Thank you Susie for your minor observation.'

Inspector Grey's dismissive response meant the moment passed without Diana questioning it, and before we had time to sit down Arthur and Asquintha walked into the room. Asquintha looked unusually scruffy and

I could swear Arthur was losing weight by the day. His clothes always had a tendency to hang off him but today his belt buckle was done up one further than the previous worn hole.

Diana gave us our orders. 'Arthur, you sit here next to me. Inspector, stay at the head. Asquintha, you sit over there with Susie.'

'How are the boys?' I said, turning to Asquintha.

'Fine thanks, Susie.' She sounded far stronger than she looked.

The door creaked open, and Mary's hands trembled as she put the silver tray on the table.

'Thank you Mary. Susie, would you mind?' said Diana.

'Of course not,' I said, getting up to reach the tray which had been put beside Asquintha.

'I'll do it,' said Asquintha, tapping my thigh.

As she filled the cups I passed them around the table. Diana was having an inaudible conversation with Arthur.

'Right, My Lady, this won't take long. I'll run through the recent statements we've taken and let you know where the case stands.'

Disappointingly, for the first part of the meeting Inspector Grey mentioned nothing I didn't already know. Antonia, May, Katy, Shepherd, Mary and Nanny could be accounted for. He rattled on in too much detail as he gave us their whereabouts.

He added that there was CCTV footage from the Yards' farm shop that showed them both behind the counter attending to customers at the time of the murder.

Diana was uninterested in this particular piece of evidence.

Inspector Grey continued, 'While it feels wholly inappropriate to suspect our Lord-Lieutenant of any wrong-doing, we can confirm she was at the commemoration service.'

'Of course she was at the service,' snapped Diana.

'Well, My Lady, it has been brought to our attention that your late husband acted outside the law. Eighteen years ago there were illicit dealings between him and the head of the town and county planners, Mr Tim Hoare.'

Arthur looked alarmed and turned to his mother, who calmly said, 'Darling, it's nothing for you to worry about.'

Having made his point about Alexander's backhander, Inspector Grey then cleared his throat. He looked down Arthur and Diana's side of the table, and then he glanced towards Asquintha. 'We have further questions for you, Lady Cornfield, and so I will be asking you to accompany me back to the police station.'

It was clear that Asquintha was considered the prime suspect. I was sure the Inspector had got it wrong.

I could see the corners of Diana's mouth twitch.

Arthur sprang up and strode around the table to his wife. He put his hands on her shoulders and kissed the top of her head with a sensitivity that made my eyes water.

I put a hand on her thigh. I wanted to comfort her, regardless of whether I thought she had done it or not. Then she squeezed my hand, with a strength I was sure would get her through whatever lay ahead.

'I have a warrant with me.' Inspector Grey shuffled through papers in his briefcase and then pushed it towards Diana, 'This morning my team, in search of mallets and hammers, will be carrying out a thorough investigation of the annex, and all cars that were stationary here on the morning of Sunday the twenty-sixth November.'

'Very well,' said Diana, passing the warrant across the table to Arthur who let it lie between them. His hands were not leaving his wife's shoulders.

Inspector Grey turned to Asquintha and said, 'You will need to be confined to the police station whilst our team carry out their search.'

She looked the calmest of us all. She nodded to the inspector with a confidence I doubted I could muster under the same circumstances.

'Can I accompany my wife, Inspector?'

'Yes, Lord Cornfield, you may. Your wife will be driven in the police car we have waiting outside and you may follow in your own vehicle once we have searched it.'

Diana got up, and with a curt 'Thank you, Inspector' left the room without looking at any of us.

Not long after, I stood in the dead-mouse-smelling hall, watching through the glass panels in the front door as Asquintha was packed into the back seat of the police car. I hoped they weren't going to drive her through Spire with flashing blue lights. Inspector Grey had said that the search team would be along in about twenty minutes.

Then I had a flash of inspiration. While everyone was agitated about the annex investigation, I could have a more thorough search of Alexander's study. But first I had to get Diana out of the Manor so that there would be no risk that she would disturb me in my nosying.

I couldn't find her in the family sitting room, and when I called for her along her bedroom landing there was no response. She wasn't in the study, the drawing room or the dining room. And Mary and Shepherd had also disappeared.

I went through to the conservatory, and, looking out of the window, I saw her standing on the front lawn staring down at the lake. She wasn't wearing a coat and she looked as if her world were falling apart.

I quickly gathered a warm coat and scarf and hurried across.

She turned around as I got closer.

'Susie, I know it's her. She would kill to have all of this for her own.'

I bundled Diana into the coat, and handed her the scarf. Softly I said, 'I really don't think it's a good idea for any of us to jump to any sort of conclusion just yet.'

'They'll find some evidence against her. Just you wait, Susie.'

I spoke to Diana as firmly as I dared. 'I know Asquintha is currently a suspect but I honestly don't think she's guilty. You have to remember she is family, and until they uncover the murderer I think it'd be very prudent if you didn't do any lasting damage to your relationship with her, or your relationship with Arthur. What if this proves to be a storm in a teacup and he feels you didn't stand by his wife? This is so important, Diana, and I'm sure it's what Alexander would have expected of you.'

There was a long pause. A very long pause.

And then she murmured, 'You're right, Susie, I know. I really must try and trust in her a bit more. I've always found it so difficult, you see, as I always thought Arthur could have done better. But she's stood by him, and she's been a good wife.'

This humbling confession was quite something to hear. Diana, as forceful as she appeared on the outside, showed a vulnerability. For reasons I couldn't quite determine, I felt sad. There was so much forgiving to be done before a true friendship could develop.

I prayed desperately that Asquintha was not the culprit. If she were, it would tear Arthur apart, and it would cut Diana to the quick.

'Susie, I am very fortunate to have you here throughout all of this. Your way of looking at things is wise, and I have learnt from you.' She took hold of my hand. 'Thank you for everything.'

Diana then swiftly changed tack completely, asking me to request that Nanny take the boys on an outing while the police were there, and for me to make myself scarce too. And then she said, 'I'm going to buy some candles for that dreadful smell. I'm quite capable of doing this on my own, before you say anything.'

This was music to my ears. Now I could search Alexander's study to my heart's content.

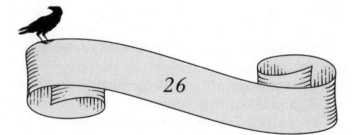

26

Looking for Nanny, I went through to the laundry room of Beckenstale Manor, which leads to the interior entrance of the annex. The interconnecting door was open, but out of politeness I knocked. There was no answer.

'Nanny!' I called out.

Michael and James shot out of a room, ran down the corridor and clamped themselves on to my legs.

'Boys!' said Nanny in jest, as she made her way rather more slowly towards me.

I ruffled their curly hair. Neither liked it and both let go of my legs.

'Sorry Susie,' said Nanny. 'Not shy, this pair.'

'How do you fancy an outing, boys?' I asked, looking down at them.

They were gripped by my presence in that way innocent, inquisitive children can be.

'Well, boys, answer Susie.'

'Yes, yes, yes, yes,' they chanted, each trying to outdo the other by being louder as they jumped up and down almost knocking one another over.

'Now you got them going,' said Nanny.

I lent towards her. 'I need to have a quiet word.'

'Michael, James, please go back to the playroom while I talk to Susie.'

Without hesitation they charged down the corridor.

'What is it? You look worried.'

'Mary and Shepherd have been sent home and the police investigation team are about to turn up to search the annex.'

'Oh!' Nanny looked concerned.

'Asquintha has been taken in to the police station while this is going on, and Arthur has gone with her.'

'Oh my Lord!' Nanny gasped.

I put my hand on her shoulder to quieten her down. 'This isn't time for the rest of us to panic'.

'What if their Ma's a murderer?'

'She isn't,' I said firmly. 'She absolutely is not.'

Nanny took in a deep breath, blinked several times and regained her composure.

'You need to take the boys on an outing immediately. You must be gone for at least three hours. This is at Diana's request, and you mustn't worry the boys by acting as if something is very wrong. You need to leave by the side entrance and drive down to the road the long way so that the boys don't notice too much police activity. And if the police take longer than three hours, I'll ring you and so you must keep your mobile handy,' I told her.

Nanny nodded gravely.

'What about money?' I suddenly remembered.

'I have enough and I can reimburse myself from the petty cash tin if I need to later. I'd better look sharp and get the boys away.'

I watched Nanny bustle out, then I headed for the kitchen, but the connecting door to the annex wouldn't close. A suede glove had got jammed under it and once I'd removed it the door banged shut.

I stuffed the glove in the pocket of my gilet. This morning's cup of coffee had gone straight through me and I desperately needed the loo. There was one off the kitchen, a dark and ancient thunder-box. Many people have had them removed from the grand old houses these days, but a thunder-box has a wooden shelf you sit on that spans the width of the lavatory, and the loo is positioned below the shelf. A very comfortable arrangement, I've always thought.

All four walls of the Greengrasses' downstairs lavatory, or Gents as those in the know refer to them, displayed an old-fashioned framed cartoon of hunting, shooting and fishing. This being a popular decoration in conventional country houses.

The best loo I've ever been in belonged to a vain actor I once house-sat for. All four walls were mirrored, making the reflection of whoever was in there go on into infinity. I think he liked looking at himself. Still, the effect was mesmerising and since then I've always thought that one day I'd like to do something similar in a house of my own.

I was about to pull the plug from the hand basin when I heard a car arrive. I rushed out through the house, on to the porch. Two cars had parked in the yard and several uniformed officers were clambering out. A policewoman walked towards me, holding up a badge in her hand.

'I'm here with three members of the special

investigation unit to carry out a search on Beckenstale Manor annex and a named vehicle.'

'Hello, I'm Susie Mahl, a friend of the Greengrasses, and I have been expecting you. Would you like me to show you in?'

'No need. Detective Inspector Grey has given me all the instructions, including a map to the entrance and floor plan of the home. Is Lady Greengrass at home?'

'No she has already left.'

'Right. We'll get on with it then.'

'Oh, okay. I'll be in the main house.'

She gave me a scrutinising look but didn't say anything, and then spun on her heel and strode back to her colleagues.

I asked her retreating back if she would mind waiting a moment while I check if the family have left.

'On you go, then.'

I raced round to the back of the Manor to find Michael and James clambering into Nanny's car.

'Some people have arrived, Nanny.' I said, and then leaned over to speak to the boys sitting on the back seat. 'But I hear there's a competition that Nanny is going to run for you, down in the woods of the back drive, over who is going to be the first to find seven different sorts of leaves from trees and bring them back to her. I think perhaps the winner can choose between lunch in McDonald's or Pizza Hut or fish and chips.'

All small boys love fast food in my experience, and these two were no exception as they began to bicker over which would be the best treat.

Nanny and I smiled at each other, and then I waved at the boys as they left.

They were only just out of sight when the police filed past carrying a variety of cases.

I now had a window of free time. The house was empty and I could search the study, although I really wasn't at all sure what I thought I'd find that Inspector Grey had missed during his search the other morning. I guess I was looking for unusual outgoings on bank statements, strange meetings in the calendar, correspondence, or anything else that would help me piece together whatever it was that had been going on behind the scenes.

I turned on the lamp on the desk, hoping that if she returned early Diana wouldn't notice it as she came up the drive. At least the scrunch of gravel would tip me off.

Where should I start? The wastepaper basket was practically empty. I tipped it out on the floor and sifted through torn envelopes and junk mail. Nothing. Alexander's desk drawers were full of stationery, unused cellophane slips, a box of biros, a blank notebook, headed writing paper and ivory envelopes to match. All perfectly kept and boringly organised. This was hopeless.

I stood in the centre of the room, scanning the shelves, and then remembered the diaries behind the door, all similarly bound and of the same size. The dates were visible where Toby had licked his finger and ran it along them. But then, tucked away on the far right, an unusual binding caught my eye. It was too high to reach. I dragged over the solid Victorian chair from the desk and without bothering to kick off my shoes I got up and reached for the book. It wasn't a different binding. The diary had been placed on the shelf with its spine to the wall.

I sat on the chair and flicked it open. Very few pages had been used. I started at the beginning, which said, Arthur's thirteenth birthday party. Just as Diana had told me, the details were dull: Mild day, twenty or so children for a tea party. Our little Arthur enjoyed himself. We gave him his first bicycle. And so on. I read as fast as I could, as page after page never rose above tedious.

Then, all of a sudden, I couldn't believe it: familiar names were jumping out at me. Right in front of me was an uninhibited account of a passionate love affair. Every last detail written down.

> *It was in the middle of a hot summer's afternoon lying beneath the shade of the chestnut tree we had gone to for many years when H. found us, bare-naked, our bodies entwined. He swore at us with the very worst language. I fear I've scarred a teenage mind forever. Why was his mother not told the cricket match was cancelled? I grabbed my clothes and ran, knowing I'd never see my love's naked body again. Our dream broken and with it my heart. My dear sweet Princess Violet.*

I ignored the purple prose but I couldn't help thinking what a bloody fool Alexander was to write it all down. But of course now one thing seemed clear.

It was Henry who killed Alexander, I just knew it.

Ben had said that Henry was always inviting himself to stay with the Codringtons since they'd moved next door to Beckenstale Manor. And then Ben had greeted Alexander by name, when Henry and Antonia and I were right beside him in the Dorset Horn, and so Henry definitely knew the evening before the murder exactly what Lord Greengrass looked like now. The following morning Henry was dealing with Situp's piece of bone and could have seized a split-second opportunity to kill the man who'd had an affair with his mother and, if Antonia was right, wouldn't acknowledge him as his bastard son. My thoughts whirled frantically. Henry's fingerprints would be all over the cross and orb...

I had to speak to Toby and it wouldn't wait.

My car keys were in my pocket. I hurriedly put the chair back at the desk, returned the rubbish to the bin, flicked off the light and ran out of the front door of Beckenstale Manor with the diary clutched in my right hand. It had to be done face to face. I drove irresponsibly all the way to the county hospital praying Toby wasn't out to lunch.

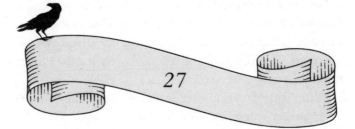

27

'Come in,' he said from behind the door.
I pushed it open.

'Susie! You've come to take me out to lunch, have you?'

Toby swivelled back and forth in his chair pleased with his humour.

I was not in the mood to be jolly. 'Toby! You have to see this.'

I plonked the diary on his desk.

He stood up. 'Susie, don't get me wrong, it's lovely to see you, but I am at work. Perhaps we could meet later?'

I was definitely on to something, I knew I was, and I really didn't want to wait.

'Please, hear me out.'

Toby pointed at the sofa with a slightly resigned look on his face. 'Go on then, take a seat.'

Instead I pulled up a plastic chair and sat down at his desk.

'I found this,' I tapped the cover of the diary, 'in Lord Greengrass's study.'

'And?' asked Toby.

'In it is a detailed account of his affair with Violet Dunstan-Sherbet. It describes her son discovering them, er, at it.'

'At it?' said Toby, a trifle amused by my coy choice of words.

'Yes. At *it*.'

'How long ago was this, Susie?'

I flicked open the cover. 'Twenty three years ago.'

'And you think it's linked to his murder?'

'Yes!' I exclaimed, longing for him to register.

It was unfair of me to presume Toby could fill in the missing gaps, I realised. 'Violet is Henry Dunstan-Sherbet's mother. Henry is her only son.'

Toby's blue eyes doubled in size. 'Are you saying what I think you're saying?'

'Revenge, Toby, revenge is what I'm saying. Antonia told me Henry thought he was an illegitimate son and that his real father never acknowledged him. And she mentioned too that Henry had invited himself to stay with the Codringtons, so presumably he knew they lived near the Greengrasses as Beckenstale Manor has been in the family for years and is well known as the family seat. But knowing is not enough – we need to find proper evidence.'

'*We*?'

I wasn't too enamoured with Toby's tone.

'Yes!'

'But you are forgetting that the police have said that Henry's no longer a suspect.'

'He is, Toby, I just know it. I don't believe you can be sure of the sound of Lord Greengrass's last breath. Ben and I came across his body a few seconds after Henry.

What I need you to tell me is whether four or so seconds would be long enough for Henry to have murdered him?'

'Wow,' said Toby. And then after a pause, he added, 'Now that is a thought.'

Toby looked serious and as if he were concentrating deeply. I didn't want to interrupt and so I kept quiet, even though I couldn't quite prevent my fingers drumming on my thigh.

'Yes, yes indeed.' Toby sounded as if he was thinking out loud. 'I suppose Henry could have murdered Lord Greengrass with the orb, but to do it in four seconds he would have had to know how, and he would have had to be quick to have seized the orb to do it.'

'Drat and damnation,' I said. 'It can't be the orb! There was absolutely no time for him to hide it in the hedge. I was by his side up until the forensics people turned up, and I could see that he didn't have it with him.'

'Well, Henry might not be your man. Are you sure it's not more the case that you want him to be the murderer, Susie?' Toby's tone was gentle, and I knew he had my best interests at heart when he said this. But still…

'Henry is responsible, Toby. I just know he is.' I could feel my face twitch with strain as I stared across the table. 'There's more.'

'Go on then,' said Toby.

'I have Henry's bag—'

Toby interrupted, 'You—'

But I wouldn't let him continue. 'Don't ask, that's not the important bit. In his bag I found a notebook, which had a record of a martial arts class at one two five Devonshire Place in it. I don't have it with me but we can Google the number.'

Toby immediately began typing on his laptop.

'Got it!' he exclaimed.

His hand shot down to his pocket, grabbed his mobile phone, typed the number in to it, placed it on the desk and pressed the loudspeaker button.

'One hundred and twenty-five Devonshire Place. Fumiko speaking.'

'Hello,' said Toby, 'I have a friend who recommended your class and I was wondering if I could sign up for the same one he attends?'

'Yah of course. Name of him.'

Toby replied emphasising each syllable of Henry's full name, 'Hen Ry Dun Stan Sher Bet.'

There was a long pause.

'Hello?' said Toby.

'Yah, 'enry come six o'clock for Dim Mak class.'

'Thank you, I'll be back in touch soon.'

Toby ended the call without waiting for Fumiko's goodbye.

We stared at each other, Toby's eyes unflickering. 'If Henry attented a Dim Mak class he'd know exactly how to end Lord Greengrass's life with one strong blow to the old man's chest. Evidence of this is what we need, Susie.'

We sat there for a while, and then I came up with another idea.

I pointed at Toby's pinboard. 'Is that Alexander's X-ray?'

Toby turned and looked at what I was pointing to. He chuckled. 'No, that's not Lord Greengrass, it's just an exposed bit of film I like the look of.'

'Oh.' I felt foolish. 'I was just wondering if there is

anything showing on the X-ray which would help us prove Henry is involved.'

In the manner of Rodin's *The Thinker*, Toby rested his head on his right hand and gnawed at his knuckles. I could hear his foot, the left one I'm sure, ever so slightly tapping the floor.

Preying on my mind was Asquintha being interrogated for something I was now certain she hadn't done, and it wasn't long before my impatience got the better of me. 'Come on Toby, we need to find something. I know we can work this out if we think hard enough.'

He snapped out of his reverie, got up and marched swiftly down the long, pristine white corridor, with me trotting along behind.

'The boys will be on their lunchbreak. We have to be quick or they'll want to know what we are doing,' he whispered.

We'd stopped in front of a door. It looked exactly like the one opposite, and every door that we'd passed and would go on to pass if we kept walking. Toby fished out a bunch of keys, loosened one and put it in the keyhole. The door swung open into a stark, white lab with a massive bit of equipment on a low table. Toby flicked a switch on at the wall and the whole machine lit up with the colour of an electric flycatcher. He handed me his keys.

'Lock the door will you, while I put some of those on.' He nodded towards a box of Nitrile gloves.

Toby fiddled with the gloves for an inordinate amount of time.

'You see that plan chest over there?'

'Yup.'

'Open up the top drawer for me please, Susie.'

We crossed the room together and our closeness made me think of words like trust and dependency. I was rather enjoying myself.

Very carefully, as I held the draw open, Toby sifted through various acetates as he checked the reference information, and then he lifted out an X-ray.

'This is the original image of Lord Greengrass's chest.'

He placed the X-ray on the flat surface of the machine and pulled the lid back down. I realised that the machine was in fact an enormous microscope and, when Toby indicated that I should come closer to inspect the image, the intensity of light enabled us to see every last detail of the X-ray.

Toby was not nearly as engrossed as I was. He was preoccupied, shuffling his hand around under the machine. It wasn't long before he produced what looked very like a pair of binoculars. 'These, Susie, may just help us; there's a tiny chance that the actual film might show something that isn't currently coming through on our computerised image in Lord Greengrass's archived file,' Toby explained.

He pulled the end covers off them, opened up a glass cabinet behind the machine and took out what he referred to as an 'astronomer's mono zoom'. He screwed it on to the end of the binocular points and, leaning over the machine, held them up to his eyes and peered down at the X-ray.

Without lifting his head he called out, 'There are some callipers hanging on the wall behind you; please will you pass them to me.'

He took them from me, and, very carefully, began stretching them out, measuring individual short distances on the X-ray.

I tried to see what he was studying so intently, but then I realised that his head was raised. 'We may very well have got ourselves some concrete evidence.' His matter-of-fact tone belied the enormity of his words.

'Really?' I asked excitedly.

'Yes, there may be knuckle imprints on Lord Greengrass's pectoral casing. They are extremely faint but as I've magnified from a life-size image, I calculate it shows the first two knuckles of a right hand as being 3.46 centimetres apart. Let's get out of here – we need to leave everything how we found it.'

Within sixty seconds we'd covered our tracks and were safely back in Toby's office.

'We should have found this earlier, Susie. But at least we know now, and it's all thanks to you.'

I smiled at the compliment.

'Now all we need to do is get Henry's knuckle spans.' It sounded so easy, I thought as I spoke. I had completely forgotten about my previous theory of the orb from the statue.

'Inspector Grey is not going to go all the way to Brighton unless his team are absolutely sure Henry Dunstan-Sherbet's the murderer.'

'Then we must prove that Asquintha and Ronnie are innocent,' I said. Then, 'I have no idea how we can do this.'

Argh. In frustration I stuffed my hands into my pockets.

Bingo!

I pulled out a grubby suede glove; the one I had found caught under the connecting door. 'This is Asquintha's glove!'

'Are you sure it's hers?'

I drew his attention to the fact that there was a nametape with 'Asquintha Cornfield' sewn inside the wrist band.

The glove was an extremely snug fit on my hand, which meant Asquintha's knuckle span was a little smaller than mine.

Toby produced a lump of soft Plasticine from his desk draw. I giggled, 'What have you got that for?'

'Feels nice, Susie. I like to mould it from time to time when I'm bored of work.'

He squished it into a rectangular lump and put it on the table.

'Stand up, clench your fist and push it into the Plasticine, will you?'

I took the glove off my right hand and carefully made an impression of my fist.

'Damn. I'm just going to get those callipers.'

Seconds later and Toby was back, measuring my imprint in the clay.

'Well, Asquintha's not the murderer, we can be sure of that.' The measurements were wrong.

I felt relieved.

'Let's visit Ronnie before we call the inspector,' said Toby. 'But we need to be quick as I have meetings this afternoon that I can't be late for.'

Toby took his corduroy coat from the back of his chair and put it on.

'Here,' he handed me the Plasticine, 'you keep hold of this, and put these callipers in your handbag.'

'I don't have my bag with me.'

Toby bent beneath his desk and popped back up

holding a green canvas shoulder bag. I took it from him and placed the Plasticine in one half and the callipers and diary in the other.

28

'The charitable donation!'

'What's that, Susie?' said Toby, looking across at me from the driving seat as we headed to Spire.

'Alexander must have given money to Gonville and Caius College in order that Henry could get a place to study medicine at Cambridge.'

'You don't think Henry's clever enough?'

'Well, Ben joked that Henry didn't have the brains he was born with. And even Diana seems to agree that Lord Greengrass paid the planners to pass his application for the new housing estate, and so it's not a massive stretch that if he made a substantial amount of money then he would secure his illegitimate son a place at university...' I trailed off as I thought of the injustice of such corrupt behaviour.

'Let's wait and prove it first.' Toby's level-headedness frustrated me but I knew he was right.

As Toby parked the car right outside the pub, a tiny little bit of me wished we could rewind back to the previous evening. I did enjoy his company, and I hadn't met a man who'd I'd instantly felt so at ease with for a long time. If I had now solved the case, it would mean the end of us gallivanting about, and that would be a pity.

'I have a plan,' said Toby. 'I suggest we go in, order drinks, sit at a table and wait for Ronnie to deliver them.'

'Yes…okay,' I said, a bit dubiously.

'I'd rather you don't know the rest. You just improvise.'

The Dorset Horn was empty. Ronnie was standing behind the bar and he looked pleased to see us. 'Hello again,' he said to me, and nodded at Toby. 'What can I get for you?'

Toby turned to me and raised his eyebrows.

'A lime and soda for me please.'

'And I'll have the same,' said Toby, handing Ronnie a note.

Ronnie rang it up on the till and passed back some change. 'Coming right up, I'll bring them over.'

Toby chose a table against the wall, tucked away and small enough for us to have a private conversation.

'Let's have that Plasticine.' Toby held out his hand.

I handed it over.

He moulded it into a rectangle and placed it on the table between us.

Ronnie arrived with the drinks. 'What's that you got there?' he asked, as if on cue, as he stared at the lump on the table.

'Oh that? It's a silly game Susie and I've got going. She's bet me a tenner she can make a deeper imprint with one push. I've told her it's the best of three.'

'It's been my party piece for years,' I improvised. 'I can beat any man.'

'That's why I've had to do the best of three,' said Toby.

'You soft, office types,' Ronnie exclaimed. 'Hefting those barrels down in the cellar is what you need.'

Toby frowned at the Plasticine and muttered, 'You may be right. Do you have a technique I can steal?'

'You two! Do I get the tenner if I beat her?' said Ronnie as he shuffled into position. The solid table didn't even quiver under the quite considerable force of him pushing his right bunched fist downwards.

'That puts me at the bottom of the pile, I can tell,' said Toby. 'It's a mighty arm you've got there.'

I realised we'd backed ourselves into a corner and it was now going to be hard to get a measurement without Ronnie wondering what we were up to. We couldn't possibly risk moving the Plasticine for fear of distorting the result. Ronnie's innocence could be a matter of a millimetre here or there.

But sometimes one just has to think a benevolent force is watching, as at that moment somebody stuck their head round the pub door and announced that some of the sheep from Beckenstale Manor had got out and were in the beer garden.

Ronnie turned to go and deal with the errant ewes, calling to me over his shoulder, 'Next time you're in here, young lady, we'll do this proper, and I'll take your tenner from you.'

Toby and I gave nervous laughs. We really hadn't thought it through sufficiently, and only got by on a wing and a prayer.

Discreetly, I passed the callipers over to Toby.

'Can you go and make sure that Ronnie is distracted for a minute or two while I measure his fist imprint?

Team work, and all that,' he said.

'Do you need a hand with the sheep?' I called loudly to Ronnie as I headed outside.

Luckily, the sheep were predictably tiresome; they darted this way and that as we tried to persuade them to go back to where they had come from.

Then Ronnie said, 'Little bleeders! I'd better call the shepherd.'

I swear the upward curve to the mouths of the sheep looked as if they were laughing at us. 'No!' I squeaked, anxious to stop Ronnie going back into the bar.

He gave me an odd look and much to my relief he pulled an ancient Nokia from his trouser pocket, and pressed a couple of buttons. As he waited for someone to pick up he told me the sheep were little beggars and that there was a small renegade group that made it their life's business to get into the beer garden. His call was answered then as he said, 'They're here again, I'll close the gate so they can't get out but I'm not helping you put them in the trailer, I've had my fill,' I saw Toby beckon me from the other side of the picket fence. 'I need to get back to work,' he called.

I nodded bye to Ronnie and dashed to the car.

'It's not him,' whispered Toby as I got in.

'It's Henry, I know it is,' I said. 'Let's go to Inspector Grey.' I blew on my fingers: they were absolutely frozen, me having been running about outside without the benefit of a jacket. 'I think we should get your car first, I can't be sure I won't be called away at any point today.'

We drove along in silence, and then as we parked in the staff bit of the hospital car park, Toby said in a mollifying manner, 'Have you got any photographs of your work, I'd love to see some.'

I unlocked my mobile and picked out some pictures of my work.

'Recognise this?' It was a painting of the Seven Sisters.

'Dover,' he said, jokily.

'That's right,' I answered, knowing full well he knew it wasn't.

'What about your pet portraits, Pet Detective?'

'Here's the latest one, a blue-eyed Jack Russell called Sky.'

'No wonder you're in demand,' he said. 'I think it's time to call Inspector Grey.'

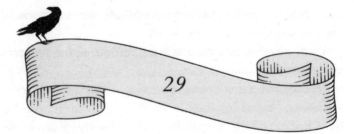

29

'Susie Mahl, I wish you'd pack up your things and head back off to Sussex. Some might say that you are interfering where you shouldn't be. Everyone – and I mean everyone – I've taken a statement from mentions having spoken to you previous to *my* interviewing them.'

I hadn't imagined Inspector Grey would have been anything other than thrilled with our news. How naïve of me.

We had gone to Toby's office, and I had telephoned the inspector, who had asked whether we could come to the police station for 2pm.

Toby had entered Inspector Grey's office first, and it was only after they had shaken hands across his desk that Inspector Grey had looked at me and blurted out this greeting.

Toby and I caught each other's eye, and then Toby said, 'I'm sorry we've surprised you, but really Susie has excelled herself.'

Inspector Grey snorted in what I could only think was contempt as he stood behind his desk, leaning on both fists. He was too small to intimidate either of us but he did his best. 'And why might that be?' he boomed. He looked rather peeved.

I was just trying to work out the best and most succinct way of explaining everything when the inspector added, 'Fancy yourself as a detective do you? It's not for amateurs. And as for this,' he looked at me sternly as he held up the *Globus Cruciger* which Toby and I had both seen on his desk, 'your red herring had my team searching for hours for something which we later discovered in the parish council notes has in fact been missing for a whole eighteen months. It was a complete blind alley, and an utter waste of valuable police resources, when the orb was very likely kicked around the graveyard by local vandals over a year before the murder.'

Whoops!

The weight of the stone caused a great thud as Inspector Grey impatiently stamped it back down on his desk.

Toby came to the rescue. 'We're here to tell you that key evidence has been discovered through a six percent magnification of the chest X-ray.'

'Very well then, go on.'

I opened my mouth to speak but then I saw the inspector staring at Toby, waiting for him to continue and so I shut it again.

'In an early diary of Lord Greengrass's – not part of the evidence that was bagged that morning – Susie discovered a detailed account of an affair he had with Violet Dunstan-Sherbet, mother of Henry Dunstan-Sherbet. Lord Greengrass recorded the whole incident, describing in detail the moment Violet's son discovered them.'

I put the diary on the table.

'And you think this has something to do with a murder many years later? That seems to stretch credulity,' said Inspector Grey as if we were fools.

Toby was undeterred. 'Violet Dunstan-Sherbet's infidelity could well have made for an unhappy environment for an only son to grow up in, and as she comes from one of England's oldest Catholic families, divorce would never have been permitted.'

'I fail to see what this could have to do with Lord Greengrass's murder?'

I couldn't keep quiet any longer. 'Having spent time with Henry, I can say there is a strange streak in him. And I'm sure the incident described in the diary when he was a teenager very probably led him to believe he was not his father's son – by that I mean Violet's husband's son. Plus, I have been told that Henry felt his birth father did wrong by him by never publicly acknowledging paternity.' My opinion was pouring out in a bit of a muddle but it didn't stop me continuing. 'I'm sure Henry believed Lord Greengrass was his father, and of course a sizeable charitable donation that Lord Greengrass made to the Cambridge university medical department that Henry attended, but which Lord Greengrass had no other link with that we can find, is indicative of a relationship between them.'

Inspector Grey spent a little time getting to the bottom of what I meant.

Once that was all clarified, Toby went on. 'Susie,' Inspector Grey's lip twitched at the mention of my name, 'reminded me that Henry came upon Lord Greengrass's body seconds before her and Ben. And so

I've revisited the chest X-ray and can confirm we have concrete evidence that neither Asquintha nor Ronnie played any part in the murder.'

'Show me the evidence,' said Inspector Grey wearily.

Toby explained. 'When studying the X-ray under an astronomer's mono zoom, I could make out the knuckle marks of the fist imprint around Lord Greengrass's pectoral casing. The span between the first two knucklebones of a right hand measured 3.46 centimetres.'

Inspector Grey shuffled a few papers and then nodded for Toby to continue.

'We took it upon ourselves to carry out a few fist measurements. We wanted to gather as much evidence as we could before coming to you so as not to waste your time.'

Inspector Grey nodded with thanks for our apparent consideration. The truth was that we had acted as we had because chasing down the evidence was fun.

'So basically,' I chipped in, 'Ronnie's fist is much too big and Asquintha's much too small.'

I put the glove on the table with a dramatic flourish. It was too good an opportunity to miss.

'Asquintha's glove gave an approximate measurement, but it's clear her hands are small as I can barely fit mine in the glove, and so she couldn't possibly have two knuckles which span nearly as large as 3.46 centimetres.'

Inspector Grey stared at my undeniably petite hands and, even though he was murmuring something about none of this being admissible in court, his tone had softened somewhat.

'In a notebook of Henry's,' prompted Toby, after he told the inspector how we had got Ronnie's fist measurement, 'Susie found record of a martial arts class in Eastbourne which we have confirmation that Henry attended.'

'And of what relevance is this martial arts class?'

I explained, 'It tells us that, combined with his medical background, Henry Dunstan-Sherbet had all the knowledge and physical strength to perform Dim Mak.'

Inspector Grey looked confused.

'As I'm sure you know, Inspector, Dim Mak is also commonly known as the touch of death,' said Toby. 'It's a very effective, silent manoeuvre that interrupts immediately the body's electrical current and leads to sudden heart failure.'

'Assuming for a moment that you two are correct in your assumptions, how can we prove it so?' asked Inspector Grey.

I thought the solution glaringly obvious, but Toby managed to say in a non-patronising manner that perhaps the best thing would be to measure Henry's fist.

'Nice work Susie,' said Toby as we stood outside the police station a few minutes later, raising his hand for a high five. 'I guess you'll be heading back home to Sussex now?'

'Yes. Back to painting. Time off from this detective malarkey,' I joked.

It was only after Toby and I had parted that I realised I still had his canvas bag hoiked over my shoulder. I was looking forward much more to finding an excuse to return this to Toby, than I had been over giving Henry his bag back.

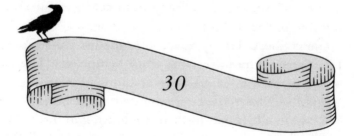

30

Three weeks later…

'Oh Susie!' Antonia gave me an all-encompassing hug. 'We've been hugely looking forward to your arrival as you really are a hero in these parts now.'

I withdrew from her embrace with just a little sense of pride.

The thought of having been the one to bag up their friend didn't outweigh the anticipation of unwrapping my drawing of Situp in front of them.

It's always a nervous prospect, being on the scene whilst delivering a work of art. I'm not sure I'd like to be the receiver either. It's an impossible thing to show complete delight at something you are seeing for the first time.

Gingerly, I followed Antonia in to her kitchen.

'Susie!' said Ben crossing the room and kissing me warmly on both cheeks. 'You are a hero. But poor Henry.'

On the drive over to the Codringtons I'd been thinking how I would feel if a childhood friend of mine had murdered my neighbour, and realised that I would feel sorry for the dreadful psychosis their damaged upbringing had bred in them.

Nevertheless, Henry was a cold-blooded killer and so I was pretty certain that the Codringtons would be at least relieved that he was now in custody awaiting trial. I wondered what Henry himself felt about his actions, and whether he was experiencing any remorse.

Situp rushed towards me, his claws slipping on the polished floor as he nuzzled me in welcome. Everyone smiled at his tail, which wagged frantically. I patted his head with my free hand as I greeted him, 'Hello Situp, how are you boysies?'

'Come on, Susie, let's get your work of art out. I've dusted the table in preparation and we're dying to see it,' said Antonia, who was standing by my side.

'I think champagne is in order,' said Ben, who had the fridge door already open and glasses standing on the sideboard ready to be filled.

'May,' called Antonia. 'Susie's here. Bring Bella through.'

Once everyone was there, I pulled the white stopper off one end of the cardboard tube and took out the drawing which was curled up in greaseproof paper.

'We could do with something heavy to pin down the corners,' I explained.

Quickly, Ben handed four mugs to Antonia and she secured the corners as I unrolled the paper.

'Oh my goodness, it *is* Situp!' exclaimed Antonia.

Ben put his arm around his wife's shoulders. 'Anty, isn't it excellent?'

I tapped the little hand, which had shot out. 'No, sorry Bella, this one doesn't like to be touched.'

Situp was looking up through the glass table, confused by all the attention.

'It's absolutely brilliant. It's just brilliant,' said Antonia unable to look away from my vast charcoal drawing of their dog.

'Champagne,' said Ben handing me a glass. 'Congratulations, Susie.'

'Thank you very much. I'm so pleased you like him.'

Antonia took a glass from Ben and gently clinked it against mine, 'We are going to hang him up right there.' She gestured her hand towards a blank wall space above Situp's basket. 'It will be the first thing everyone sees when they walk into the house.'

I felt happy to the core. One sip of champagne and my nerves settled completely.

Antonia couldn't stop staring at my drawing. 'Oh look, you've even got the fleck of white under his right ear; it's so tiny that I always think I'm the only one who's ever noticed it.'

Later, Ben and I were standing by the wood-burner when he reached into his pocket and handed me an envelope. 'We knew we'd love your drawing Susie, and we're sorry for the dreadful business we had to put you through.' I held the envelope tight in my hand. It felt thick with cash.

'Ben's being Father Christmas,' said Antonia happily. 'The joys of village life.' May was helping Bella into her best clothes as there was going to be a party for the little ones in the village. 'We've been doing all we can to make local friends since Lord Greengrass died. We didn't want Bella to be thought of only as the girl whose parents introduced a murderer into the village.

Thankfully everyone's been very forgiving. The best of the bunch are a couple called Yard, they're our favourites, aren't they Ben.'

I pointed out that Henry had been exceptionally charming, and that he certainly hadn't seemed like a man on a murderous mission.

Antonia smiled at me, and added, 'I know Ronnie would love to see you. He found that whole punching the Plasticine game very amusing.'

Ben smiled at Antonia. He looked well. He must have handed in his manuscript. But who on earth was going to buy a definitive history of private banking? Not me, that was for certain.

'How's the book?' I asked.

'Done,' said Ben, with a huge smile.

'Tell her Benji,' said Antonia, with anticipation.

'I've already begun the next one. It's a family biography I suppose, but a novel and with a crime angle inspired by recent events...'

'So who solves the crime?' I asked.

'That'll spoil the ending,' said Ben. 'But if you really want to know it's the best friend of the murderer.'

'Have you seen Alexander's headstone?' Antonia changed the subject.

'Yes, I walked through the graveyard to here. It's a nice touch, the engraved cocker spaniel under his name.'

'Isn't it? It reminds me of *Greyfriars Bobby*. That was my favourite book growing up.'

'Me too,' I said, remembering the sadness I felt when I first read it.

I gathered my things to go and Antonia smiled at me.

'We'll be sure to spread the word about the brilliant Susie Mahl amongst all our friends.'

As I walked across the frozen grass in the graveyard to my car, I was filled with nostalgia. It felt as if in the few days I'd spent here in November more drama had occurred than ever before in my entire life.

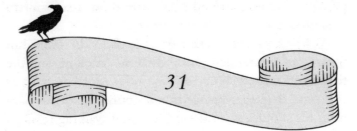

31

Toby and I agreed to meet high on the cliffs at the ruins of Sweetheart Abbey. It had been arranged in an exchange of letters. We hadn't spoken in the last two weeks, which I found very romantic.

As I waited for Toby it was absolutely freezing, but a serenely beautiful day. The sea was calm and the sky clear blue, with not a cloud in sight, other than a wisp of white scrolled along the horizon.

I knew that he would recognise my car when he arrived at the lay-by and so I decided to walk the short path over to the ruin.

The chalk was soft underfoot. There was a pale red stone at my feet and I bent down and picked it up. It felt smooth in my hand and fitted snug in the cup. I slipped it into my pocket. I almost always pick up a stone that catches my eye when I go to a place I want to remember. They line the shelf around my bathroom, where the wall joins the slope of the ceiling.

When I reached the ruins of the abbey I looked back towards the car park and could see him coming my way. I pretended not to notice, and stared out at sea. I timed perfectly turning around again just as he was about to reach me.

'Toby!' I said, as if surprised. Of course I wasn't but the coil of excitement inside me made it come out like that. I suddenly felt very hot.

'Susie,' he said placing the two bursting canvas bags from his shoulders on the ground and walking towards me with his arms open. 'It's great to see you,' he said, as he held my shoulders and lent in to kiss me on both cheeks.

The sun shone a golden glow over us as Toby unwrapped our picnic.

'How did Situp's portrait go down?' he asked, handing me a cup of steaming parsnip soup.

'Couldn't have been better. I think they loved it.'

'I was telling a friend of mine about you the other day, and he asked if you drew horses. I said if you didn't I bet you could.'

'Very loyal.'

'So you don't want to give up and become a detective?'

'I don't see why I can't do both. Us pet detectives like to multi-task.'

Toby had drizzled the centre of a sourdough loaf with oil, layered green olives, sundried tomatoes, tomatoes, spring onions, chopped parsley, crushed capers, artichoke hearts, emmenthal, beetroot and grilled pancetta, and put the loaf between two chopping blocks under a stack of books to compress overnight. It was delicious.

Toby put his hand in his bag and produced two small water bottles. 'I mixed up some lime and soda for old time's sake, but I've also got some sloe gin to warm us up. I knew you'd be driving otherwise I would have bought a bottle.'

He fished out from the side pocket of his bag a little jam jar of purple gin.

As Toby looked out to sea and told me something about the curvature of the earth I couldn't help but hope we would meet again. I liked him and he'd been such a great help with uncovering the murderer. I thought that it was hard to beat a doctor like him as a sleuthing partner in crime. I hoped he felt likewise.

Later Diana and her new puppy greeted me as I knocked on the door to her new home.

'Susie dear, meet Ferdinand Humphrey Cuthbert Daniel John the Seventeenth. I've nicknamed him Alex for everyday.'

I bent down and picked the little spaniel up in my arms. 'He's so soft, what a cutie.'

'Look, here's that sketch of him that you did.' Diana was already through the next door, where I could see above the roaring fire my framed picture, looking surprisingly good for an off-the-cuff sketch.

'I never thought it would be the case but I'm very happy living off the estate. And you know what, a small house isn't as bad as I imagined it would be,' said Diana as she jiggled a poker about in the log fire.

Small!

Diana's new abode, the Manse, was at least three times bigger than my cottage.

'It's a lovely house,' I agreed as I continued to stroke Alex, now happily dozing in my arms. 'How are Arthur, Asquintha and the boys?'

'They're very well. They are now fully settled in the main house and have left the annex free for the future generation. We all wanted a fresh start and to put what was said and done behind us. I was able to move in here as soon as the estate had arranged my things. Two days after Alexander's funeral in fact. It was so kind of you to be here for that.'

Of course, I had returned to Spire for the funeral, even though it was very soon after Henry's arrest. It was a long journey to go all the way there and back in a day but I hadn't wanted to stay over.

I was given a reserved seat in the church next to Diana, who held my hand throughout, only flinching once with disapproval at the stand-in organist. Diana didn't shed a tear, and was almost cheerful that finally Alexander's body could be laid to rest.

Asquintha had looked stunning in a pillbox black hat with a veil. Her eyes were glassy as she held the hands of her smartly dressed boys tightly. When it came to the eulogy they all glued their eyes to Arthur, and while he spoke about his father, Lord Greengrass, I felt very, very sad.

The staff lined the balcony tier of the village church, and when Diana and I left our pew at the end of the service, Nanny, Mary, Shepherd and Sid were there. I looked up with great fondness for them all. It seemed as if everybody was where they should be.

Acknowledgements

With special thanks to my brilliant editor, Jenny Parrott, for conceiving the idea and believing in me as the one to write it. Great thanks also to my parents for the upbringing they've given me; and Susan Bacon, for introducing me to barrister, Thomas Seymour, whose advice was unconditionally given and which enabled me to tackle the complexities of a will. Emily Carter, and all my family, for casting an eye over hidden truths. Richard Cohen, Gordon Hopkinson and many friends for their support and encouragement. To my husband Sam, for letting me laugh at my own jokes. To all at Oneworld, for their help and hard work every step of the way, and to Fr Edward Corbould, for being a loyal friend.

© Jack Warrender

Ali Carter was born in Scotland and read art history at St Andrews. She first followed an eclectic career in investment management; then in 2011 she had a catastrophic bicycling accident. After major brain surgery and a long recovery, she set herself a challenge to walk alone from Canterbury to Rome, a three-month pilgrimage she wrote about in a book, *An Accidental Jubilee* by Alice Warrender. From then she decided to follow her passion and become a fine artist. She specialises in oil paintings from life with an emphasis on colour. Ali also draws pet portraits to commission and works from her studio in East Sussex. *A Brush with Death* is her first novel.